THE LIFE OF KIM

AND THE BEHAVIOR OF MEN

HUMAN BONDAGE IN THE
AFTER-MARKET OF WAR

Praise for *The Life of Kim and the Behavior of Men:*
Human Bondage in the After-market of War

Thoughtful, with dark, more-than-entertaining humor and a good, sad ending might best describe *The Life of Kim and the Behavior of Men*. Rod Davis calls on his own experience as a first lieutenant who found himself in South Korea instead of Vietnam, and he writes convincingly about the rocky relationship between LT Thomas Jefferson Hobbes and Kim, a young working girl who almost survives what can be called the "after-market of wars." This is a better read than *Catch-22*.

—Bill Helmer, former *Playboy* editor and
author of *St. Valentine's Day Massacre*

War is hell, but it's also a trap as Rod Davis eloquently demonstrates in his novel *The Life of Kim and the Behavior of Men*. Davis's narrator—LT Thomas Jefferson Hobbes—finds himself deployed to Korea, not Vietnam as he had expected. Although the assignment may guarantee that Hobbes won't witness mass slaughter (or be killed himself) he witnesses another kind of slow, methodical slaughter of people's souls. The economic system that thrives around a war machine crushes and kills, and as Hobbes narrates his own story we can only hope that by telling it he can salvage himself and make some sense of the fate of the bar girl—Kim—whom he loves. He is presented with a true Hobbesian choice—the necessity of accepting one of two equally objectionable alternatives—and one must wonder how we ourselves would fare under those circumstances.

—Helen Thompson, writer and associate editor for *Texas Monthly*; founding editor of TexasMonthly.com; and author of *Marfa Modern*,
Texas Made/Texas Modern, and *Santa Fe Modern*

It's 1970 and LT Thomas Jefferson Hobbes is shipped out not to Vietnam as expected but to Korea, where GIs have way too much time on their hands. And more importantly for this compelling and unflinching portrait of Ugly Americanism, where temptations for grift are irresistible. Hobbes watches fretfully while a supply officer peddles pilfered PX goods and runs a drug ring, a mess sergeant sells steaks on the sly to local restaurants, and an army dentist treats local women for sexual favors. A chief attraction to the soldiers is bar girls rented by the hour or, better yet, set up in hootches for a pittance per month. Hobbes has a moral compass, but he's also part of the crowd, and his agonized attachment to "Kim" is the twisted heart of his story. The tragic consequences that follow make this novel march at double-time to a very big ending.

—C.W. Smith, author of *Girl Flees Circus* and other books.
He is a former Marine and a Dedman Family
Distinguished Professor Emeritus at SMU

Thomas Hobbes is deployed to South Korea during the Vietnam War... Davis' story is well paced, its descriptive prose deftly conveying the setting and the culture of life in the camp: "Whiskey at thirty cents a glass, opium and heroin in cigarette packs, switchblade knives sold by amputees and hustlers in the alley, dice slammed against mud walls..." The author is unafraid to highlight the flaws of his protagonist... once Hobbes and Kim do have a deeper bond between them, he struggles to commit to her because she is not of "the World." Davis' story... presents an impressive and engaging tale of love in a rough setting.
A moving and well-written war drama.

—*Kirkus Reviews*

THE LIFE OF KIM

AND THE BEHAVIOR OF MEN

HUMAN BONDAGE IN THE
AFTER-MARKET OF WAR

a novel by

Rod Davis

Lake Dallas, Texas

Cover Design: Kimberly Davis

ISBN: 978-1-956440-79-9 paperback,
978-1-956440-80-5 ebook

Library of Congress Control Number: 2023950530

For those who didn't make it.
And those who did.
And those to come.

And for the many Kims,
business girls, and sex workers
of the world,
and hope for the day when
they all will be safe and free.

In the end, there were not many things worth wanting—for the serious man, the samurai. But there were some. In the end, if the serious man is still bound to illusion, he selects the worthiest illusion and takes a stand. The illusion might be of waiting for one woman to come under his hands. Of being with her and shivering in the same moment.

—Robert Stone, *Dog Soldiers*

Everyone believes in the atrocities of the enemy and disbelieves in those of his own side, without ever bothering to examine the evidence.

—George Orwell, *Looking Back on the Spanish War*

I

Kim

(The GIs)

1

It must have been her only way of getting back at us, sitting at that fence outside the Kimpo airport, skirt pulled high. I remember thinking that the last time I saw her. Not the first time, curious and fresh on the rumbling bus to my new station, where she leaned against a wall outside the sentry gate. I just felt sorry for her, glad I was born in America, where she couldn't sit in public like that. I felt like that, indignant and curious and separate, the first time.

The last time, when she was dead, I saw her watching me. I was going back to the World, where Korea was *M*A*S*H* and *The Bridges at Toko-Ri* and fading old soldiers with corn cob pipes and where she could not exist, either.

The grapevine said she was crazy, that she would rise from the fence and wander aimlessly. The spirochetes that had destroyed her flesh had done the same to her mind. Sometimes a truck would let her sit in the back and drop her at the local village. Children seeing her ran. Older ones taunted her. Women pretended not to notice as she drifted through, begging for food and clothes.

They said she talked about things no one could understand. Wild gibberish, strange cries, laughter. Everyone knew the story of when she danced like a pro in a dirt road, cutting her bare feet on glass and rubble, luring men in a bar to come out and throw coins before chasing her away. They said she was possessed.

GIs had a running joke: "She's somebody's *yobo* from 1950 who told her to wait for him outside Gate 10."

In time, she was forgotten.

2

I am here. Fall '70. Stepping down the Northwest Orient ramp in the harsh late autumn light, striding quickly across the cold flat runway. I squint at Kimpo airport, gray and metallic, alone and indifferent. Officers and enlisted, two hundred of us crowd cattle-close. A rope cordon separates us from five NCOs who tell us where to stand, what to do.

Numb with lack of sleep, we enter the In Processing area. A sign says: "Welcome to Korea." The DC-8 jet, called a Stretch-8 because the middle has been elongated to carry more of us, had wiggled in the high atmosphere as it sailed all night above the moonless clouds over the Pacific and past the anti-aircraft batteries when it touched down in the Land of the Morning Calm, as a stewardess called it on the intercom.

In the terminal, an NCO barks out and the enlisted men stumble toward their green duffle bags to hunt their stenciled belongings. I hear a staff sergeant say to another sergeant who has returned from mid-tour leave: "Hey, Willis, your damn yobo's out there, waiting for you."

"Whadja expect? She misses me."

"Yeah, you got the PX card."

Willis, a stocky man with a New Jersey accent, lifts his bag and steps out into the cold. As he pushes open the terminal door, I see her, my first yobo. Her eyes, which the GIs and most Americans call "slant-eyes," as compared to our "round-eyes," hide behind her sunglasses. Her black hair glistens with hairspray. She huddles in her coat until her sergeant appears and hugs her and they slide into the back seat of a black-and-white cab with a PX Transportation sign on the door.

I turn to a major beside me who wears a Ranger patch on one shoulder and the black horse head of the 7th Cavalry on the other. "What does yobo actually mean?" I ask, one man to another. "That's not his wife?" He laughs and buttons his coat. "Wife? That whore? Hell no." He adjusts his reflecting sunglasses and looks at me like I'm a fool. A colonel standing nearby smirks.

I walk to a window and rub frost from the glass. Outside, the enlisted replacements trudge through the bitter air, tugging their green caps over their short hair. I look back inside at all the signs and instructions.

On the far side is the most pertinent: Out Processing. Dogs sniff the luggage-loading lane. GIs are laughing and horsing around. Some of them cry and hold their yobos, who somehow have gotten in. The rest of us, the ones who haven't been in-country before, are mostly numb to the emotions. We're aliens. Alien. I turn the word over and try to stay awake. I know the ones leaving will get onto the same plane that had brought me. My Stretch-8 becomes their Red Tail.

The officers begin moving. We get on gray buses and ride to the sprawling Army depot and compound near Bupyeong, a growing city not that far from Seoul. At the compound drop-off, officers are taken to their quarters and the enlisted men are sent to an overheated tin building for the KAMUP lecture. KAMUP stands for: Korean-American Mutual Understanding Program.

Unfortunately, an artillery captain steering the officers notices by my orders and Adjutant General insignia that I will be a personnel officer, what the Army calls a battalion S-1. The captain says I should go with the enlisted men to hear the lecture. Probably because he will be giving it.

I nod off through most of it, like everyone else, but I remember him saying, "Don't think of *when* you get out of Korea, think of *what* you get out of Korea."

He offers some functional advice; the kind soldiers need. He says something about the clap, and a few people laugh. I am thinking about Beth. There are wisecracks, the kind our fathers heard in *The Sands of*

3

Iwo Jima. When the KAMUP lecture is over, and the papers have been processed, the enlisted replacements file out the door. Me, too.

Some will be unlucky. They will go to the DMZ, the 38th parallel, the approximately 160-mile long, 2.5-mile-wide country-splitting garden of mines and barbed wire and tanks and hilltop outposts that turned one Korea into two. They will be Spartans until they leave, commanded by Calvinistic generals who believe comfort is sin and privation strength. A few may become MPs at Panmunjom, the city of eternal negotiation, where they can be killed if North Korean guards catch them at night. Others will go to Seoul, home of the 8th U.S. Army Yongsan headquarters garrison, smug in the capital city. They will find dope and women and become ugly American GIs. We all will.

Still others will go to lonely mountaintop missile sites where the only roads are dirt, everything is at least six hours away by Jeep, and the only females are in magazines under mattresses. Or they will go to the smaller cities like Daegu or Busan from which U.S. Army posts reach out through the hills like green tentacles to rocket batteries and other forms of military presence. There they will live in a nether world of comfort and isolation. But all of them spend their first night in the transient barracks, attend the orientation class, learn of KAMUP. None of them, nor me, care.

*

Before I came East, when I was still safe and well-scrubbed in the West, I believed my only foe in the ROK would be time. Some of the lifers said I'd enjoy it. Said things like: "It's a ball, no shit. Get it? A ball?"

To which I groaned.

Sgt. First Class Bottham had another approach. "Anyway, it could've been Nam. Depends on whether you'd rather fuck gooks or kill them," he quipped when I received my orders from Maj. Weston that Thursday at Fort Leonard Wood, Missouri, where combat engineers learn their craft.

Maj. Weston enjoyed telling me he thought I had bad morale.

It was true. I was in charge of a personnel office for the basic and advanced training units. Vital records for a lot of soldiers, often younger than me, passed across my desk. I hated the war, which was a constant challenge. I couldn't do much about that, but I was able to cancel the enlistment agreements of a half-dozen soldiers, because their recruitment contracts were hokum and bullshit, and because I was a commissioned officer, and I could.

That was enough to put me in bad standing with various commanders and civilian admins and negate any career aspirations I might have had, which were none. So, I had to add something else. In part of the personnel office, where we also recruited for Officer Candidate School (OCS), I hung a photo of Second Lieutenant "Rusty" Calley, of the My Lai massacre. I had ripped it from a layout in a story in *Esquire.* On the photo I had stapled an Army ad that said: "Be a Leader of Men." My artwork stayed up a couple of months, bright and shiny. Until a particularly gung-ho colonel stuck with a basic training brigade came through, noticed it, and somehow restrained himself from punching me.

"Lieutenant Hobbes?"

"Yes, sir. "

"This is Major Weston."

"Yes, sir."

"How's everything down at the shop?"

"The shop is fine, sir."

"Good."

"Yes, sir."

"No more of those magazine pictures that pissed off the colonel?"

"No, sir."

"Good."

"Yes, sir."

"Um, uh, Lieutenant Hobbes, I'm calling to tell you we have received orders for you. The levy just came in for this month."

Vietnam, I thought.

"It's for Korea."

Shit, Vietnam. "Did you say Vietnam?"

"No, Korea."

"Korea?"

"Yeah, South Korea."

We talked only a little longer.

Know what I found out later? I was the only one of 23 officers from my former training class sent to Korea. It was certainly the last place I expected. Vietnam, of course, the first. And I can't say I hadn't become a little curious about Vietnam. Not enough to volunteer.

I had a week's leave before exiting the States. I took it in Dallas, where Beth had moved after college. At 8 a.m. on Oct. 21, she drove me to the airport and told me how much she'd miss me. But without tears. I pondered that without results on the flight to San Francisco. The terminal there was crowded with people in uniforms. All branches. Multiple destinations.

My flight departure changed and now I had a twelve-hour wait. I hunkered down in a plastic seat and read a book by James Baldwin that I hadn't gotten to before giving up my grad school deferment at LSU. I thought staying in school was wrong after learning one of my college friends had been killed in Vietnam. What right did I have to be safe?

Finally, the Stretch-8 took off for Anchorage, Honolulu, Osaka, and then Kimpo, where I saw the sergeant's yobo. I was talking about yobos, wasn't I?

In Korean slang, and especially in Korean/GI slang, yobo, means a lot of things, I was told, along the lines of friend, but mostly we heard it as something like a girlfriend/boyfriend. It could be the man or the woman, like each calling each other sweetheart, or baby. But I learned fast that when a GI said he had a yobo, the meaning was downgraded, and usually meant a kept woman. Long-term contract. Although even a one-night stand from a bar could be a yobo. And just to complicate it a little more, *yoboseyo* seemed to be some kind of greeting, because I would hear it all the time on phone calls.

I concluded that "yobo" itself, and what it meant, was really a matter of circumstance. It was like a utility infielder. Neither the long- nor

short-term yobos selling sex were whores, exactly. But plenty of GIs
thought so. Whore/yobo, or yobo/whore. That line is called a slash. In
the Army you would say: Whore slash yobo, or yobo slash whore. It
means they are interchangeable/identical.

Like our time in Korea. Waiting out the truce/occupation. Keeping
the peace/war.

3

Spec. 4 Charles Edgar Sansoe, a clerk in what would be my office, and First Lieutenant Howard Scott Travis, on compound "escort greeting" duty, met me after the ride from Kimpo airport. It was a Saturday morning, almost noon. Everyone else was off. Because I was an officer, Travis and Sansoe were to take personalized care of me. They had prepared for the task by drinking coffee and PX bourbon in the 12 x 15-foot room that would be my new home.

"Welcome to the Hermit Kingdom, the Republic of Korea, Land of the Morning Calm, Flower of the Orient and Gateway to Heaven," Sansoe hailed down from the broken screen window as I unloaded my gear from the Jeep that dropped me at the BOQ. It was really an old hospital, a two-story concrete and plaster L-shaped box known as the White Elephant. It had a tar-and-gravel roof known as the Beach. The whole thing was built by the Japanese, who once occupied Korea, and remained forever hated for it. Compared to them, we were knights in shining armor. It wouldn't take me long to learn that was a title we hardly deserved.

I waved to Sansoe and carried my baggage up to the second floor. It was good to see him again. By one of those coincidences, we had also been in the same unit at Fort Wood. There, too, he had been a clerk in my office. He got his orders to Korea two months before I did. "Could have been Nam," I had said at the time. Which is why he said the same to me as we now shook hands.

Although he was an enlisted man, we had become good friends. He had gone to college at Virginia but got drafted in his junior year.

He was a couple of years younger, and although he was from North Carolina, the Southern accent was almost imperceptible. He was also part Spanish, but only about a sixteenth. He'd told me the whole story over beers at a bar back on the post one night. His great-grandfather was from Barcelona, got to America as a teenager during WWI, and changed his name from Carlos Sansolero to Carl Sansoe in New York. He thought it sounded more American, or even Scandinavian, and someone on the boat told him it would be better and would work because of his red hair.

He married a dark-haired German girl, Inga, who also had fled Europe, and they never again shared their origins, fearing deportation. Their two offspring went to New Mexico, and later returned to the East Coast, where Sansoe was born. Nobody along the family tree had ever married any Latin blood again. But the current Sansoe, who every so often when shit-faced called himself "the king of green-eyed Spaniards" and wanted to go down to Mexico if we ever got out of Korea. Maybe learn the language. Wanted me to join him. Maybe live there.

He always seemed out of place in a uniform, and sometimes I thought his only real function should have been to walk on back roads or beaches in the Carolinas, or ditto in Mexico, strumming a guitar and talking quietly to small children and pretty girls. And now he was drunk and swearing, trying to squash a cockroach in the corner behind my metal frame, lumpy mattress bed. It had already been de-bugged and smelled it.

Travis walked in and introduced himself as executive officer of Headquarters and Headquarters Company of the compound's Quartermaster Depot. "That means I make sure all the supply clerks get tucked in at night and write home twice a month," he said. "Sometimes I deal with you fucks in personnel, but we have a different chain of command." He was six feet, thin and graceful, with coal black hair and matching eyes. He said he was from Connecticut, Dartmouth '68. He liked tennis and once worked for Bobby Kennedy, he said in an anxious, rambling way. He thought my name, Thomas Jefferson Hobbes, was funny: "American founder and English sourpuss philosopher

9

combo. Way to cover all the bases." I'd heard variations back at Mizzou plenty of times. Mizzou was where I met Beth my senior year. We had gotten scholarships, but we were both from Texas: Corpus Christi for me, San Antonio for her.

Travis and Sansoe weren't much alike, but close enough, and had bonded from the time Sansoe helped Travis get some paperwork through 8th Army. They helped me unpack fatigues and underwear and itchy socks. I was tired and jet-lagged, but my "escorts" insisted I plunge into my new environment immediately.

"To Korea!" Sansoe said. "You know, Hobbesie, and I can't say this too many times, 'Could've been Nam.'" He passed me the bottle. "Here, this will wake you up."

I gave him the finger and drank the toast.

"All right, newbie, let's go to the ville. We can't let you sit around your room, you'll get instant depression."

I took another swallow. "They didn't tell us that at orientation."

"You can sleep tonight. It's only four now and you've got to get started before it's too late."

Travis pushed my luggage next to an olive drab wardrobe that was the only furniture other than the bed and a desk. "Sansoe's right. You can put all your shit away later. Meanwhile, you're the only officer coming in today. And since we've had to waste a glorious Saturday on you, let's at least go out and raise a little hell. Goddam, it's my actual fucking job to make you welcome."

I took a long breath, hiccupped from the booze. "OK, show me the sights."

*

Outside Gate No. 8 we stood like musketeers in the dirt street, yelling for a kimchi cab, which were the Korean cabs, not the PX. I could see most of the sprawling compound just above the concrete and barbed wire walls that surrounded it. I could smell the brisk if slightly polluted air, hear the clang of rickety bicycles and the blare of outside storefront speakers playing what sounded like a mix of rock, soul, and country. I coughed as an old bus passed by, sputtering blue monoxide fumes from a broken tailpipe.

We got our cab and wound through streets I had never seen or dreamed of. The sightseeing took maybe five minutes and then we pulled up to a concrete brick building with a hanging sign in Korean and English, the latter of which said: Blue Dragon. Inside, we had a few more rounds of cheap bourbon. Ear-breaking Temptations and Jethro Tull blared over the mounted Japanese loudspeakers. At one end of the room, GIs in black silk windbreakers played pool. One wore a jacket with luminescent orange map of Korea on the back and the words "South Korea, 1968-69." Another jacket said: "I'm on my way to Heaven 'cause I've spent my time in Hell." It, too, had a map of Korea, with a big green star at Incheon, which was only a short drive from Suchow, the real name of the ville.

As we made small talk about Korea, mostly things I should look out for, I watched the bartender, a small old man in a white shirt, fill glasses and draw beer. He carefully counted the money turned in by the waitresses in tight pants and blouses. Behind the bar a long mirror was lined at the bottom with shelves of amber and green bottles.

Other girls drifted in and out, playing pool with GIs, talking to them at the cracked tile-topped tables, leaving with them. I thought of Beth. I thought there was virtually no chance she would wait for me to come home.

"Hey, Hobbes, you want to get laid?" Travis asked. "I think I can arrange it."

I had thought about it, getting laid over here. I mean, it was a long flight. And that's what everyone said at Fort Wood. But looking at them now, it was different. They were business girls, whores, fetching enough, but still.

I was looking around, not answering.

He nudged me. "Well?"

"I don't know. I mean I just got here."

Travis laughed. "Takes some getting used to, doesn't it?"

11

Meanwhile, a girl was talking to Sansoe. He was my size, about five-ten, and good-looking. He had a habit of continually brushing a shock of hair from his forehead. The girl was maybe five-two, in a tight blue dress cut low in front, with long, coal-black hair she constantly brushed back, too. They had something in common. Sansoe was ready to leave with her.

Travis noticed and shouted above the music. "Hey, forget that, man. Let's get Hobbes laid. Cherry Hill!"

I said I was tired, but the idea was an immediate hit to them both, like taking your cousin on a snipe hunt.

Sansoe told the girl he'd be back later and slapped me on the shoulder. "You've got to see Cherry Hill, man. It'd be a crime not to take you."

"What's Cherry Hill?"

"Well, it's not an orchard." Travis drained his shot glass. "To Cherry Hill! To the Yellow Peril!"

We were on our way. Another taxi dropped us off out in the countryside at the head of a one-lane dirt road. I had no idea where we were. We staggered along drunk-warm and singing some song from Woodstock about the war. Right away we came to a long, checkered series of rice paddies connected by mud banks and narrow dikes. On the other side of the rice paddies a small group of brown huts up a slight incline huddled in the cold.

"There it is," Sansoe said.

"You mean Cherry Hill?"

"Yeah, that's it." He scrunched his hands into his field jacket.

"That's Cherry Hill?"

"Beautiful, isn't it."

"Shit." I hiccupped as I sized up the walk across the dike. And I was drunk. And it was cold. But the reward was women.

"Come on, Hobbes." Travis in his best New England good cheer. "Nothing to worry about. Just walk along. There's nothing to it. We do it all the time. And Jesus, wait till you see what's over there."

Sansoe was already on the dike path, bobbing along.

"Next," Travis bellowed like a jumpmaster, pushing me along. I was navigating the dike, nasty bourbon my only stabilizer. Twenty feet out, I slipped and while trying to get up lost my balance and was sitting in a rice paddy.

Sansoe and Travis, one in front of me and one in back, were bent over, laughing. A few villagers watched.

"If you could see yourself," Travis said.

"A one-and-a-half with a double-gainer." Sansoe held up both hands to show a seven-fingers rating.

Travis held up eight. "And Hobbes moves into first place in the inaugural annual Korean outdoor rice paddy diving competition. Damn, that's hard to say when you're shit-faced."

I threw them a finger. It was covered in mud. "Assholes." I managed to stand and started to climb the slippery embankment as they walked toward me. "A little help, you fuckers." Sansoe got to me first and I held up my hand.

He reached out.

I pulled him in.

He landed on his butt, scrambling until the final sploosh to avoid it. Then he looked like a melted fudgesicle, too. "God damn it, Hobbes. Try to help and you fuck me over."

We had a mock battle with mud and what may have been fertilizer shit.

Sansoe made a sudden try for Travis's leg.

Travis dodged and stepped back. "Fuck you. Three's a crowd."

Sansoe and I made it up the side of the dike, tried again to grab Travis. Missed. "They think we're crazy," he said, waving at the villagers as he got back on the trail and moved along.

He beat us to the dry clearing at Cherry Hill. We were carrying our shoes, which had been sucked off our feet by the goop.

It was then that the girls attacked us. First only a few, then at least a dozen, pouring from unseen doors, beckoning from iron-barred windows.

"You makee love?" they begged, dragging us down, pulling on our arms, utterly indifferent to our appearance. "You wanna fuckee? You want blow job?" They fought over us, screaming, laughing, pulling us apart, competing for customers.

They hoped to take us inside, clean us, please us. It should have been a fantasy. Every man's dream. Scores of women fighting for him, wanting to take him to bed, to make love to him in any way he wanted. It should have been the great dream. It wasn't.

They peeled us away. I saw Travis go and then Sansoe. I was next. Alone and drunk in a foreign country with girls all around intent on sex. Okay, that doesn't sound terrible. I'm just saying it was beyond what I could have imagined, and not in a good way.

I staggered through a gate with a girl I couldn't see, and we entered a courtyard, then a small room. There was a step up and I tripped over it. Inside, I crawled a few feet to a bed, propped myself up, and asked if she spoke English. I passed out.

Beth? Is it you? You have come now. At last. You'll love me now. It's okay. It's not wrong. Do you love me? Don't you know? Here. Touch me. I love you, Beth . . .

*

I wake up. I'm in a hootch. Naked but clean and shivering under a thick quilt. All my parts are still there. The sliding door opens, and a girl walks in, carrying my clothes, mostly clean and folded. Just a little damp. I smile. Should I say hello?

"Hello."

"*Annyeong-hashimnikka.*" I learn later it is a greeting. She places my trousers and shirt neatly on a chair. It is a Korean girl. I am with a Korean whore.

I look at her slowly. I see her eyes. What does slanted even mean? Her skin is brown, not yellow. Her black hair is long, with bangs framing a grinning, delicate face. This girl is gorgeous. She speaks but I do not understand, nor she me.

She points to herself. "Susie." Smiles. "Susie."

How funny for her to have an American name.

"Hobbes." I reciprocate. "Hobbes."

Then, slowly, as though that will help her understand, I ask, "You speakee English?" She giggles and pulls the covers from me. *"Anyo."* Which means no.

Then she unfastens the buttons on her robe and slips it off. Her body is small, slender. "Susie," she says, sweeping her hand across the view.

I will get laid. A whore. My first whore.

She looks at me, feels me, caresses me. It's cold. I shiver and I touch her, run my hand along her side and stomach. Along her breasts.

I don't want to call her a whore. And I don't know yet anything about what that really means. I don't know, yet, that she is likely to turn twenty-one on Cherry Hill and thirty-five in Seoul or maybe farther down in Daegu, her body converted by the post-war economy into a government issue, aka GI, machine for every drunk American with ten bucks who comes down the Stretch-8 gate, eager to rent happiness. Because it is the right of the soldiers of the occupation. Not that any of the brass will ever say that. They never have. From any war. Any time. Any place.

She kisses me, warm lips. Her only words are, "Let's fuck," spoken softly, the only English love words she knows. She kisses me all over, but I am still drunk and definitely wary, and don't know why yet.

Something is wrong. I can have her. No petting, backseat necking, tortured pleas. Just fucking. Now. Here. She wants me. I can have her. It is here. No convincing. No stubbornly unyielding refusals. No Beth. Just fucking.

She still kisses me, caresses me. I feel the smooth thighs, the soft bottom, pushing against me. I smell her.

"Let's fuck. Fuck Susie, yobo."

I laugh, but it's not funny. Why? What says this is wrong?

"I guess I'm still too drunk, Susie."

She understands. Then she revives me with her lips until something comes out to spurt warm on her breasts. She smiles like women do when that happens. Pity, something, I don't know. She says my friends left her money to call me a cab and she already has.

I dress and give her another ten dollars U.S. I don't have any Korean money. She says no problem.

4

Like Travis, my job was to take care of my clerks, while they took care of the 8th Army. A mother hen for mother hens. The only difference was that my hens were personnel clerks, Travis's were supply clerks, and I was adjutant for a battalion, while Travis was at company level. We weren't in glorious positions, but we were exactly the kinds of links in the chain that no soldiers in their right minds wanted to fuck with. We had their pay, their supplies, and the only records they had that could make or break a career or a posting. I couldn't complain.

When they gave me my ROTC commission as a second louie, they said I should be an infantry officer, that I had what it took. I said, you mean eight quarts of blood? I wanted a desk job. Hell with twelve o'clock high. I wanted five o'clock. That's 1700 in Army time.

Maj. Astor, a training officer, said, "Can you tell me any profession that has more dignity than the combat soldier?" The way he said it, I wasn't supposed to answer, and when I didn't take infantry, he didn't speak to me again. But that was all back in the World.

Sansoe agreed I had bad morale, especially for an officer. We were talking in his wing of the personnel section one morning when nobody else was around. He was doing a morning report, which he hated. So, he was a little edgy. Maybe he also had a hangover. He said that with my attitude, I should've been an EM, an enlisted man. "If you're an officer, you should like the Army. All the EMs think you do anyway."

"Bullshit."

"Not even."

"Give me a reason."

"Officers suck. That's all the reason we need."

"You sound like that goddam Maj. Weston. I guess no one ever stops to think an officer isn't necessarily a company man," I said.

"Nope."

"Well, think about it."

"Why? You didn't have to be a fucking officer, wearing little bars and ordering people around. If you didn't want it, you wouldn't have done it. Shit, at least be consistent."

"It's just easier this way," I said. "You'd have done the same if you hadn't been drafted out of UVA like that. Besides, if I were consistent, I might be in Canada. So would you, you little malcontent."

"At least I'm doing as little as possible."

I picked a file out of his In box. "Oh, glad you finally got this done. Now finish the morning report. Mister Voice of the Enlisted."

"Yes, sir." He might have muttered something else.

But yes, sir, he was right. Bad case of morale here at my end. All kinds of namby-pambyism, inconsistencies, half-commitments, lack of decision. But less pretense.

*

Forty-five young men, a platoon, are in fatigues running down the road. We are at an ROTC training camp learning to be officers. A sergeant who has his last chance at pre-second lieutenant begins a Jody call, an endless rhyming song matching the military double-time cadence of 120 steps per minute. It always starts on the left foot, which is why it is sung, to tell the left from the right.

"Ain't no use in goin' home."

"Ain't no use in goin' home."

"Jody's got your girl and gone."

"Jody's got your girl and gone."

"Sound off."

"One, two."

"Hit it again."

"Three, four."

"One, two, three, four."

"One, two . . . three, four."

We sing it, with other verses, for two miles. It lifts our spirits, makes us a team. We sacrifice while Jody's back fucking our women. We gotta stick together here, forget our problems.

Doc never sings Jodies, just mouths the words to stay out of trouble. On the bayonet course, when we are to scream "Kill" with each slash and vertical butt stroke, I know he says "Kleenex."

Doc is in his early twenties, a few years older than the rest of us. He says the singing is ridiculous. We try to cover for him on that and also because he finds it hard to keep up with the younger guys on PT. We wait for him frequently, his glasses flopping against his thin nose, his steel pot clanging against his scarecrow head.

He had gotten a late start in college back in Kansas, and talked his way into ROTC because he'd heard he could get deferrals for grad school later. And he was about to be drafted. So, he's a kind of oddity in our training cycle, and while friendly enough, he exudes an aura of knowing more than we do about what we are up against.

Doc gets schooled himself in the middle of our training in the hot summer sun of Oklahoma. A battle drill has us running and skirmishing for five miles. Just as we reach a clump of trees and brush and shade, he falls to his knees, then collapses. I'm near him and turn him over, pull off his helmet and start loosening his boots. He looks half-dead and can't talk. I actually slap him on a cheek, so he won't pass out. His face is red, then starts going pale. He is dry as a burned radiator.

"Heat stroke," a cadet says. "That can fuck up your brain." Which we learned in first aid already. A stream is nearby, and we plunge him into it, force-feeding him salt tablets and water from his canteen.

Doc's temperature goes down, and his color changes a little for the better, but he still can't talk. Can barely move. A field ambulance summoned on our PRC-10 radio arrives, spewing up the red dust of the artillery range as it approaches.

We lift Doc into the ambulance and as we do I see him look at me, as if he has something to say but can't. As the medics slide the stretcher into place, he shuts his eyes.

Our training officer, Capt. Clark, will tell us later that Doc was "recycled" by medical to go into a later class, but for the last four weeks we are there, no one sees him. No one hears anything about him.

Our last week, as we're pretty much indoctrinated into the feel of what we're to become in the jungles once we graduate, Capt. Clark drops in during a field exercise about mortars. We're breaking for lunch and latrines in the itchy tall grass. Something is on the captain's mind. He rarely shares his actual feelings. For some reason he does now, maybe because he'll never see us again after next Friday.

"You'll be good officers," he says, getting our attention. "But even with all this training here—you can keep eating—I think there's one more thing I need to teach you. It's not in the field manuals or the schedule." Slight laughter. But not from him.

"Knock it off. This isn't a comedy bar. What this is, is why, to me, the Army is really having you do this here. Now. You're getting a taste of the tactical stuff, for sure, but you'll get a lot more of that, way more intense, before you actually get sent off anywhere. Like Nam." A few shouts from the gung-ho factions.

"Save your cheers for later, too. The thing I want you to absorb, if nothing else, is this. The more shit you can take, the longer you will live. Got it? Remember it."

Some chuckles start up again, but he stares them down quickly. He had been a Ranger in Vietnam. Two tours. He is only 28. His favorite part of training is taking us through the mock Vietnamese village where we supposedly learn to dodge booby traps: Punji sticks, snares, staked pits, swinging dead weights with spikes.

"My point is I want you to be ready. You gotta take shit and give shit. It's how you'll survive." He notices a broken, prickly branch, leans down to pick it up, and slaps his open palm hard, hard, hard until it bleeds. We watch. He's never been like this. He looks at his hand, squeezes the branch harder. "I want you to be animals. Animals."

He throws away the branch and rubs the blood from his palm onto his face. "You'll be fighting animals."

Nobody talks. Nobody moves. Nobody eats.

"So," his voice rising, "are you animals?"

"Fuck yes," in scattered cries.

He stares.

A rumble begins, grows unanimous. Like on the bayonet range except real. "Yess, yesss, yesss."

"What are you?"

"Animals."

"Damn weak ones, eh?"

Louder. "Animals! Animals! ANIMALS!"

The Ranger looks us over one by one. At the time, I didn't know about the "thousand-yard stare," but I'm pretty sure that describes the expression on his face. After a long moment, he salutes, walks over to the company Jeep, and drives off. We don't see him the rest of the day.

At 0500 the next morning we come in from night attack maneuvers. The trucks unload us at camp. Our eyes, ears, noses are caked with red dirt. We are horribly thirsty and have only red water with purification tablets to drink.

The mess sergeant decides milk and cookies will lift our spirits. The cookies are spread on a small table in the mess tent. We stampede, crowding the table, grasping for the chocolate chips, pulling them from each other's hands in the halo glow of the mess hall lantern.

The next morning, I'm sick and don't eat breakfast. In the afternoon we go to the shooting range to practice with our sidearms. Capt. Clark pulls me aside. He says I have promise but I should go to Ranger school so I'll have a better chance of staying alive.

Soon I will be an officer.

5

The compound: Tin barracks and Quonset huts painted green among yellow hills and brown mountains. It was built by the Japanese in WWII, overrun by the North several times during the Korean War, gradually re-taken by the U.S. Army, massively rebuilt to hold huge supply warehouses, various Army units and commands, even an evac hospital. And a processing center. My battalion is the gateway for any GI going in or out of the Hermit Kingdom. Barbed wire fences surround everything. MPs at every gate, keeping Americans in, Koreans out.

The weather: Cold, cold winters. No skiing here, but many mountains with trampled footpaths instead of Swiss T-bars. Humid, pungent summers, with old sweat and new smells, ending with monsoons of sideways rain and after the rains we will look out our windows through layers of steam. Spring and fall are considered the best. Maybe not fall, as I will find out.

The ville: Blocks of mud-brick houses line jagged streets and alleys, forming a kind of town. Except on the main drag, facing the compound, where wood, tin, and concrete storefronts weave a maze forever inward. Tailor shops, record and music stores, various other businesses convenient to the GIs. Also a string of bars and clubs in easy walking distance. The women wait for us there, their conquerors/defenders. Their customers. They grace the dark in alluring ardor and junkie attire as loudspeakers from the bars blare Rolling Stones. "Love, sister, it's just a kiss away, kiss away."

Neon signs advertise Sam's Place, Soul City, Acid Bar, Blue Dragon, Homestead, Hawaii Heaven, and more. The love sisters owe

21

their livelihoods to us, and we fill them with semen and junk, and they trip from back doors to small beds covered with olive drab blankets and the white sheets bought second-hand on the black market, usually from the PX.

Their world, and ours. Whiskey at thirty cents a glass, opium and heroin in cigarette packs, switchblade knives sold by amputees and hustlers in the alley, dice slammed against mud walls, black GIs hanging around together at funk and soul bars, not that the U.S. Army is in any way self-segregated, eyeing white freaks and hijacked hippies in jeans and work shirts and all wondering if they can just hang out and get through the whole thing.

And there's more. Meat hors d'oeuvres, possibly canine, on steaming two-wheeled carts, stolen and always fake Rolex watches lining back-alley arms, stoned soldiers eating Indian corn, old women's faces smiling under shadeless bulbs, and, for those who become lost in the dark alley maze, sewer ditches in which to bleed and drown after the snickety-snack vorpal blade of the eye-patch slicky boy has done its work.

The ROK is considered hardship duty. True enough. But the hardship is on the Koreans.

6

I fell in. Got used to it. Rise each morning, fumble into wool socks, scuffed boots, down to the BOQ second-floor latrine. My daily adventure. Tedious, trivial. It took thousands of us and left nothing but the past. Perhaps a photo album, sterile and aloof. Glossy remembrances from Sammy the Photo-Man with the faded "Press" stick-on patch, who recorded our nights with his battered, ancient Kodak, only 100 won, far better than the Polaroids that other hustlers used. But GIs had the best cameras, via our own technological lechery (Capt. Plato said) with freshly ordered Japanese Nikons and Canons. A surprising number of us strode Korea like Matthew Brady's rendering of the West. Something we could put in scrapbooks and reach for when we became old men in hospital beds, shuddering and ringing the nurse's bell.

I was indignant at Marty, the lieutenant I replaced. He had a yobo, a strong, pretty woman of about thirty. He gave her $140 each month, plus food and occasional splurges on clothes. He shared her one-room hootch and her body. She fed him as he went to her each night. When he was packing his BOQ room to leave Korea, I asked what would happen to Miss Katy. He smiled in a stupid, inane way, and never answered. I wrote to him once, to send some paperwork he'd forgotten to fill out, and told him Katy found a new yobo, but he beat her and robbed her, and she had moved back to her home down near Busan. I asked if I should send her address, if I could find it, but he never wrote back. For some reason I thought he had loved her.

By comparison, I suppose, it could have been worse. At least Miss Katy had her health, and her life, and never burrowed like a mole through the junk tunnels, or lay gasping for air in pointless defeat. Or trudged through the snow like Mr. Jo, the Outside Diesel Man, who brought fuel every night to keep us warm in our barracks and Quonset huts.

I saw him in the ville sometimes, where he slept in a one-room hovel heated by charcoal briquets, a common but dangerous method that frequently killed people from toxic fumes and poor ventilation. Mr. Jo had lost an ear to frostbite years ago. His cast-off fatigues were oil-stained, and his gloves had worn-out fingers until someone, in pity, gave him a new pair that a transit Air Force pilot had left behind. He always grinned.

*

Vast Army. Hunkered on the Land. In it we endure. Pass the time.

Endurance is greatly admired.

Surviving, even more. It is all. Sayeth the survivors. The writers of history.

They say Korea endures. Soldiers come and go, but the Land, the Race, endure. Interim happenings—my life, Kim's life—are trivial in context. That's the deal. All else is but preparation. There will be tomorrows. If not for me, then for the Race, the Land. For Time.

But Korea does not endure, any more than I endure. I survived, true, but I am now lost, my future passed, become the now, reduced to blood visions of a single night which I had not seen then but was to see in the endurance of time. A night that was not a single night but many nights, dependent on those that came and went and were the only truths and measures that endured.

I cannot see how they fit together, all those nights, yet I know they are not separate. And so, they come back to me in components, random visions of what must be, or were, or could have been.

To endure is not enough. I endure, and I am not enough. I will be dead one day. Can I care then if Korea *endures*? If anything does? My time there, all of our times there, however else they might have unraveled, carried us into dark nights and crisp green mornings and returned us damaged goods, tainted meat. Damaging others. But did we affect time? Will the mountains fall? Streams dry? Rice grow? Will the children eat more? Will Kim smile? Women hobble less?

Who will strut and fret? Will we take the Red Tails home, pick up again our knives and forks? Lay down our chopsticks? Say: Hey, mom, pass the fucking salt? Will we laugh at cabbage leaves that will never be kimchi in Safeway? Forget not to piss on the curb? Dare to eat a peach?

I wait for the moment. I snatch the lucidity. I see her. I see Kim. I hold it, the lucidity, and it, her body, her laugh, her frown, and take the only vision left to me in life. As life. As enduring. As not. If only I could see the Buddha, not just the statue in a garden in Seoul surrounded by people with cameras.

Of course, if I could really hold lucidity—and who can, other than the monks in the temples and caves? And they cannot hold it for us, not really, not really share it although they want to, calling it enlightenment. If I could really hold lucidity, enduring would make no difference. I could choose my own time. My own life. My own yobo. And she would not fade away, as in the song.

There is no madness except in metaphor. Where where *where* is the World? All of it happened. As has what is about to happen, that of which I am telling you, and also the one final vision to be formed by the many happenings that preceded what we think we know.

There is no war story to recount afterward but that's been done. What about a love story? That's been done, too. All are the same, even with different players. What hasn't been done? Eyes were ripped from sockets in Greek dramas and amphitheaters. Top that.

So, when I thought that I'd be doing it all new, and that negotiating Korea, military style, was the Great Experience waiting for my challenge, I got a surprise.

With no armies to battle, troops to squander on every side, a distraction was needed for legions of males, ergo moi, who had been taught basically to do one thing. Fight. And only in one way: the Army Way.

So, the distraction we evolved into was but a fable of pleasures. It lets us create wild escapades and dark tales to recant later to friends and strange audiences in whimsical horror.

If the stories seemed too little, or too much, or not enough like the odyssey of combat, people just had to listen goddam harder. So, press your eyes until they streak red. Gaze into the yellow watts of the lamp at your thread-worn chair. Grin until your gums flash dark crimson over the hardening plaque.

Read on, pilgrim.

Endure.

7

I met Kim at the Homestead, a couple months after I'd been in-country. I had gone with Sansoe, Travis, Nick Banyon—a dentist that lived down the hall from me in the BOQ—and Robert Halua, a buck sergeant from our supply room who had been wounded in Vietnam and was finishing his Army time in Korea. Halua had invited us, saying the first three rounds were on him because I had helped him with paperwork to receive the Purple Heart and Bronze Star before he rotated back home. We sometimes called him "Glory Halleluiah." He was 6'3", beanpole thin, and came to us from the hospital at Seoul, where he had been sent for special treatment after a helicopter crash in Quang Tri, South Vietnam.

He grinned broadly most of the time, and said he was an "Arkansas mountain man," but we knew one reason he grinned was because the face muscles had been severed on one side and his right lip was hiked up as if on a string even when he didn't smile. He told us his helicopter had come under heavy ground fire, and when it crashed into the jungle, a metal strut in the rear compartment had slammed against his ear. He had been a door-gunner, strapped in the open chopper bay, cradling a .50-caliber machine gun. Straps let him swing out the door and shoot with wider range.

When the helicopter went down, the two pilots were burned alive because the seatbelts welded shut. Halua was pitched about fifty yards. Three other people, including an intelligence officer who specialized in interrogation, died from the explosion.

Halua said he was lucky to be alive and he wanted to go back. To Vietnam. To finish the job, he would insist. GIs said stuff like that more often than you would expect. But the doctors wouldn't let him. He couldn't hear well, and his eyes sometimes flashed wildly for no reason. And in his right thigh, a steel pin.

Nick said Halua should have been sent home, but when the Army saw he could walk and talk again, and still had four months left, and it looked like he might be the type to re-enlist, it sent him to Korea. He was to convalesce, taking light duty, nowhere near the DMZ.

But when he found he couldn't be a door-gunner again, Halua lost interest in re-upping. He decided to get out. As soon as his Korea bit was over. All things considered, he was lucky, he said. They might've amputated his leg.

He put down a whiskey shot. "Enough of that, lieutenant. How you like this place so far?" He was shouting above "Fraulein" on the Homestead's Sansui tape system. It was a favorite in the ville, especially for the older soldiers.

"Not worth a shit, just like everyone else says," I shouted into his good ear.

"That's what they all say. But lemme tell you something. It ain't all bad. You know, I'm even starting to like the fucking gooks." He poured an OB beer into a small, spotted glass. The waitress, who also worked as a yobo on weekends, had set four bottles in front of him, because she knew how fast they'd be gone.

"They kind of grow on you, you know?" He took a long drink. "And they ain't nobody shooting at you here, neither." He nodded in agreement with himself. "Nobody fucking shooting at you."

"I guess you're right," I said, trying to agree. "I suppose I just haven't been around long enough."

"Shit, yes," he half-shouted. "You'll get to it. You know, I even want to get back over to Nam. Or, fuck, I mean at least I did." He slapped his leg. "You think it's good here, you should be there."

"What?"

"I mean that's where the action is. I mean it's exciting, lieutenant, in spite of getting shot at and all. You ask anybody. You guys are just pissin' in the wind over here."

I looked around Halua's shoulder at the bar, where a small, middle-aged man in civvies shouted energetically at the waitress and poured five drinks from the same bottle for his friends. He looked familiar, although I didn't know him. Maybe a spook or maybe just one of the USAID field guys. The ROK was full of all types of round-eyes.

"I suppose."

Sansoe waived to me that the place was too crowded and pointed to the door and signaled that he and Travis were heading out.

"Fuckers. Probably looking for some other girls," Halua said.

"Too many civilians in here. Not even a table to grab."

"Yeah, might be. What the hell. Got this one to ourselves, eh?

"Works for me."

We sat for a while just looking around and listening to the country music that had replaced the pop and R&B. It was loud.

"You know, you ought to put in for a transfer," Halua said, leaning in so I could hear.

"I have." Raising my voice several decibels.

"No kidding?"

"Sure, I want to go to New Orleans."

His head tilted toward the waitresses. "I mean, you seen one gook, you seen 'em all. Right?"

"It's what they say."

If he was puzzled, it passed, and he clinked his glass to mine. The conversation lulled again. Buck Owens on the sound system.

"So, you been laid by a slant-eye yet?"

I looked down at my drink, suddenly embarrassed, I told him, sort of, about Cherry Hill.

He shrugged. "You just had the wrong girl. You gotta have the right girl. There's no two ways about that," He peeled the label off his bottle. "Hell, one time when I was in Nam, at one of the out-of-the-way bases, me and this little gal got hooked up. She come to my bunker every day and just fucked my poor brains out. Vicky, that was her name." He paused and looked up at the ceiling. Like he was lost for a minute.

"One night there was an artillery barrage about a mile away and we was out fucking under our water tank. We finished up and was just, you know, laying there, and sooner or later she had to piss. Well, hell, I was pretty messed up. We'd been smoking and all, and what'd I do but get behind her and lift her up and hold her legs apart and while she pissed. I squirted her around like a damn fire hose. Funniest thing you ever seen."

We finished another beer, chugging it, as I tried to take in his story. "Know what else?" He wiped foam from his chin and shirt. "About two hours after that, those Charlie fuckers hit the goddam water tank."

He clinked my glass. "How's that for some shit? Anyway, what you need is a good woman. Like that one."

He pointed to a slim, beautiful girl in white bell-bottom trousers snug around her hips. Her loose blue blouse was tied up and knotted just below her breasts. She had just walked in.

"Hey yobo. Over here."

She recognized Halua, smiled erotically and came to our table. Her gait was unconcerned, almost swaggering.

"Hello, yobo," she said, stroking Halua's dark hair. "You buy me drinkee?"

"Well, now I might not, but the lieutenant here might. That right, lieutenant? You buy a drinkee for Miss Kim?"

"A drinkee for the lady," I called out as our waitress passed by.

Miss Kim stared at me with piercing, deep black eyes. I had never seen anyone quite like her.

She sat next to me.

Halua made the introduction. "So, Kim-san, this here soldier is Lieutenant Hobbes. He's kind of a newbie. He needs a good woman. You know any?"

She rubbed her hand over mine. Electric, at least to me. An enchantress, in a grass skirt on our island, alone with me and her coconuts, echoes of hollow drums, volcanoes, Bali Hai, pearls, and blue sea.

Flashing sober, I was piqued at Halua for ID-ing me as an officer. You're not supposed to tell them that, everyone said. It raises the price. Not that it made any difference. I couldn't take my eyes off her.

"What you think, yobo?" she asked me, but laughing and looking at Halua. "I pretty good woman, huh?"

He grinned. "I know you are. He don't. Yet."

She turned her face to me and smiled again in that enchantress way. "Yeah, sure," she said, and kissed me on the cheek. I had never felt lips like that "He gonna find out most skoch." She pushed her chair back and stood up. "I be back. You stay here." She walked away.

"What the hell? Where is she going?"

Halua grinned. "She'll be back, lieutenant. Don't worry. You got it made. She just went to get rid of somebody who thought he was going home with her tonight. She likes you; I can tell."

"Yeah, she does." I grinned triumphantly. "She could have gone with somebody else, couldn't she?"

Halua laughed. "You betcha, lieutenant."

"Goddam pretty slick of me, wasn't it?"

"Slicker 'n owl shit."

We toasted again, this time so hard our glasses cracked. Or maybe they were just worn out.

"Ouch, shit. Cut yourself?"

"Fuck no," he said. Actually, there was a little blood, which he sopped up with a table napkin. "But I wasted a beer. Hey yoboseyo, another round."

"I mean, you know, she's good-looking and all. And I'm her guy? Damn!"

He nodded.

"I mean, I mean I just can't get it. I mean it just doesn't seem like they're whores."

"Who whore?"

It was Kim. She had snuck behind me and hugged me around the neck. She whispered in my ear. "You come home with me already?"

I turned up to kiss her. "What do you think?"

"Come now." I stood and hugged her, like we were close-dancing.

Halua tilted his head back, slumping over his chair. Drunk-dreaming.

"Come on, old buddy." I let Kim go and pulled him upright, and

31

then to his feet. "You brought me to this fucking place, and I'm gonna take you out of it."

Kim and I led him to the door, and we were out in the cold street. He leaned against the building, steadying himself.

I pulled him forward. "Come on, man. Walk. Those damn MPs will be on your ass in a minute."

We helped him across the street. How I was sober enough, I don't know.

Just before he was to pass through the compound gate. Halua stopped, leaned against me. He thought he was whispering. He was as loud as his breath was foul. "I'll tell you, lieutenant, she's it. The best lay you'll ever have in your life. I ain't kidding. I been all over this fuckin' world, seems like, and I've had a lot of women. They ain't none like these, and especially her."

"I hope so." I sagged under his weight.

Kim pulled at my free arm. "He right. I *it!*" She seemed agitated. "The *best*. You hear?"

Halua made a thumbs-up gesture and stood free. "And you know what else?" He shook his head frantically. Instead of what he was going to tell me, he just mumbled, "Shit, what the fuck," and weaved sloppily toward the gate's moth-swarmed lights.

8

Actually, Kim hadn't left the Homestead for a few minutes after Halua introduced us so she could ditch another yobo. Maybe Halua knew and didn't want to tell me. Maybe he didn't know.

What she left for was to sell Time. As in a way to pass it. It didn't take long for her to get it or for someone to buy it. Not just Dope. Time. And Space. And business. Big business. All about Time. Entire weeks could vanish in a trace, a whirl of colors, a memory of sex. It was an alternative to drinking. Juicing was for the lifers, the red-faced light colonels of eighteen years struggling for rank, the twice-busted SFCs, the sergeant majors in their carpeted suites, dreaming of dangerous times, when they would be needed again.

It came as a dividing line. You could tell someone's idea about the Army, about politics, about the war, about life, by whether he or she drank or got high. And it was snobbish, and it was petty. But it was for real. You weren't forgiven if you lined up the wrong way.

Then there were the other levels, like the speed freaks in the DPU, the data processing unit. Going there to get some orders printed, I would see them, gaunt and grinning. Hey there, Lt. Hobbes, they would smile. For all I knew, they really meant what Sansoe said: Fuck you, fuck all officers.

Sansoe's friend, Spec. 5 Thornton, got assigned to the DPU. He came to Korea chubby and gregarious. When he left, he was thin and pale, paranoid. And there was Silas Gordon, the staff sergeant who ran the printing press. Tall, lean, from South Dakota, part Indian, the speed made him a new man.

He got so loose, so confident that one night he forgot to take off his ring and when the clackety-clack shuttle from the press whizzed over the blank paper, it caught the ring and ripped away his third finger and knuckle. Shrieking in horror, he ran to the headquarters Quonset hut, where I was duty officer. The buck sergeant on duty with me, Dubose, helped me put Thornton in the back of the battalion Jeep, which wasn't easy, and get him to the evac. Thornton went into shock. He just "freaked the fuck out," Dubose told the doctor.

They sent Thornton to a special ward in Seoul and later sent him home. The DPU press was down for five hours because no one would pull finger bones and flesh from the machine. Sergeant First Class Sellers, who was NCOIC of the DPU, finally came in early and removed the mess. Col. Samuels busted Sellers to an E-6 for negligence when he learned the story, and I had to fill out a report.

And there were the stone junkies. Opium mostly, or heroin. The same trade that went on in Vietnam was no stranger in Korea. It was hard to tell who they were. Sure, you figured there were a lot in the Acid Bar, some more in Panther Alley. But other places, you never knew. You couldn't tell, until you found yourself in the wrong place and someone you maybe vaguely recognized was hitting you up for money or your watch and sliced you with a razor if you didn't cough up the goods. Or maybe just knocked you to the ground in an alley and disappeared before you could stand up and by morning had probably forgotten or laughed at what they did. Preferably to an officer.

In Washington, they got concerned at all the crimes, and especially the crimes with racial motives. In Washington, even with a war decidedly racist against the people of Vietnam to worry about, and with plenty of racism in our own ranks, the pols and the Pentagon still had plenty of time to wonder how law-breaking could be happening in Korea as well. I mean, fuck. They really approached things that way.

So, the answer was to just crack down on the GIs, never mind the context, like race riots in mess halls, fights out in the clubs, shout-fests over at the PX and in the barracks. Court-martials and stockades could straighten all that shit right out. And what better way to catch the addicts and stoners (rarely the boozers) and the malcontents than through drug testing.

Everyone was surprised when Maj. Will Barton, the well-liked battalion XO to Col. Samuels, got caught after he forgot some opium mixed in with hash cigarettes at out-processing shortly after I arrived. They let him go with an alibi, but it meant he'd never make lieutenant colonel because word would still get around. Enlisted men were rarely that lucky and the testing went on. None of it solved the drug trafficking let alone the internal race war, here or in Vietnam. Nor maybe anywhere in the military in those days.

I bring this up because the first night with Kim, we smoked her opium. I didn't really like it, or more accurately I didn't like how it just zoned me out. Kim didn't go for it that often herself, but knew it was good for business to do a little sampling, to get buyers to trust her. And there were times when it passed the dark hours after curfew.

It took me a while to realize that, at least at first, she saw me as a possible addict, a customer, a steady source of income. Coletti, a black-market captain I'd heard of but not yet met, and for whom Kim secretly (at least to me) worked, told me later I shouldn't have been so naive.

It just never occurred to me. I was blessed with finding this international angel, also one who wanted to fuck me whenever and wherever and get me anything I wanted. All I had to do was stay with her and pay the bills. Like Marty, the lieutenant I had replaced, had done. Which was not difficult. At least at first. And so what? I wasn't in the World anymore.

9

The colder cold came quickly. Buttoning my field jacket, I wondered how they'd done it in those years twenty years ago. How they'd trudged through the snow, up the numbered hills, in their *Life* photo faces, bleak and hollow from fear of death. Just to establish another ridge line that wouldn't last and kick a frozen enemy corpse. Larger ideals or rationales no longer had any meaning. Same-same now, in the jungles not so far away. And in residue you could still feel here. Nowhere in this part of Korea was their land—including the compound where I stood—that had not been taken, lost, taken, lost so many times that it was drenched in blood and suffering. The Land of the Morning Calm was now home to the souls of millions of dead, counting both halves of the country, and almost no truth about what really happened.

Sansoe and Travis and I went looking for quilts to keep the cold off at night when the diesel heaters died and the Outside Diesel Man didn't come. We wanted the thick, nylon ones in orange or yellow with dragons and flowers. The kind we had seen on beds in the enlisted hootches, snug among the stereo sets and *Easy Rider* posters and more bikini babes than I could identify. And locked drawers filled with dope. Or hanging outside shops in the ville.

We took a kimchi cab from Gate No. 8 to Bupyeong, which I was told went by variety of names and boundaries, including Bupyeong-gu and Bupyeong-dong, the funny version, but only the Koreans knew the difference and GIs just simplified it to Bupyeong. It was a suburb of sorts to Seoul, and the closest actual Korean city to the compound. As for GIs and camp followers, there was Suchow, but mostly its zone of sin, the ville.

Bupyeong was where you went for real things that normal people would want. Usually to the town circle at one end of the long main street. The circle was next to the railway station, where trains connected to Seoul for less than $1 U.S. or MPC (Military Payment Certificate). Along the main street area were long stretches of small shops. Even more shops were behind that, on the north side. A maze of streets, including an open-air market of dirt alleys and canvas-topped carts, lumped together like the land-locked river flotillas of Indochina.

We started on the main street, walking and gawking. Of course, we had our cameras. The sky was clear and the temperature relatively mild, and if we kept our fatigue jackets snapped and zipped we were plenty warm. Some of the people were only wearing sweaters or long-sleeved shirts.

We passed store windows with Korean words, and some English, vivid in red and blue. At one corner, businessmen and laborers clustered around tables in a café, eating dishes we had never seen, smells we had never sensed.

Across the street a movie house strutted against the skyline with its marquee of Korean films, beckoning customers with re-touched color posters of sex, tae-kwon-do fighting, villains and heroines with torn skirts and blouses, violence, and mayhem. School children stopped to look and walked on. Tailors selling suits stood in their doorways, calling to us. Come inside, they said, good deals.

GIs bought a lot of clothes they'd never be able to afford back home. Cut from Korean cloth to the styles of last year's *Gentleman's Quarterly*. Ever so dapper, even special underwear patterned by *Esquire*. In the bigger clothing stores, salesmen often gave us condescending looks if we came in wearing the wrong tie or cheap shoes or a Madras shirt that did not bleed. Bleed meant fade. You bought shirts that faded and jeans that shrank. It reminded me of fashion trends back home.

We walked on. Bicycles clanged by. Old men shuffled along in papa-san suits or sat in doorways playing Go. Leather-faced workers squatted under A-frames. Children with books tied on their backs ran past, maybe to school.

We still looked for quilts and turned back onto the main street until we saw some. They were $30. Travis insisted we could find them for $20. Just to prove him wrong, we looked, turning one corner, then another, deeper into the market maze, absorbed in the gleaming metal pots and iron stoves, tinware, copper, rugs, twelve-foot stacks of wicker baskets, knife-grinders, menders, fixers, clothing hung on wires across the narrow streets, so you pushed them aside or bought them.

*

A half-hour later we are at another open-air market and totally lost.

Forget the quilts, we have discovered a photographer's paradise. Yellow afternoon sun filters through gray clouds in swatches. Canvas tops yawn over a seafood bounty on land. Sweating fish, row on row, glistening with mucous, sticky to the touch, cold and dead. On bamboo poles over the carts hang strings of dried seaweed, shriveled and tough. Water buckets of squid are underneath.

Old women sit behind the carts, yelling, cursing, selling. What are they saying? They wear green and black dresses and jackets, always moving, talking, hands reaching for this, that. Every eye marked by crow's feet of age and exhaustion. But it is a kind of beauty.

They look at us, GIs in their world. We take pictures. Snap. Exposure f/11 at 1/60. Enlarge to 11x14 print. Look, almost no grain. It will hang well in the den, years from now. Friends will ask about it.

I use a roll and replace it, opening the Canon in the shade of my body. A child watches, looks nervously at the inner works, the sprockets, shutter, winding spool. I see him and when I am finished, before he knows it, I have his picture, too. He stares and says nothing. My fingers are getting cold.

Around us are smiling teeth, eyes that really don't slant, allegedly yellow skin. I frequently ask why these people are called yellow. Never an answer that makes sense.

They know we're lost, these old women. We hurry about, getting our last shots, laughing to tell ourselves we'll find a way out soon. But we remain bewildered. Here is the food we do not eat, the people we do not see in the ville, the people whose life is the ocean, not the Army.

Travis says he is sick. But mostly he is lost. It is a terrible feeling, really. Where is the air that doesn't smell of fish and salt? The surface from this strange new depth? I want to scream at them all, the ones around me, hit them all, push their fucking fish to the ground and them with it. I really am in a day-nightmare: in a closet, four years old. Someone has locked me in and says, "come out, come out, your mother is dead." I can't. The door does not open. Push, push. Let me out. Let me out. I push and cry and then someone opens the door and laughs and thinks it is very funny that I'm crying and afraid.

We walk faster, trying to reckon our direction in the encroaching dusk and chill. I almost bump into an old woman sitting on a crate at a cart in front of me. She holds a long, silvery carp by its gills and runs her knife along its stomach. The entrails pour into a bucket through her red, raw fingers. She laughs as we watch.

Come closer, she motions. I do.

Give me your hand, I know she is saying. I do.

Her eyes look into mine. She puts the entrails in my hand and squeezes.

Then she laughs. And everyone around laughs. And I stand with cold fish guts in my hand. She holds me with her eyes and her hand, even colder than mine. I stare and try to smile and look quickly to the side at Sansoe and Travis. Unable to speak or even knowing what to say, I pull my hand away, dropping the entrails to the ground. I have nothing to wipe my hands on and use my pants. Now everyone around us is laughing.

It's funny, kind of, but I walk quickly out of the alley. Travis and Sansoe say we should get out of here no matter what. Travis says to follow him, and we hurry through piles of dried salmon, rows of squid, shells and scales of all kinds and fly-covered fish heads. And people and their carts. We never get the quilts, but nobody cares.

At last, we come to the small river at the edge of the market and the town. Across the river are open fields. I climb down a small bank cleared of brush and wash my hands in the cold, muddy water.

Travis says the river will lead us back near the train station. It does. Sansoe flags a cab to take us to Gate 7. In the cab, the driver, who speaks some English, puts his fingers on his nose. "P.U. chingu, you smellee number 10. You maybe get stinko and go to fish market?" He cracks his window.

I slump back, wiping my hand on the cab seat. "Yeah, fuck you, too, chingu."

Sansoe and Travis laugh.

The driver laughs.

I just roll my own window half-down. I might be smiling. Might not. Nobody says anything else the whole way home.

I am now calling it home.

10

Korean women. Ugly. They said. Flat cheeks and broad nose. Slant eyes. No tits. Small, yellow. No blue eyes. Ugly. Is what they said. The round-eyes said. The men, yes, because they are pigs, and it was necessary to de-humanize them in order to buy them like animals or used cars. But the round-eye women, too. The nurses, donut dollies, officers' wives, hot and young and chic. It wasn't hard to sense—the smirks, cat-glances. How they walked through the ville. If they went to the ville.

But I saw Miss Kim. Smooth, olive brown skin, peaches, cream. Stunning cheekbones, large, coal-black eyes. Mysterious and beckoning. Thin, fine nose, pouting mouth that whispered softness like morning dew on a ripe peach. Heavenly body, small waist, hips. The most beautiful woman I had ever seen, I thought then and do still. And she was on sale, every night, having sex with strangers at twenty-three while girls back home held hands at *The Graduate* and wore pom-poms at homecoming.

I say this, describe comparative anatomy, because I grew tired and angry at the put-downs and lies. As for Kim, queen of them all, she didn't care. Caring had stopped many years ago. She knew what was what.

She became my yobo. For $150 U.S. a month. Meals, a hootch for two on the far side of Suchow, and her. A good price for an officer.

"Why are you doing this?" Sansoe asked me at the happy hour bar. "Lots of amazing chicks here in the ville. Like a parade. Why get tied to one like you were married or something?"

"Well, for one thing, it's a good way to keep from getting the clap. Just fucking the same person you know you'll be safe."

"For a hundred-fifty a month you could use a rubber."

"Yeah, but even so, look at it this way. If I got different yobos all the time, it would be ten dollars U.S. a night, right? I could only fuck fifteen times all month for a hundred-fifty, where this way I can fuck any time I want. Like a bulk rate. Plus, you know, it's cold and I don't have to roam around so much. She said she would be my winter yobo, but with a renewal option for the rest of my tour. It's a good deal."

"She said that? That way?"

"Yep."

"Okay, she's smart. But to live with a chick, man, that's something. No matter where you are. Whether she's a yobo or not."

"I'm not living with her. I just go see her at night."

"Every night."

"Not every night."

"Damn near."

"But not every night."

"But damn near."

"A lot of guys do it."

"Do you love her?"

"What?"

"Are you in love with her?"

"Don't be stupid."

"It's not stupid. Would you live with a chick back in the World you didn't love?"

"I never lived with anybody back in the World."

"But would you?"

"That's ridiculous."

"Just answer. Would you?"

"Probably not."

"But you can here."

"Yeah."

"How?"

"What do you mean, how?"

"Just 'how'?"

"I just do it. Look, she's just a yobo. I mean, sure, I like her and she's beautiful and fun, and way smarter than I would have guessed, but that's all. I mean it's just a convenience, that's all it is."

"You don't love her? No shit?"

"Of course not."

"Liar. Not even a good one. Especially for a louie."

"Fuck you."

"Uh huh."

I was sure of it. I didn't love her. Sansoe was wrong.

We changed the subject.

11

So, I didn't know why I did it. Bought a yobo. I only knew things to tell people when they asked. I didn't know why Kim did it, either.

"Why do you do this?" I asked as we lay stoned in a hootch, much bigger and nicer than ours, that Nick rented in Bupyeong for his yobo.

Kim said nothing, just slipped her hand into my pants. She could have said: I do it to support my family. She could have said it simply, without seeking pity. It would have meant she did what she did because she had to, not because she wanted to. Probably any yobo in Korea could have said that, or something like it.

"I mean, really, does it bother you?"

"What bother me?" I remember that smile. It is part of the preferred vision, not the real one, that will never go away.

I looked at her, not wanting to actually say it. But I did.

"This." I gestured around the opium-filled room. "You know, all this. I mean, wouldn't you rather do something else if you could?"

She put my hand on her hip and rubbed it. "I like this."

"No, Kim, I'm serious. Wouldn't you like something different for yourself?"

She stopped rubbing and tilted her head to me, shaking the long hair out of her eyes. "I like this. I told you already. What you want?"

"Why don't you just give her a fucking CARE package?" Nick interrupted. I'd almost forgotten we were in his hootch. He was from New York, an NYU Wonder Dentist, egg cream and all. He could be hilarious, hitting the point in that Manhattan way. Or he could grate like a bad file. But he was there when you needed him, and he weathered well. I missed him later. If he was rough, he also smiled a lot. I could see now he was stone fucked-up.

"What the hell kind of shit are you laying on her, Hobbes? What, do you want to save her? What a load of shit question to ask—whether she wants to do something else. Jesus Christ."

Nick delighted in attacking what he called my "lack of total perception." Later, especially after I agreed to help his midnight dental clinic, he would say that I had learned a lot, that I was coming along.

I rolled to one elbow. He was holding his yobo, Marilyn, because guess who she resembled when she dyed her hair. They were sharing an opium joint Kim had brought.

"Hey, I'm only asking. I mean haven't you ever wondered? Doesn't this stuff bother you or anything?"

He exhaled a cloud of smoke through his sandy-colored mustache and leaned back against the lone wicker chair. He clucked his tongue and shook his head, like a smug professor. "A lot of things bother me." He took another hit. "For that matter, damn near everything does at one time or another. Especially crabs and the clap. But that's not the point, is it?"

"What do you mean?"

"I mean the point is that it's still not your business."

"Maybe I care about her and want it to be my business."

"Oh, you care about her? Bullshit."

"What's that supposed to mean?"

"It means your question isn't for her, it's for you. You want her to say something so you won't feel guilty about fucking her."

Kim was looking at Marilyn.

"What's the bullshit," Nick said, "is that you're going to fuck her no matter what she says, just like I do this one." He looked at her. She rolled her eyes at Kim. "And you'll do it because you like to fuck Kim as much as you like to feel guilty. You can't turn it down, man."

"You're fucked up," I said. Kim was pretending not to listen. Or maybe actually wasn't.

"And most of all you can't stand it that you're just like every greasy slob redneck lifer who's been here the last twenty years. You want her to say she doesn't want to be a whore, so you won't have to face what you are, paying her like you do and screwing her for a few months and then leaving her ass high and dry when you go back to your homecoming sweetheart. Or what-the-fuck-ever."

I was getting too pissed off to talk about it. Kim shook her head at Marilyn, then gave my face the once-over. Especially my eyes. I tried the same with hers. I couldn't see anything I could understand. She tickled me under the chin like I was a kid. "Come on, yobo, you no worry about talkee, OK?"

I kissed her. Everyone was quiet. Zoning on the shit.

Then, feeling calmer, I told Nick, "I mean, it just bothers me that she's so perfect, and smart as hell, and is doing this. If it's being an asshole to let that bother me, I guess I am. If it's just for money, I mean, maybe we could help her. I mean me. I could help her, is all I'm saying."

He sighed. "That's still shit talk. What the fuck are you going to do for her? Marry her? Is that it? Sweep her away to the World to be Mrs. Thomas Jefferson Hobbes? Is that it?" The irritation in his voice was obvious. "Because that's the only thing you can do, you dumb asshole."

Marilyn tried to distract him. He smiled, touched her cheek, but then got back to it.

"And Our Miss Kim knows it as well as you. You're just a new kid on the block, goddam it, and she doesn't want to talk about it. And hates that you keep bringing it up. Do you fucking blame her? Christ, Hobbes, wise up."

He took another hit. He did that sometimes, went on dope binges, drinking and smoking all weekend. He said it cleared him out. Other times, he talked of his ex-wife and of starting his practice, maybe in Vermont.

He passed me a joint. I stared at the glowing end, then trapped the sticky smoke in my lungs. I blew a heavy cloud and looked at Dr. Nick Banyon, Army captain and pride of his mom.

"Sometimes it depresses me. Doesn't it depress you?"

"You're a dumb asshole. Like I said."

Marilyn kissed him for a long time. We all relaxed, dreaming our stoned dreams. No idea what they dreamed, Kim and Marilyn, but they did swap a long look at each other impossible to translate into American GI. It made me feel sad and stupid.

After a few minutes, I said, "But I still don't see why she has to do it. A yobo."

Nick leaned forward, Marilyn put a finger to his lips, and he slouched back. He chuckled, or some sound like that. "Hell, if I know." He faked a smile, waved his arm lazily as if to wipe away the conversation. "Maybe she just likes to fuck. And make money. And goddam, it's not like the girls back home don't come with a price. All the shit we buy to impress them, take them out, tie them to us. Shit, you can spend more on a Saturday night date in the World than you would for a week of a yobo. And don't even get me started on the fucking money deal between husbands and wives." He glanced at Kim. "Am I right?"

She did her jungle-cat smile. Looking at Nick, then at me. Winking, I'm pretty sure, at Marilyn. "Maybe Nicky right. And you pretty dumb spend all that money at home just to fuck some round-eye. And now you got me. Better, huh? So maybe I be yobo for you, Mister lieuten-tant-san, because I just like fuck."

Nick and Marilyn laughed.

"Also, I like to have a job. You know? Money, right?"

She looked at me in a way that was overpowering. Possibly a tint of resignation that maybe only I could see. I adored her. Even if I was a walking wallet. And I think there was something else. I know there was. Maybe that was the catch-22. I had read Heller.

12

One frigid night a DPU speed freak dragged all the empty beds in barracks 3728 into the street and set them on fire. No one knew about it until the flames were spotted about 2 a.m. It was lucky the whole place didn't go up. When we learned who did it, PFC Williams, the colonel had him court-martialed, and then sent to a stockade.

But that's how I formally met Coletti. I had to requisition new beds for the barracks and that meant going through Capt. Patrick Coletti, a procurement officer for the supply depot. That was the same outfit Travis was assigned to, so I got Travis to call him and arrange a meeting.

Coletti was the kind of cog in the Army machine that if you needed something, people would wave you off and say, "You gotta go through Coletti for that." He had a blustery, cocky-confident Chicago way. He was Irish and Italian, with a red mustache and black hair. He was only a captain, true, but he was smart like a master sergeant. He knew all the angles.

Most of all, as I came to find out, he had his deals. Deals with pimps, slicky boys, gamblers, black market hustlers. Deals with yobos, with GIs. With pretty much anybody who had a need that a quartermaster finagler could deliver.

At the colonel's table in the officer's club, they said he had more deals than he really did. But they were wrong. Commanders and MPs sometimes tried to catch him, but he had deals for that, too. Word was he would be getting a promotion to major if he'd re-up.

And he had a deal with me. "Sure, we got lots of beds in the old warehouse, me bucko," he assured me, sitting at his desk, propping his feet on a supply book, drinking coffee from a mug that said, "Mayor." He called everyone "me bucko."

"But look here, think of it this way. I got beds, and I'll be happy to get them for you. Nice rusty mustache you got there. Although mine's better. I'll be happy to get 'em."

"Good, thanks."

"But there's one thing, dashing young lieutenant. Hobbes, isn't it? Travis told me about you. Anyway, Hobbes, maybe you can help me, too, you being in the personnel battalion and all."

"Uh, sure. What is it you need?" I could envision a 45-day leave, TDY to Tokyo, an early out, baggage allowance for 5,000 pounds. Personnel favors came in all kinds of flavors. It dawned on me that Coletti and I were kind of in the same business.

"Well . . ." He looked at me like we were old pals. "What I'd like is I would like an extension to stay here two more years."

I thought he was joking.

"Right. How about five? Great place, isn't it?"

"I'm serious. That's what I need. Two more years."

He sipped coffee and tried to read my face. Which probably looked awkward.

"Well, sure, okay. Just come by my office some day and we'll fill out the forms and I'll see that they go to the right people." He kept staring at me. I asked again. "You really want an extension?"

"That's right, me bucko." Finally, his mask-face dissolved, and he winked. "You truly think it's pretty odd, don't you?"

"Sort of."

He took his feet off the desk and leaned towards me. "Come here. I'll tell you a secret." I leaned in, too. *This guy is crazy*, I thought. *Definitely crazy.*

"I've uh, sort of taken root here, me bucko. I've been having dreams about it. They say not to leave. Dark, horrible dreams, me bucko, and I break out in sweats at 4 a.m. I get this warning. This terrible warning. Know what it is?"

"What?"

"The warning says if I leave, I'll become a fucking Kinney shoe salesman in Terre Haute."

His eyes, dark, granite-hard, did not betray him. But then his mustache twitched, and he rocked back with a con man's laugh.

"Shit. I fucking believed you."

"You're okay, Hobbes, for a kid. Listen, you want those beds today or can I wait 'til tomorrow?"

"Tomorrow will be fine."

"Come see me sometime out in the ville. The Homestead. I'm usually there. Or the Blue Dragon. My home away from home. Hell, you can find me just about anywhere, come to think of it."

I began to see him often.

I don't think Coletti was using me, not even back then. I was someone who would listen to him, and he never called Kim a whore.

I can still remember when we were friends. Some of his "supply trips." The time he was in Seoul with pneumonia. How those memories stay, I don't know. But they're there. Small, sacred units of time, insulated from the Fear. Joking about the barracks beds, and the other times he did a deal for me, and how I got him his two years.

I don't always see in my memories what erupted in the later times, sweating and weaving before his burning eyes, toying with the scream in my blood-caked mind.

13

Sometimes we pretended not to be in the Army. The dope might be bad, or you might wake up in the morning with the shakes, and hold yourself near the line, the junkie line. The crazy boredom but what can you do about it? You could hold back. Where there's a will, dig it? Or we could play fuck-around-with-the-locals. In the mornings, when I came across the mama-sans piling dirty clothes on the washing machine and scrubbing them by hand instead, I said, look, plug it in. They always laughed and kept slapping and pounding them on the stone floor, drinking tea and gossiping. Lieutenant Maytag, one of them named me. They could play fuck-around, too.

Once a month we put on our $30 civilian suits and went to Seoul. So, we booked a PX cab, a 1962 Chevrolet, instead of the usual kimchi. It cost more, but there was more room. Sansoe, Travis and I all sat in the back, drinking Sansoe's martinis, which we called Santinis, mixed in a canteen. The driver kept an eye on us in front through the rearview mirror. GIs did not always behave on such trips.

We were not in the Army then. Our hair was short, our mustaches trimmed at lip's edge, but our clothing was beige or blue or anything but olive drab. Our shirts were never khaki nor our ties black. We still couldn't wear jeans, which were banned under the off-post dress code.

We leaned against the broad back seat of the cab and pretended not to chug the Santinis, but to savor them. Which was a joke since they were awful. But effective. We looked out at the slums of Bupyeong and outskirts of Seoul as we passed, at the children on the crumbling curbs, at the tattered men groaning under ox-cart loads. We were buzzed and smug. Poor devils. Wretches. We should have been drinking gin and tonics instead of martinis. Wasn't that the way of the Brits in the Raj? Part of Kipling's burden to sort out? I won't say this was our mindset, but it was our drunkset just to show off like we were some kind of deranged tourists.

"To the Korea Club," Travis told the driver. "And don't spare the horses. Hey, chingu, want a drink?"

The driver laughed under his short-billed cap and checked us in the mirror. "Anyo. I no can be stinko while on duty."

"Then turn your meter off," Sansoe said. "And have a drink with us. We're just fucking around. Bet you'd like to as well."

"Sure," I added. "We won't tell anyone."

"Ha, ha," he laughed in a high-pitched nervous way. "No can do, GI. Then I be take you Seoul for free." He said it: flee. We always thought the "L" and "R" thing was funny. While we mangled every possible word in the Korean language.

The rice fields and coastal hills zipped past the windows. "Hell, we don't mind a freebie," Sansoe said. "Really."

"Oh, shit no," I said. "We could make a deal. You don't tell anyone we rode for free."

I started on my third Santini, but Sansoe botched the pour. "Fuck, you missed." I adjusted my cup. "And look, there's an olive stuck in the back seat. Jesus, they'll think we were going to a Triple Fucking A meeting."

"Tell him," Travis elbowed me. "Tell him why he has to keep quiet."

"What? Oh, yeah. Listen, chingu, you can't tell anyone you drove up here for free or you'll get in trouble. And in return, we won't tell anyone you got stinko with GIs. What do you say?"

He was looking into the mirror more than at the road now, which was bad because we had crossed the Han River bridge and were nearly in downtown Seoul.

"But I no stinko. I just told you."

"Right. And we won't tell anyone you were."

"But I no stinko!"

"Right," Sansoe said. "You're not stinko and so we don't have to tell on you."

"What you mean, tell on me?"

"You know, about being stinko."

"But I no stinko, goddammit."

"Exactly," Travis said. "But only we know that."

Soon we were on a narrow street outside the Korea Club, just a few blocks from South Gate, Imperial Treasure No. 2 or 3, or whatever. The driver stopped in the drop-off circle. Travis patted him on the shoulder as we swallowed the last of the drinks.

"And believe me," Travis said, "as far as anyone knows, you never touched a drop the whole fucking trip. Not a drop. Right, Hobbes?"

"Absolutely."

"Not a drop," Sansoe said.

The driver turned to look at all three of us. Expression somewhere between pain and anger.

"Won't tell a soul," we all whispered in unison.

"But I no stinko. I no drink. Stop saying this."

We got out of the cab. The meter was in won and MPC and said $5.10 in the latter. Travis handed the driver an MPC fiver. "Mum's the word, chingu. We won't tell a soul." He leaned in toward the window. "But listen. You gotta promise not to say you took us for free or we'll all be in trouble. Okay? Keep the change."

The driver crumpled the MPC in his fist. He looked at the meter and he looked at us.

"You bullshit me too much, you know? Not funny now."

Sansoe stiffened indignantly. "Well fuck you. I'm going to get a cop. We'll see if you double-cross us."

"Ungrateful bastard," I laughed.

"Heathen," Travis said.

Sansoe concealed his thermos under his jacket and headed toward the Club entry.

The driver watched, looked us over again, then the $5.10 on the meter, and said something in Korean. Just as he was about to finger us, I pulled a $5 U.S. bill from my pocket and gave it to him.

He took the money but looked at me like he'd had enough of

Americans for forever, although he knew he hadn't. "You no fun, you know?" He peeled off. Now I felt like shit. Definitely gone too far, even if I did pay him.

We went into the club, dark, traditional, and full as usual for the weekend. We followed the reception boss to our table. She knew we'd been drinking but didn't care. Pretty much everyone in the room had been doing the same. On the way, we passed a table with Eileen Rush, the wife of a West Point colonel. You weren't supposed to bring wives or families to Korea, being a hardship post. Some people did, though. It helped to be a senior officer. But we were glad, in this case. Her brunette and golden-highlighted hair and honey breasts were fairly easy to see. As we were seating ourselves and ordering drinks, we moaned and fake-fantasized as if she were a pin-up goddess.

It was easy to see that she thought we were asses, which was true, and thus gave us the consequent stare. Like her other GI fans, we thought that the real reason she was over here was that the colonel knew if he left her back in the World, she wouldn't be his wife for long. Which kind of made me think about Beth. Which probably everybody in-country with a girlfriend or wife back home also thought about at the slightest prompt. Or one tardy letter. Or one strange reference to a "new friend."

"Fuck her," Travis said. "Can't take a fucking joke."

We had stopped toying with her, rather than risk a colonel's wrath, but she was a trophy wife. Up to a point, he liked it that she drew attention. We were close to that point, but reined ourselves in. Mostly because the club manager came to our table. Not about the goddess, but because a cab driver out front had called the MPs and claimed he had been harassed by some drunk GIs. Very bad for the club, the manager said. He assumed it was us. We denied it and the manager let it go.

Just after we placed our orders, a young MP, who actually seemed stoned, showed up. He came to our table and picked on Travis, maybe because he looked more like an officer than I did. The MP sat at an empty chair to seem less intrusive and explained the problem. Community relations kind of thing. He said it wasn't anything important if we wanted to leave ten bucks for the driver to pick up as amends, it would all go away. He said we could finish our meal if we just behaved.

Nick started to object, but Sansoe and I gave an OK signal and said we'd split the bribe. Travis gave the MP $10 U.S.; Sansoe and I dropped five MPC each. We toasted the driver in absence since we were drunk anyway and had to give the guy credit. Of course, he'd never give us a ride again, but no matter. On his way out, the MP gave a good look to Eileen, which probably made his drop-in worth it, or miserable, depending on his girlfriend situation. Over our steaks, we speculated if the MP had kept some of the bribe for himself.

For the trip back to the compound, we nabbed a kimchi cab since there were no PX rides around. I gave the driver ten MPC without trying to bargain. Before I fell asleep in the passenger seat, I kept thinking about what kinds of ugly Americans we had been with the first taxi driver. Especially Travis. He was supposed to be a little more refined, or at least thoughtful and progressive, than the rest of us.

Was it out of boredom, frustration, resentment at having to be here in the first place? Whatever, it was wrong and was making me feel like a total asshole. Which probably applied to a lot of what my life was becoming.

My dream in the taxi was about naked older women washing our clothes in a dazzling snow-covered creek in the mountains, and how they all froze into statues.

14

I needed a woman, *the woman*. Perfect, ideal. I met her once. Before I could know her. In the womb, the doctor says, you knew perfection there and your first word, your template, was "mommy." But there was more to it. There had to be. There was a time when I thought the perfect woman was Beth.

"I can hardly wait to be with you," I had written to her while stretching on the green wool blanket on my bed in the BOQ. "I put your pictures on a shelf, so I see you just before I go to sleep each night."

Beth didn't cry the morning I left Dallas, but she did a few nights before that, tiptoeing in her nightgown, holding me, promising to love me forever. Whispering with her kisses. I don't want you to go, I don't want you to go.

And me, not crying. Being stoic. My role. I had to. Not cry. I had to. I belonged to the Army now. Two years minimum. In exchange for being an American. In exchange for a duty. I had to be gone. From those I knew. From the World. The young man's obligation.

Mrs. Parker from tenth grade said we were lucky to be Americans and had to fight for our way of life. What is our way of life? Peace, she said, and honor. Peace and honor. But the time would come when I would witness a night in Washington, cold and rainy, candles in the rain, people in the streets. I would know that the president, for whom I did not vote, who had no honor, would ignore the candles and the people in the rain and watch football in the White House.

But I would go to Korea. Or anywhere I was sent. I would go. I was not strong enough not to. And there was this: I wanted to see it.

Yet there was no roar here, no war roar. Tigers with nothing to snarl about. I would manifest absurdity these two years, taking and giving orders. Because I had to, because I wanted to. Maybe that formula is what made us what we became here.

We were soldiers. Trained, or selected, to move forward, explore, challenge. To be aggressive. Enough to kill. There was none of that killin' here, as in Vietnam, but when that is over there will be other places. So, we channeled all that into what was around us. Other people, cultures, ways of living. We stirred up trouble because it gave us something to do, to figure out.

I know why Beth didn't cry. Maybe the women got it worse. Maybe they are the realists.

I wrote: "I haven't heard from you in three weeks now. It's only been four months since I left. I know you're probably busy, but I really wish you could write more often. It makes me feel good to hear from you."

I guess I was thinking of this because Specialist Alvarez was in my office. Again. Again. Sansoe knew him slightly and had sent him to me because he didn't know what else to do. Alvarez wanted a mid-tour emergency leave. He said his wife was going to leave him and she was running around with other men. Alvarez was 19. Lucy, his wife, was 18. They had been married a year when he got shipped to Korea.

"Lieutenant, you just gotta get me a leave. Tell the old man what's happening. Means nothing to nobody. She's leaving me. Don't that matter? The Army is just fucking up my life. I'm going home if I gotta go AWOL to do it."

It was a conversation Alvarez had had with me a half-dozen times in the last three weeks. He would sit in the folding chair by my desk, slump down with his cap in his hands, and tell me of Lucy and her passion and his loneliness and jealousy. I always listened. I was an officer.

"Come on, Alvarez. It'll be all right. Look, she's probably just lonely, but I'm sure she still loves you. It'll be okay. Just wait and see."

He slapped the cap against his trousers. "It don't matter if she *loves* me. She's *fucking some* other dude. I know. My sister told me what's going on back in the World." He shifted to a new slump. "Listen, Lucy don't know how to wait. I mean, how would you like it?"

How indeed. But I said, "Look, you've just got to be mature about this and accept the facts. The facts are that you're here, 7,000 miles away from the World, and you can't go home for seven months. You can't get emergency leave for marital problems. You know that. Everybody in the whole 8ᵗʰ Army would be on leave. Just try not to think about it. Tell your sister not to tell you so much."

His eyes were too many miles away. "Maybe I'll just go to the ville or to Seoul."

"Yeah, right, That'd be real smart, wouldn't it? Go AWOL in Korea because you can't get leave to see your wife in California." I leaned across the desk. "What the hell good would that do? You can't get out of the country, and if you go AWOL, when you get caught, you'll just get put in the stockade and have to stay in this fucking country longer." I was tired of this and probably sounded like it. "Jesus, use your head if there's anything in there."

He didn't answer, just stared ahead, running his hands through his hair, fidgeting around like a canary in a cage.

I twisted and turned a paper clip into six pieces trying to decide something. Finally, I said, "Okay, look, I'll talk to the old man. But it won't do any good. It's just against the regulations. You know the AR's."

"Yeah. I also know Lucy."

That one hit a nerve. I knew nothing of Beth. Evidence: "Beth, I got your letter yesterday. It was good to hear from you after six weeks. Listen, I just want to know one thing. If anything is going on, please tell me. I really miss you, but I feel like something is wrong. I hope I'm wrong. I hope all this is just in my mind. But just tell me if there's somebody else now. I keep thinking of holding you that last morning. Please wait for me. I'll be home by next winter."

I went to see Col. Samuels about Alvarez. He had an "open door" policy. That meant he would always talk to anyone about anything, the modern Army way. I asked Sansoe if he knew anything else about Alvarez that might help.

The next morning, Spec. 4 Alvarez reported to battalion HQ at 9 a.m. He saluted but marched straight through to the colonel's office, shutting the green wooden door behind him. He was in there thirty minutes.

When he came out, he paused in front of my desk, put on his hat, looked at me resolutely, and left. Didn't say a word. I turned to Sgt. Frye and shook my head. "I guess it didn't go too well."

Frye nodded. "Hell, I could've told you nothing would come of that before he went in. Sar'nt Major Russell told me the colonel is having lots of trouble with his own old lady. He knows he can't go home and he ain't likely to let anybody else go."

"What?"

"Yessir. Colonel just found out yesterday. He told sar'nt major while they was having a few beers. Hell, you think the old man's been a bear up 'til now, wait'll you see what's to come. I seen this happen time and time again. Only bad thing is, we're the ones have to suffer 'cause of his old lady's bullshit. Never get married, that's my advice, yessir." He stretched and folded his arms behind his head, making that "tch tch" sound.

"Why didn't you tell me this before Alvarez went in? I feel like an idiot."

Frye sat up. "I'm sorry, Lieutenant. Hell, I guess I just didn't think about it, to tell you the truth."

I knew he was telling the truth, so I said, "Forget it. But Jesus do I feel bad. I bet Alvarez got chewed up one side and down the other. Shit."

I headed for the colonel's office.

"Wait, lieutenant." I stopped, looked back. "Alvarez would've gone in anyway. Hell, he didn't expect no good news. He just wanted to give himself an excuse."

"Yeah, maybe," I kept going and knocked on the colonel's door. He told me to come in. He was sitting in his swivel chair with his back to the desk, looking at a framed 8x10 of himself, his wife, their two daughters, a dog, and an old wooden house. I cleared my throat, and he spun around.

"Sir, I was wondering about Alvarez. Should I do anything about the leave request?"

He said nothing, just looked in my direction, but not really at me. More like a memory of a home in Arlington. Maybe wondering if his wife was with someone.

I waited for him to answer.

I tried again. "Sir?"

The cold blue West Point eyes focused on me. Shit.

"Don't you knock, mister?"

"I did, sir. I'm sorry to have disturbed you. I just—"

"Forget it."

"Yes, sir. I'll knock louder next time."

His eyes were out of focus again, looking at Virginia.

I cleared my throat. "About Alvarez, sir?"

"Forget it."

I saluted and left.

"Dear Beth: From your last letter, I guess you've changed most of your feelings about me. I just want you to know I didn't change mine. Wait 'til I get back, okay?"

A week later, Friday morning. I was just getting to work.

"Lieutenant?"

"Yeah, sarge."

"Did you hear about the report?"

"No, why?"

"Alvarez is AWOL."

15

"To tell you the truth, I don't see how you can spend so much time around her," Travis said, crunching his cabbage salad. We were grabbing early dinner before one of the occasional Saturday night music shows at the O Club. It would also give us a good table before the place got crowded. Every show was filled because there was rarely anything better to do. I was starting to wish there had been.

"Why do you say that?"

"Two *bulgogis*. Watch out. Super hot." Miss Che, the waitress, set our plates on the blue tablecloth. The thin beef strips sizzled in the metal pan. Travis ladled the meat onto his plate of steaming rice.

"Why do you say that?" I repeated.

Travis scooped more rice. "I don't know, really. I mean it just seems like you'd get bored spending a lot of time with a whore."

"Depends on how much you like to fuck."

"When you're not fucking, I mean."

I picked at the meat with my chopsticks. "Oh, I don't know, she speaks pretty good English and all when she wants to. It's just nice to get away from the Army and assholes like you."

"But what do you talk about?"

"Kim and me?"

"Yeah, I mean, what do you talk about? Politics, books, or music or what? I mean what do you have in common with a Korean whore?"

"Yobo."

"Okay, yobo."

"We just talk about us, I guess, or about Korea or when she grew

61

up or GIs or the clubs. Sometimes the mountains she liked to walk in. Sometimes music. She really likes Joan Baez."

"Well, then."

I tried to concentrate on using the chopsticks with rice, but switched to a fork and pointed to Travis before digging in.

"Well then goddam, what the hell do you talk about to girls back in the World? Do you have discussions about detente or the stock market or Shakespeare all the time?"

"Not all the time. But we do talk about more than when I'm going to get my next blow job."

"Ease off, man."

He eyed me like I was on a stretcher. "I'd hate to see you get fucked up like the other guys over here."

"You mean over a girl?"

"Over a whore."

I pushed back my chair as the busboy cleared the table. "You've slept with plenty. And you have a yobo, sort of. Remember?"

He shrugged. "So?"

"So why do *you* do it?"

"Well, to get laid. What else?" He attempted a laugh.

"You never talk to her or anything?"

"Yeah, I talk to her, but it's just whore talk."

I looked off around the room for a moment to stay calm. "So, you just treat her like a train ticket? Soon as the ride's over you disappear?"

"It's not like that."

"You just said that's exactly what it's like."

"Look," he said, "I'm not saying it's not fun or that these women are sub-human or anything. I mean Miss Wu is fine. So, I mean I like her. But only so far. That's why our deal is only for three months. You know?"

"Not really. Or maybe I don't want to."

"I'm just saying they're whores. We give them money—they fuck us. It's business. Not love."

"Jesus, Travis."

"I mean don't think they're going to love you, either. Don't project your feelings onto your yobo just because she happens to be right here next to you. This isn't the World, Hobbes. You'd better remember that. You'd better fucking remember you're going to leave it someday, so you better not get tangled up in it."

We both fell silent, avoiding eye contact again.

"Okay, okay," he said. "Do whatever you want. Just don't come running to my ass."

I was about to tell him not to fucking worry about it when Miss Che slipped up at my elbow.

"You boys talking a lot, huh? You likee dessert?"

"Dessert?" I knew she had timed it perfectly. "Wow, do we get dessert?"

"Please, please, do we?" Travis said.

We slapped palms. A peace gesture.

Miss Che smiled indulgently.

"What are our choices?" I asked.

Miss Che started to speak, but Travis stopped her. "No, let me tell you. Thank you, Miss Che. It's either ice cream with chocolate sauce, or chocolate sauce with ice cream!"

"Is that right, Miss Che? All those choices?"

She smiled, technically, because it was part of her job. "So, you like ice cream with chocolate sauce?" She hated saying "chocolate" because it was hard for her, and frequently said so. Really, she hated the whole routine.

"Travis will order for me."

"Lieutenant Hobbes will have the ice cream with chocolate sauce," he sniffed. "As for myself, I'll have the chocolate sauce with ice cream."

She rolled her eyes, went to the kitchen. She came back to set a bowl of vanilla ice cream swimming in Hershey's syrup in front of each of us.

I shook my head. "I'm so sorry, Miss Che. You've got it backwards. He wanted the chocolate sauce with ice cream. I wanted the ice cream with chocolate sauce." The required pause. "But that's okay," I switched bowls. "We'll still leave a tip."

"You better leave a big tip from now on," Miss Che said.

"I wish I'd ordered what you got," I told Travis.

End of performance.

Around us, the club was filling and getting louder as showtime approached. Travis and I clinked beers at our genius for already buying our tickets. Tommy the Korean manager began clearing the stage area at the far end of the room. Two young Koreans with long hair set up sound equipment.

The club bulletin board had said: "Saturday Night, February 27. The Fabulous Lee Brothers Band. Direct from Hong Kong." A photo of the Lee Brothers was above the writing. There were four of them and two girls, probably Lee Sisters.

The O Club had "top quality nightclub acts" every weekend. Sometimes on weeknights. The biggest attractions were the Australian bands with the round-eye women, curvy and tan. Everyone crowded around tables to be near the stage and pass notes to the babes. Please marry me. Come have a drink. They never did, of course. Except sometimes, according to gossip, for $200 a night.

Tommy introduced the band: "Tonight, ladies and gentlemen, the Fabulous Lee Brothers from Hong Kong." The red lights came up and the Lee Brothers sprinted onstage. Whirling in Motown mimic, they hit the first licks: "If you go down to the leever . . ."

There must have been 100 people in the club by then. Colonels and yobos at the long table at the side, warrant officers and yobos at three round tables pushed together. Young captains with the young wives they brought over at their own expense, but with a lot more expense and paperwork than the colonels had to go through. The extra waitresses for the show squeezed through the crowd, expertly collecting empty glasses and setting down new ones, fifty cents per drink. Travis and I had a couple dollars' worth.

"Lollin', lollin', lollin' down the leever . . ." I was starting to wonder if they pronounced it that way on purpose because it always got some laughs.

They shook in red fringe dresses, pumping ass like jackhammers, or swirling suggestively, pushing imaginary lovers slowly with their hips. Imperfect choreography, copied from old variety shows on television, or from the big American bands that came, infrequently, to the Chosun hotel in Seoul. But they want it to be right. To look American. Creedence Clearwater Revival. Ike and Tina. Temptations .

They mouthed the words, not always knowing what they meant, with that incongruous hollow sound of Western syllables on Oriental tongues. But they were actually pretty good. We drank at fifty cents or a dollar and applauded and loved the pretending that it was back home and the smug knowing that it wasn't.

The second band, clearly inexperienced, was less fortunate. Off-key guitars and ear-splitting speaker feedback kicked in with the third song. If an O Club band screwed up, the audience, drunken officers, laughed and threw harmless things at the stage. And so they did. The girl singers cried. All of them walked off the stage. They'd come back for their instruments later.

A notice was posted on the Club bulletin board in the hall the next day that there wouldn't be any more shows if "such behavior" continued. But it was signed by the club manager, not the compound commander, so no one paid it much attention.

16

There were definitely things Kim and I did, getting back to Travis's interrogation on the subject. On weekends when I couldn't look at Travis anymore, or Sansoe or Nick or the Army, I stayed with her in our hootch. Long Friday nights blended easily into Saturday noon, and we cooked dinner and maybe took a walk and rolled into bed and awoke in the soft light, dry-mouthed and bare.

It was good to lie with her under the heavy quilt, her face cuddled against my arm. It had not been like that before. Back in college, sometimes on weekends there were dates that went into overnights, and the results were shared later, in dorms or frat or sorority houses, by all participating parties.

And it was different. Different rules, expectations, levels of confession or bragging. Different boundaries. Courtship limits. Three-date finish lines. I was never any good at it and never really understood it, or the entire nature of relationships between male and female that those templates generated. And Beth? We got along fine. She just always said no. For the entire semester before graduation. Not doing it—waiting—was what she wanted, for reasons she never really could explain and made us both miserable. And then it was a habit. Not really talked about anymore. It only changed a few months before I posted to Korea. All my male friends thought I was a fool. Maybe they were right.

So, Halua, that's how Cherry Hill happened. From no going past second base to wanna fuck me, GI? Pretty great, huh? No—swell, that's the word. Swell. A careful way of putting it. Not mutherfucking A or goddam straight. Just swell. And Kim, what she did, all she did, was fuck me. Not make love to me or screw me or sleep with me or be one with me or meld me into her total being or any of that. She fucked me. For money.

I liked it. An entirely new way of looking at things. I could turn to her at night and say, let's fuck, and she would hold me tightly and say yes. Or she would be the one to say it: let's fuck. That word. Probably why I used it all the time. It was THE word. In the bars, she always said fuckee, like the other girls, and drinkee instead of drink, and so on. She said it sounded better and made the GIs easier to catch because they thought it made the girls sound more nasty and more fun. Or something. Sometimes she said "fuckee" to me, but with a kind of laugh, and in the sin and complexity of it all, we fucked. We sweated, and smoked pot and drank and sat naked in the middle of the day playing cards and once she beat me off on the train from Seoul and jesusfuckingchrist I couldn't believe it.

There were afternoons of picnics and walks at night and stargazing towards Nam-san and quiet dinners and even running through fields, and hiking the foothills, but you could get that in the World. All the clean fun you wanted.

17

All I could think was how cold I was. Everybody was cold. The week the fuel ran out because winter weather was lasting way too long, the White Elephant was an icebox. They issued extra blankets and said only go to your rooms to sleep, but it was cold anyway. Capt. Plato got pneumonia, and so did Coletti. They were quarantined in the hospital, and then more days back in the BOQ. Three people at the compound, including a visiting donut dolly, died.

"Beth: I guess it's been a while since I've written. I just haven't known what to say. I don't know whether to say I love you and will you wait for me or just say I'll see you when I get back if you like. I expected you to write before now. Maybe I'm a fool to hang on to what I left. Everyone over here does, though. Too bad you'll never know what I mean."

Shit, that's as far as I could get, and I tore it up. My hands were cold. I took a bottle of bourbon from the top shelf. It was next to a photo of Beth and me. I turned the picture down and took a long, burning swallow that made my stomach churn and my head buzz.

If only they'd given us enough fucking electric heaters, at least.

I did have a goddam electric heater with a frayed cord for three days, and I was going to sneak it out to Kim, but the BOQ building manager snagged it while I was at work. He taped up the fray and gave it to a doctor who out-ranked me. Capt. Plato, a lawyer, told me it figured, doctors were fascists.

So bitter, Lieutenant Hobbes, for such a young man. I took another, smaller drink, and felt warmer. Fucking doctors.

Kim already had a heater, though. Actually two. Wasn't the first Korean winter/early spring she'd been through. The hootch we'd rented in Suchow was reasonably warm. I'd put my foot down (as if) that she couldn't use the charcoal stove that came with the place. She stayed in the hootch when it was "freezee my ass, Hobbesie." No outside business. She said she wasn't going to lose her toes or get pneumonia. I stayed in with her as much as I could, at first, and brought food so she wouldn't have to. I planned to go back on our regular schedule as soon as it seemed warm enough. But turned out I didn't want to. I was actually missing her the nights we were apart. Not the sex. Her.

Someone pounded on the door to my room. "Let's go, Hobbes."

I told Nick to come in and stayed slumped against the frosted ledge of my only window.

"Beautiful sunset," I said. "It's like being in Aspen."

"Uh huh. Get off your ass, you Texas pussy. Let's go see Coletti."

"I don't know. I was having a pretty good time here."

"You got two minutes." Nick sat in the chair at my desk and thumbed through a PACEX catalogue. He had ordered something from nearly every page. He was saving by buying, he said. Fucking dentist. He had an electric heater, too. But at least he had to buy it from the catalogue. He was a dentist, not a doctor.

I gave him the bottle for a swig and put on my jacket. I examined my face in the hand mirror tacked to the wall. "Okay. Let's go get the girls." We bounded down the hallway to the back stairs and cut across the alley to Gate 7. The MP looked at us like we were idiots.

The Blue Dragon was plenty warm inside. Blaring rock music as I opened its door. A GI in a purple fishnet shirt was dickering price with a whore. It was plenty warm, which is why Coletti spent most of his time there, even at night when it was noisy.

"Hobbes, Nick. Over here." We waited for our eyes to adjust to the dark and went to his table, dodging dancers and GIs holding yobos by the ass. We hadn't seen Coletti in two weeks. He looked completely recovered.

"Double bourbons for my friends," he told a waitress.

As soon as Nick and I sat, two girls joined us.

"Hey-ey, yoboseyo, long time no see," one said to me. I looked closer in the red darkness. It was Kim II.

"Looks like you got a good one," Nick grinned. "Want to trade?"

Kim II nestled close and kissed my ear.

"No thanks, doc. Yours looks in need of a Geritol fix." It was difficult for us to judge the ages of Korean women, but the one hanging on Nick's shoulder had to be at least forty. Not old, just old to us.

"Geritol?" Kim II asked. "What that?"

"Geritol?"

"Yeah, what that, yobo? Some fuckee trick?"

"Yeah." Three girls I'd never seen had surrounded Coletti. I asked him why so many. He winked. "Wouldn't you like to know, me bucko?"

I told Kim II I wanted to go home with her later. She asked me where Miss Kim was. My Miss Kim. What the fuck do I care? I said. Except I did care. Somewhere in my soggy brain something finally had ticked during this weather separation. I wasn't going to think about it. So that only left the option to act it out.

Kim I and Kim II were friends, as much as can be among the business girls in the ville. And I had been Kim II's customer right after I got here, before even meeting Kim I. Nothing more, but we always joked a little with each other when we happened to cross paths. Kim II said we should dance, and we joined Nick and his new girlfriend and a few other couples on the linoleum floor. When the songs changed to slow country ballads, she looked at her watch, said she had to go over to the Acid Club, and took off. Neither of us had really planned to join bodies.

Coletti darted briefly in and out the back door every thirty or forty minutes meeting Koreans in the alley. I knew that despite the cold, and his recovery, he was making deals. Nick didn't approve and looked the other way. They had similar outlooks on how to deal with what we had been dealt. Not so with Travis, even though once Coletti had gotten Travis a rare antique pitcher for his mother. Coletti dismissed Travis as hypocritical. Actually, that's not what he said. He said Travis was a "spoiled snot-nosed rich kid who needs to grow up." He said the same held for me, except I wasn't snotnosed or spoiled or rich.

*

I could never decide about Coletti's deals, although I made an issue of them more than once. The last time was just before he got pneumonia, when I ran into him one evening in the alley behind the Homestead. I was hurrying to the hootch and Kim. He was wearing a parka and half-hidden in a drainage ditch between two buildings. Saying something to three Korean men inspecting a stack of cardboard boxes. The top one was open. PX radios. The Koreans, one of whom I recognized as the owner of the HiFi Heaven shop, picked up the boxes and walked off quickly and silently, cloaked in the fog of their own breathing.

I gave them a few steps and then called out to Coletti. He was surprised and squared away as I approached. "What the hell are you doing here?"

I held up my hands to show I wasn't a threat. "Hey, man, I'm just on my way to Kim."

He studied me. Longer than I liked. Then, "Okay. No sweat. Want a drink?" He pointed to the Homestead's back door and started to walk off.

Now I was the one that was pissed. "No."

He turned back to stand directly in front of me.

"Say it."

"Say what?"

"Say it, goddam it."

All right. Fuck it. "Okay. What do you want me to say? That you're stealing from the Army and you could go to Leavenworth? That I know it?"

"And?"

"And." I stopped. "And, oh hell, I don't know." I threw up a palm, shook my head. "No need going into this again. Just caught me off guard to actually see it in action, that's all."

"You think it's wrong."

"You know the answer. Hell yes."

His expression, even in the breath clouds, was unmistakable.

"I mean no." I wiped cold moisture from my face. "I mean, damn, Coletti, it's just, you know. I mean what can I say?"

Now his expression said I was wasting his time. "So, is it wrong or not?"

Wrong. Wrong. I tried to focus on the word. The concept. Words wouldn't come out.

"Don't brood on it all night. It's fucking freezing. Just answer."

I coughed. Spit to clear my throat. "I wish I'd never come this way."

"Business is the key word, Lieutenant Buttinsky. And it's my business not to have to take a lot of cheap shit. Because it's none of your business. Am I getting it from you?"

"Getting what?"

"Getting what?" He breathed out a cloudbank of lung air, then theatrically slapped his palm to his forehead. "Getting what? Getting this attitude like I'm somebody who sticks needles in babies' arms to hook them and then lives off the profits. Like I'm some fucking dirty wop scum."

"That's not it. Mick scum, more like."

I was going for a laugh but got a hard stare. I was ready to dodge his fist. "Oh, that's not it? It's not? Well excuse the fuck out of me, asshole of a friend. Then what the fuck is it?"

I backed up against the building wall, hoping to show a look of truce. "It's just, you know, I mean I know it's just a little black market and all and not really any big deal and what the hell is morality considering what we are even doing in this country. It's just—shit." I kicked a heel against the wall. "It's just, like, something in me has trouble justifying it, but something else says I don't have the right to justify it, but something else says I don't have the right not to justify it, but, like, deep down, even though it's not that much, something says, well it's not right."

Coletti was probably rolling his eyes, but I couldn't see clearly,

I was getting nowhere. So, I kept at it, of course. "Like, you have to draw lines or something, and if you draw one, you have to draw a lot of them. And if you don't draw one, you don't draw any. Right? I mean philosophically?" I was pretty sure the look on my face had warped into exasperation.

He folded his arms across his big chest. "Hobbes, you fucking tangle of human brain cells, if God gave you a question, and said, 'Brother Hobbes, if you answer this properly, eternal happiness is yours, but if you answer it wrong, you'll just stay as you are,' know what you'd say?"

I shrugged. "I don't know."

"That's exactly what you'd say."

Would I say that? Really? Of course, I would.

Coletti re-crossed his arms. "Well?"

"Well, what?"

"Does it bother you? You gonna get contaminated by evil here?"

"Forget it. Forget it."

"Are you sure?"

"Are you kidding?"

Coletti shook his head, just a hint of a smile. "For Crissake, Hobbes, you've got a big problem. But it ain't me, me bucko, it ain't me. Let's go in. I've sold out my inventory and my balls are turning to ice."

I followed him into the club. The rush of warm air only sharpened the sense of cold. He went to his usual table and bought us beers. I drank about half while he got into a conversation with a warrant officer from his unit and waved to a bouncy young yobo over by the juke box. It was Kim II.

I reminded myself I had been on my way to see my Kim. I shook hands with Coletti, because what else was there to do, and zipped up my jacket.

Kim II sat down. Coletti smiled. I said adios and left for my hootch.

Kim I wasn't home.

18

Eventually it started warming up for spring. Coletti and I had gotten back to normal, and, like Nick, I just ignored what he did with his own private supply chain in unrestrained international capitalism. So, I was a little surprised with what he told me playing pool and downing happy hour shots at the Blue Dragon. After missing an easy side pocket, he stared at the balls left on the table. Then stared at me. The words came out, slowly, then fast and hard.

"I hate this fucking compound, I mean I hate it, Hobbes. I hate the shit we do all day and the shit they want us to do at night. I hate the O Club and I hate the PX and the PX snack bar and the PX concession stand and the PX massage parlor and the mess halls and the motor pool and the White Elephant and the Top 5 and the Lower 4 and the whole fucking thing. I hate it. I hate the officers and the fucking happy hours, and I hate the EMs and their chickenshit mustaches and their music and I hate the lifers."

He slammed his cue stick into the wire holder. A few people looked over from the bar. He glared and they stopped. He took a few breaths and turned back towards me, then slumped onto a metal folding chair.

"But I really like the Koreans, you know what? I bet you think that's stupid. Yeah, over on the compound they tell us how everybody in the ville is a low life out to rip us off. I even believed that myself when I first got here because that's all I ever heard."

He signaled the bartender to send us beer and *ramyun*. "But then I found out something. Know what? They don't rip you off because you're a GI or even because you're an American. I'm not talking about just doing business. I'm talking about ripping you off. They rip you off because they know you think they're shit. That's it, me bucko. They see GIs come and whore and shoot craps for thirteen months and leave. You never speak to Koreans except to fuck them or cheat them. You don't learn the language or the customs. You take what you can get. So how are they supposed to treat you? Like a goddam conquering hero?"

He tipped back his chair to lean against the well. "You're shit to them."

A waitress in a red silk dress brought our beer. Coletti pointed to an open table. She put the beers on it as we went over. "There's only one reason us and them get together. Know what it is?" He poured his glass to the brim.

I shrugged.

He took a drink and smiled. "Greed. Pure and simple greed, me bucko. Money, won, dollars, MPC. It's the universal language."

"Maybe."

"Maybe my ass, That's it, motherfucker. I know." He looked at me as if for epiphanic recognition. "Look, Hobbes, there's a lot of things I don't know, but I do know greed." His teeth flashed in the whirling chandelier. "It's my business. It's my fucking business."

A teenage boy from the kitchen brought the ramyun. Almost spilled it when a GI bumped into him but made a miracle save although hot broth burned his fingers. He cursed the guy who'd hit him but could do nothing more.

"Take somebody like Travis," Coletti said, taking a quick bite with the chopsticks. "For all his bleeding Yankee heart, he'll be gone when his tour is up and never back. He thinks Koreans are a bunch of half-civilized saps who need American money and his goddam Boston morals. But Koreans know Travis. Know what they think of his Boston morals?" He dug in for more noodles. "Fuck his Boston morals. He's just another parasite on vacation. Taking from him only evens the score." He took a quick sip of beer after forgetting the ramyun was so hot. "Rotten shit," he said, wiping his mustache. "Not the ramyun. The Travises." More beer. "Don't you see it?"

I toyed with my bowl while it cooled. "Sort of. But you know, it sounds more like you're trying to defend your goddam deals by claiming that since we fuck them, they have a right to fuck us back or something. I mean, I agree in a way, but—"

"But what?"

"But, well, it's like, it's all been said. You can say what you want, and it makes a certain amount of sense. And Travis or Corporal Yu or Kim say something, and it makes a certain amount of sense. But it's all things we can't really know, isn't it? I'm just getting worn out with explanations. I fuck you, you fuck me. No matter who starts it, we all get fucked in the end, don't we? I mean we all have our horseshit little reasons. I mean, that's what I've begun to think, so—"

"So why explain it?"

I looked at him with surprise.

He grinned. "At long fucking last, you said it. I mean in a roundabout way, but still. Why explain it, right? Instead of 'I don't know' and your endless doubt." He flashed a thumbs-up. "So, no more explanations, eh, brother Hobbes? Friends are friends. Period. Explanations are for others."

I resisted his conclusion. But yes.

I clinked his glass lightly. "So just tell me this. Forget whether it's right or wrong or any of that. Just tell me—all that about Koreans hating GIs. What gives you a ticket in? Aren't they just taking advantage of you to get the black-market things they can't get in the PX? I mean you're just a tool, not any kind of special friend."

He looked through his glass like it was some kind of magic prism. "They're not taking advantage of me, me bucko." He put the glass down. "I'm one of them."

He grabbed my wrist. For some reason his grip felt dangerous, foreign. But it was just Coletti.

"You know what they call me, right?"

"What?"

"Are you ready?"

I shrugged, pulled my arm free. "The mayor?"

"Hell yes the mayor. The goddam Mayor of Suchow."

He rose and gazed majestically around the room. It wasn't danger I felt. It was power. The kind I would never know. He really did carry a presence. A charisma.

"Come on snotnose, let's grab some women." He waved toward a business girl talking to the bartender. "Hey Miss Po, bring some friends over. Drinks are on my lad Hobbes." She waved.

"I thought Travis was the snotnose. Not me."

"Fair enough. Toast to the not-snotnose."

"Yeah, well, we'll split the tab."

Miss Po and two others, maybe the same I'd seen him with before, quickly joined us. I didn't have to see Kim every night. Nor she me. Just not go around fucking other people. Wasn't that what I told Sansoe back when I was defending having a yobo?

Which reminded me, we'd barely talked about Kim all this time. Now that it came to mind, he never really talked about any of the girls any of us knew. He said it was a good way to lose a friend.

But Kim was different. Coletti had met her before I arrived, and the Mayor of Suchow was the kind who kept track of people and details. So, he should know where Kim was when she wasn't with me. She was never gone long, always back around curfew, and always had an explanation, like that last night when I was looking for her. That other night when she wasn't at the hootch. Maybe a couple of other nights. Even that one where she and Kim II were trying to trick me. And how they had a laugh about the trick but that she was also glad I hadn't gone through with Kim II's flirtation and offer. I bought it.

I had bought it all along. Just seeing friends. Just doing a couple of "no fuckee favors" to make a little money. She tried doing her all her "no fuckee" business during the day while I was at work, but sometimes it had to be later. When she had to drop something off or do something for mama-san to help barter the rent while she kept her old hootch.

All the girls did that. Yobo deals, too. It was up to me to decide what made sense. Whatever "what" was. And up to me to get clear on why I had let it all ride. Ignored it. What did I know about how to treat a yobo. Or her side-deals. It wasn't like we were married. Or in love. Or even dating. It just wasn't. Anything.

"Just drink!" Coletti boomed over the Allman Brothers before I could pin him down. "Drink to the Mayor of Suchow!"

So, I let it ride a little longer.

19

Kim and I were "almost stinko" on black-market bourbon after hitting a few bars in the ville. She said she'd try not to stay out with her friends anymore and I accepted that because she said she also doesn't want to break up. So, we were trying to get out more together, stick to the contract. I was ready to go back to the hootch, or maybe get something to eat, but she wanted one last stop, at Hawaii Heaven, a semi-private NCO club in the ville I'd never entered. Somehow connected with Hi Fi Heaven, and maybe even with Coletti, rumor went. She wanted me to meet Miss Han the War Bride. She was legally married to a GI who was killed in Vietnam. Everybody knew about Miss Han.

Even with a dead husband, Miss Han was still a dependent. So, she still had perks, like using the PX. But she also still needed income. Her solution was to snag other GIs as long-term yobos, keeping them a year, taking successors. Kim said Miss Han was between yobos now and trying for a new one. Kim said Hawaii Heaven was "too old" for her and most of her friends but just right for Miss Han. It was full of senior NCOs who made good money and the juke box was all "old songs." Miss Han and her latest yobo had a big hootch with a PX television, a PX Sanyo refrigerator, warmed by two PX heaters, and cooled by a PX three-speed fan. Miss Han told Kim that her PX card was worth more than her life. It was her life.

In Seoul, there was a general's wife who didn't like the surviving spouse agreement, didn't like Koreans with PX cards, didn't like mingling with an NCO's slant-eyed whore at the Yongsan PX. One day, in the PX, the general's wife fumed when a Korean PX widow, not Miss

Han, crowded in front of her in the cash register line. She overloaded, as Sansoe put it, and hit the Korean wife on the head with a large portable radio. The blow was strong enough to crack the widow's skull, and she died.

The general's wife was taken away, furious and screaming because the cash register was closed, and the MPs wouldn't let her check out. The general and his wife were transferred to Japan within three days because otherwise she would've been tried for murder in a Korean court. I knew because I saw the transfer order.

It all had to do with SOFA, the Status of Forces Agreement. If we were arrested, we would present our SOFA card to the Korean police. It was printed in Hangul, the Korean alphabet, on the back, and English on the front. Kind of the reverse of Korean won, which was Hangul on the front and English on the back.

SOFA was supposed to protect Koreans from the corrupting influence of a two-decade occupation, a reaction to the previous outrages from Japan. But it had become corrupt and perverted in itself. It was another link in the black market now and used to restrict goods and sell justice. It was complicated and boring, and most GIs didn't know much about it. The only thing to remember was: Don't get in trouble on the streets.

I always kidded Kim about SOFA. I called it the whore's defense against the heathen GI. For some reason I didn't know yet, Kim had brought up SOFA just as we got to Hawaii Heaven.

"I still think it fucking sucks that you could hit me and nothing would happen but if I hit you I could go to Korean jail," I said as we walked in. Numerous heads turned since we weren't regulars, but Kim saw Miss Han, dancing to an old country song with what I assumed was one of her new yobo candidates. We did introductions and then went to Miss Han's table while she stayed on the dance floor.

"I fuckee-suck you, SOFA boy," Kim said, as we sat down. "So that means now you got to do same to me when we get home." She put her arms around my neck.

"Not with SOFA around."

She kissed me and twisted slowly in my arms. We play-wrestled in our chairs, tickling each other and demanding surrender. We drew too much attention.

Miss Han's yobo saw us. He was a fat, mottle-faced, motor pool sergeant I might have seen around. I don't know what Miss Han might have said to him, but he stopped dancing and marched over to ask me if I was trying to beat Kim up.

"Sure," I said mockingly. "She deserves it. She refused to go to bed with me."

Miss Han's yobo looked back at Miss Han, who had come over to the table, too, and was laughing in a funny way. She said something to the sergeant. He turned back to me. "Forget it, son. Shit, go ahead. Tune her up if she deserves it." No one knew what to say. But then he added, grinning toward Miss Han, "What the hell, I knocked the piss out of this one last night."

He backed away, smacking his lips like he'd just eaten something. Waved at some of his friends at other tables.

So, he didn't see the beer bottle that Miss Han threw at him, cursing in Korean. It ricocheted off his skull.

"Fuck you, bitch," he yelled, holding one side of his head and reaching for her.

"Fuck yourself you pig GI," Miss Han shouted. She dodged his grasp easily and pulled down a scarf she had been wearing. I could see a large purple bruise at the top of her left cheek. I realized why Kim had brought me here.

I stood up.

Kim latched to my arm. "No, Hobbesie. Stop. We go to hootch. You just get arrested in here."

"Can you see the mark on her face?"

"I see. And I no like him. Fucking GI. But, listen me. Not worth it." She motioned to Miss Han, who was heading toward the sergeant with another bottle, and called out something in Korean. Miss Han stopped.

The sergeant was right in front of her, still holding his head.

I yelled out. "Hey, buddy, leave her alone."

He turned my way. "Get the fuck out of here, lieutenant. This ain't your affair. You ain't paying for this. Just get the fuck out." A couple of older NCOs rose. They weren't going to help me, or get in trouble by hurting me, either.

Everyone was frozen in place. Probably, to get back to my point, because they knew how this would play out with SOFA. Not to mention with the MPs.

Then Miss Han walked away from her no longer yobo candidate to stand beside me. She said something to Kim quickly.

One of the other NCOs was blocking his friend's path. "Look, Ralph, let it go. This ain't going nowhere."

Ralph tried to push him away, but almost made him fall. "Goddam it, Terry."

"I can't let you go over there. Just leave it and sit over here with us," Terry said.

"I'll let it go when that shithead is lying on the floor bleeding," Ralph said, slurring his words. But he didn't move toward me.

Kim and Miss Han flanked me.

"Ssssh, yobo. Missy Han say he have gun." Miss Han nodded. "She get rid of him tomorrow for good. She say to thank you and we leave now and she take care of him and meet us outside." Miss Han nodded again.

"Yeah, like she took care of him last night," I mumbled.

Ralph was following Terry back to the long table where the NCO pals were watching like a wolf pack. But it was pretty clear the moment had passed.

Kim tugged at my arm. "Come on, my yobo yobo. We leave now. Come on. It okay, Missy Han she get new yobo most skoch." She looked into my eyes. Hard. "You no make trouble now. That man stay over there with friends, okay?"

I got my senses back, and we started for the door. But Miss Han broke away and walked over to Ralph. Kim pulled me along anyway. Outside, she kissed me, said she was sorry, and she hadn't thought it was going to get that bad helping Miss Han. We walked toward our hootch, but halfway there she said we had to go to Miss Han's hootch, to make sure she was okay. And we did.

It was in a relatively nice street, better than ours. After a half-hour, and no Miss Han, we went back to the club. None of the people that had been involved were there. Kim talked to a waitress and then told me that Miss Han would be okay. SOFA would protect her. She probably went to some other bar and not back to her hootch right away in case her ex-yobo Ralph would get more drunk and try to push his way in.

Whatever happened, Kim never told me. We never went back to Hawaii Heaven.

20

"Choose."

"What?"

"Me or her."

"Why do I have to choose?"

"I no stay you take her."

"Jesus Christ."

"Yeah, sure, jesu' chris' motha fucka you always say. So whatsa matta me?"

"Fuck your GI talk. Talk right."

"Sure, like you talk Korean."

"Go to hell."

"Why you take her last night? You my yobo or not?"

"Right, like I haven't seen you butterfly around before."

"Not when I have yobo."

"Oh yeah, like that night last week you weren't home? You said you just hang out with your friends. Ha."

"He my old yobo."

"What, does he have residual rights?"

"What that?"

"Nothing. Just stop giving me shit for seeing the other Miss Kim."

"You mean Kim Two ."

"Yeah, Kim Two."

"Who Kim One?"

"I don't believe this."

"Who Kim One?"

"What the hell difference does it make? Is this a contest?"

"You just answer."

"Answer what?"

"You know what. I Kim One or Kim Two?"

"That depends."

"What you mean, that depends? You answer."

"First you answer."

"What?"

"You going to fuck your old yobo anymore?"

"Who say I fuck him?"

"Funny."

"I say no, don't I?"

"Yeah, you say it."

"I no bullshit you like you bullshit me. I tell you truth. I no see my old yobo no more. Anyway, maybe I see him and not fuck him."

"My dying ass."

"Oh, Hobbes-san, you jealous?"

"Jealous? Of you? Hell no. But you're supposed to be my yobo and you're screwing someone else. And then you give me shit just for seeing Kim Two."

"Well, I only see my old yobo, too."

"Fuck your old yobo, you mean. We have a deal, right. You don't fuck other guys."

"We have a deal, but I no slave. I might have other business, too. Right? You don't own me, right? Like that song they play at Homestead?"

"You know what I mean."

"Well then it also mean you no fuckee Kim Two."

"Fuck you."

"Well fuck you!"

"That's what I tell you to do." She cocked her head to look at me like a dog, then giggled. "So shut up, Hobbesie, and just fuck me."

I laughed, too. How did we get into such arguments? "But first tell me if you're going to fuck your old yobo anymore."

"Not if you fuck me. Not if you stop fuckee Kim Two."

"So back to our deal, then. Yeah?"

"We always in the deal. You the butterfly cheater."

"Oh, for fuck's sake."

"You wanna fuck me?"

"What do you think?"

She pressed against my groin. "I think yes. But also I want to know."

"What?"

"You know what."

"You mean who is One and Two?"

"Yes, yobo."

"Okay, you're Kim One. So what?"

"So, if I Kim One why you see Kim Two?"

I was frantic for an end to this. "Because I felt like it."

"Well, if you feel like it, maybe you like her better. Maybe she better fuck."

"Did I say that?"

"Sure."

"Oh, the hell if I did."

"Goddam hell if you did."

"I said stop talking GI talk."

"Fuck you I talk GI talk. You go fuck Korean whore when you my yobo and you not tell me, but other girl, she tell me, so I find out and then after you fuckee when you my yobo you goddam tell me not to say dirty GI talk. Goddam fuck you number ten bastard!"

"Oh hell, why don't I just go see Kim Two again."

"Okay, why not?"

"Okay, I will,"

"Okay. Maybe I see old yobo while you do that. Fuck him like GI John."

"Okay."

"Okay."

This went on until Kim had the last word.

After, when I lay next to her and smelled her and rested my fingers on her thigh, I knew things were different. This was not the way it was supposed to be. Quarreling and pretend kidding was an obvious lie. And I knew why. And I should have told her.

21

In North Korea, the DPRK, above the 38th parallel, Kim Il Sung ruled with an iron hand. He was an autocratic communist. China was his back-up. In South Korea, the ROK, below the 38th parallel, Park Chung Hee ruled with an iron hand. He was a democratic capitalist. America was his back-up.

The Z, the DMZ, the Demilitarized Zone, was the only place real fighting still occurred, at least on land.

We could visit the Z on special tours.

So, I did. Wearing my best Class A uniform, as required when I made my reservation, I caught a ride to Camp Casey and I assembled with a group of other visitors, military and civilian. An MP got on the bus to give us an instruction sheet. The bus headed to Panmunjom, the truce city. American MPs supposedly had to be over six feet to be on duty there, to be sure they were taller than the North Koreans.

We saw the layout. The North Korean guard houses that look like ice cream parlors, the UN conference table, shiny and soulless. The air of conflict was tangible, or at least it felt that way. Struggle, death, endless irrational hostility. We couldn't take photos of a lot of things, including the Freedom Bridge. It was good to return to the compound and the bars and whores of Suchow.

Arnie Pearson told the best DMZ stories. He was attached to my battalion for four months. He was one of the obvious minority of Black guys in the entire compound. I liked him but didn't get to see him much. He took a three-year hitch, so he could make captain and then decide whether to go regular Army. He had a degree in history and often said the Army offered a better deal than a history teacher. I didn't agree but he was damn smart, and I thought he had a way of making sense of this whole mess, while I just thrashed around in it.

He didn't do the ville much, and then only for drinks, because he was married and meant it. He was a good-looking guy and the yobos always swarmed him. We caught happy hour sometimes in the O Club in the White Elephant, but I guess we got into the habit of going our separate ways in the night. Far as I knew, he stayed true to his wife back home. That was another obvious minority.

I was glad he was at our compound, even for a while. But I knew why he was more eager than most to get out of the posting. He'd originally signed up for Nam, but first they sent him to Fort Sill, and then his orders came through for Korea. His first eleven months here were spent as a platoon leader on the Z, in the 2nd Infantry Division. That was the division that, when people were assigned to it, a lot of us smiled sympathetically and thought "poor fucker" inside. But also gave them serious respect. The career guys went for it. Arnie made captain, and things were looking good. Until the incident at the Z.

Unfortunately, that led to the story everyone liked to hear, and that he would tell once in a while, usually the sign he was pissed off or depressed about something. Which was pretty much everybody's state of mind most of the time. It happened late last October, about the time I got here, when Capt. Pearson and five men were patrolling in No Man's Land. The Z was in three parts: the South Korean side, No Man's Land, and the North Korean side. No men were supposed to be in No Man's Land. When men were there, and met, they fought.

The evening Arnie told it to us for the second time, in a lot more detail, was at O Club, as we watched some pilots try Flaming Hookers, and waited to see who would take the legendary Miss So to his room. As soon as Arnie started talking, though, everyone moved in closer. No one interrupted, except me, once, and a major from some rocket battery near Daegu.

"It was about two in the morning," Arnie began, moving a stool aside to lean against the bar. "It was colder than shit, and we're fiddle-fucking up this path on the side of a hill. The wrong side, but I can't tell you more than that. It's just a routine patrol, see, and nothing's supposed to happen. Just a night out with the boys.

"And Christ, all of the sudden, out of nowhere, these fucking walls of light come on. Here we are, practically in Kim Il Sung's backyard, and wham with the fucking searchlights. I was scared shitless. And you shoulda seen this Spec. 4 with us. He just kept saying 'Oh Jesus Christ, oh Jesus Christ, oh Jesus Christ.' So, I say, 'Stop saying his name and start talking to him.'

"Anyway, we all froze where we were. It's like the book says, 'cause at first, we figured they were flares. But then they didn't die out and I turned to Sgt. Rotach and he looks at me and says we're all dead men.

"'Hell if I am,' I said and then we all spread out behind some rocks. We wait maybe half an hour and the searchlights go off. So, after a few minutes I round everybody up and we're off again. Wham! Back on they come. I mean right on us. Ever shit in your pants?

"Again, nothing happened. By now we could tell the light was coming from a couple of portable rigs on the north. We couldn't shoot them out 'cause we weren't supposed to be there in the first place. And they could have shot us and got away with it. Hell, they killed three GIs in a Jeep a month earlier and those guys weren't even all the way across the Z.

"So, what do you think happens? Do they shoot us and give us an honorable death? Hell no."

He paused, gulped his gin and tonic.

"All the sudden these loudspeakers start playing 'Buffalo Gals.'"

Dazzled looks and whaaaas? from everybody. I had to ask. "Buffalo Gals?"

"Yeah, you know—'Buffalo gals woncha come out tonight and dance by the light of the moon.'" He paused again, shook his head like the whole picture show was back in his body.

"So, they're playing this and I figure, they're just fucking with us for some reason, which they were, but anyway I figured we could get away. So, we make our way back to the entry point and all the way zigzagging down the hill these two spotlights follow us and this goddam song is blaring away. All the way down the goddam hill."

"Go for it," the overserved rocket major listening in from a nearby table called out. Arnie saluted, then went on.

"No sooner do we get back than here's old GravelAss himself, a two-star, at the fence. Everybody had heard about it 'cause we were stuck over an hour. Shit, he got out of bed to come down. I was a combination of scared to death and happy to be alive, and the first thing I say when we're through the fence is, 'Well, General, you never seen an act like that in vaudeville, did you?'

"Let me tell you now, that wasn't the thing to say at the time. To make matters worse, next day somehow those gook assholes were circulating pictures of us in their searchlights.

"Well damn it all, it wasn't my idea to do all that spy shit. I mean, you'd think old Gravel-Ass would have liked it better if we'd all been shot instead of made fools of.

"So, a week later I'm transferred down here for my last four months 'cause he figured I wasn't good enough to freeze my ass off every day on patrol and risk getting killed. So, to punish me he sends me to this goddam supply compound where there's a village of girls, not like those cunts at Dongduchun, and a good officer's club, and a warm hootch to sleep in. It's a good thing I didn't fuck up any worse or I'd probably have been sent home."

He raised his drink. "Here's to you fuckers."

We all toasted and laughed. Then he put up his hand for silence.

"But that's not the ass-kicker. You'd think they would've sent me to Nam to serve out my tour, but my CO knew I'd been asking for a transfer there, to help me make major. So, say what you will about this man's Army, they really know how to fuck you over."

He raised his glass for another toast and then shook a few hands and picked up a drink the bartender had set in front of him. Not one, but at least two dozen in a line on the bar top.

The officer audience had been buying for Arnie during the story and Billy the bartender was having fun lining them up. Arnie

91

saluted Billy and told everyone to split them and he was going up to his room because he had to do a Jeep run over to Incheon first thing in the morning.

The row of free drinks was gone fast, and soon the club was unusually quiet. A lot of people went back to their rooms, too, including me. It was one of those stories that was full of danger and bravery and a little dark humor just so what happened could sound manly understated, and that wasn't supposed to happen, but everyone knew those kinds of stories did, and didn't really want to think about it, because if the shit ever hit the fan and the DPRK ever swarmed over the Z, none of us would make it home. And that would just be the start.

22

Suchow. The ville. Me. Too often. Stumbling along this damn line of mud walls, monsoon rains soaking me to the bone. Lost, lost in these fucking alleys. It's dark, where the hell am I? Shit, another goddam pothole. Oh, shit again, almost break my goddam leg. Goddam fucking miserable fucking road.

Down, you asshole, sit down. Okay, I'm sitting.

Whew, sitting. Fuck, probably fucking drown. What the hell. What is this? Fucking mud. Aren't there any sidewalks? Even a goddam plank to sit on? This crap oozes into my pants.

It's backward, it's all backward. Don't these people care about anything? Streets fucking torn up, walls and barbed wire around all the houses because everybody steals. Yeah, walls. Jesus, there aren't any goddam yards. No yards to play football. Shit. Shit in the sewers. Shit, shit. Shit in the fields. Everything shit, shit.

I've gotta throw up. Oh, Jesus stop still. Be still. Shut my eyes and it all spins in all colors and doesn't stop. Tighter and faster. Jesus. Oops, goddam, my head, what is this? A fucking wall right here in the middle of nowhere. Fucking wall in the street. Jesus.

Look at the wall: Solid mud, growing and towering to mountains, continents of mountains, gray and massive, and they are hollow. Ooh. Splat. They fall apart, smaller than the walls again. Inside, look, there's blood now, stored up, good for how long?

Now stop that. Not blood. No. It's a mud brick. Melting in the sun, now a vast blue lake. Now the waters are black. Two frog eyes from the bottom, skimming toward me. Shit. Running, racing in quiet wakes, the frog eyes. For me. Closer. And wait. They are snake eyes. Snake eyes, devil eyes, come for me. What the hell was in that joint?

Go away, go away. Mud. Here, take fistfuls, that will keep you away. But they are closer, pulsing, blinking rhythmically under heavy mucous lids. They open again, serpents. And the black pupils glow and glisten.

A woman steps from them, walks across the shore to me. To me.

"Hobbes-san? Hobbes-san! You come with me. What kind of stupid shit are you, sit here in rain? You drunk or what?"

"Go away bitch."

"Why you call me bitch, you bastard." She slaps me across the face hard, harder, until I fall over into the mud. Lying there, I drink a mouthful of the black water.

"Why are you fucking everyone?"

"Jesus Christ, you GI bastard, stop that." She raises my head. Coughing, I spit out slime.

"Why you always ask me that? Aieee! You fuckee me, don't you? You want me stop fuckee you? Oh Jesuschrist, look at you face!" She wipes away more muck. "You like me stop fuck you, huh? Aieee! You just number ten bastard."

She pushes me away, stands up. She kicks at me but misses.

"Fuck you, you bitch," I yell. "You whore. And fuck your old yobo. But you already did that, didn't you? I saw you. Didn't you?"

She kicks again but slips and falls. We're both in the mud.

"You still think I still fuckee old yobo. I tired talking about that. You fulla bullshit." She sobs, sees a broken bottle, picks it up. I get ready for the hit, but she throws it away. "I fuckee nobody but you."

She rubs the mud on her hands on her blouse. "You no give a shit anyway. You never give a shit."

*

The next day, Sunday, we picnic. It's not raining. I must buy her a gift. Or just give her some cash. She would probably like that better. Fifty bucks. Maybe that would cover the laundry. Maybe I should give her more. A lot more. Maybe I should just leave her alone. After that little show of drama and filth and abnegation.

Under the backdrop of the beautiful day in the hills, we make up. We become yobos again. Real ones. We promise not to butterfly anymore. Not cheat. I'm not sure we even were doing that, but once that mistrust starts in your head, or at least in my head, it's hard to stop. I know she is right. I don't know what is wrong with me. Which is to say I probably do. I just can't get it out.

That night in the hootch, she sits quietly next to me as we listen to Joan Baez and Bob Dylan and sip brandy. It tastes nice. We belong. We are being with someone. Not alone. Before we go to sleep, she says it: "Hobbes, my Hobbesie, I love you, yobo."

I tell her she doesn't mean it.

23

Her convenience could not be denied. I sometimes caught myself thinking of her for no reason. Remembrances of small things. Opening a cab door, touching the smooth warmth of her back as she stepped inside. Those cosmic eyes in the night, taking me and making me over.

"You not same no more," she told me.

"What do you mean?"

"You nicer."

I smiled. "I must be getting used to this place."

She put her arm through mine as we walked toward the hootch.

I pressed her hand.

"Maybe you see. Maybe someday you see."

"See what?"

"Maybe you wish you have Kim when you oop-soh." It was some kind of slang for "gone or go away," and I was told it maybe came from the Korean word *eubseyo* but as with most slang took on a meaning of its own. When Kim said it, she always did the eyeroll to make fun of our failure to learn Korean.

"Let's don't talk about being gone, okay?"

"Later, huh, yobo?"

"Okay, not now."

"You see. You will," she said and squeezed my arm. We got to her hootch, where she changed into some clothes she had left there, and we went to dinner at the O Club. It wasn't something to do often, even though the club accepted regular yobos, or mice. The other officers pretended not to notice.

Kim said it made her feel like she wasn't even there, the way she was ignored. I said never mind what they do. Which got us started again on "mind your own business." Started as a tease but went rogue. What does the Army say? A need to know? I lacked it. And then I didn't want it.

It was about Coletti. What had been going wrong. Even if I knew it, I really didn't. Or didn't want to. And so, I acted out. Which explains the butterflying, at least on my part. Maybe hers. It wasn't the only thing going wrong, but it was big. Another thing about Kim I needed to stop evading.

I knew she had gotten to know Coletti through Halua. And before. They seldom spoke of it. But "getting to know Coletti" had evolved. Not just delivering or selling black-market PX goods for him in the ville, but with coaching by Halua from his experience in the jungle and around Cam Ranh Bay. That was enough, and at the root of my beef with Coletti, like the stolen PX goods, and I had learned to let it go. Kim was doing the same. Again, she said most of the yobos made side deals, kept it to themselves, to make a little extra. She said their bodies weren't their only business. Again, she said she wasn't a slave. No big deal.

Sometime in late winter or early spring, Coletti had branched out. He seldom sold junk to junkies, but there were new profits to be made, and there he was. I suppose I knew about that business, too, in a vague way. It was just there, part of the surroundings, like the air, like the working girls. I looked the other way. For Kim, I said to myself. For us.

Coletti knew Kim was smart and knew the ville. He offered her an upgrade, to move $10,000 worth of opium, a lot by Korean standards. She was to deliver it to Lee Chae-Sing, a half-Chinese gangster with ties to Seoul and Incheon. Her cut was 15 percent, which was considered generous, but Coletti liked her, and it ensured trust.

More deals evolved.

She developed a semi-regular run, mostly in the ville but also in Bupyeong and even Seoul. She was extremely careful and valued her life. If the CID found out, they would steal her money and kill her. Worse if she ran afoul of the gangsters.

This is what she told me, almost in a whisper, in our corner of the O Club dining room, no one close enough to eavesdrop. She said she wanted me to know and be honest and that's how it would be for us so we wouldn't have to lie or always be having fights about minding our own business or butterflying or any of those things. Ever.

I can't remember the rest of the dinner or even walking back to our hootch. Later, in bed, early for us, and in my near silence, she said she didn't want me to be afraid and had told me about what she was doing back in the O Club only because she had to let it out and couldn't wait and thought telling me in public would make her brave. I asked why she had to be brave to talk to me and then we kissed like we meant it and held each other. I relaxed, just looking deeply into her eyes, and almost fell asleep. But her lips were at my ear, and she said the words. She waited for mine in return. She didn't get them.

No matter. There was still something I had no need to know. Still a business of her own to mind. On her own. The size of her savings. Her determination. Her love.

Still a part of her business that when I would tell her no, get out of the black market, that when I would tell her that what she really wanted for us could never happen, that she would not cry. Because she had prepared for that, too.

24

She was a girl once, had not always been a yobo. GIs rarely asked yobos about their previous lives. Were seldom told. The histories had always been there. Would never change. Why bring them up?

That kind of memory, of permanence, had no place in the GI/yobo existence. The gap, the hole, the invisibility, were hardly opaque. GIs came and went. Literally and figuratively. Tragedy. Adventure? Business? Or just the stage on which we strut and fret and are no more? That was definitely the storyline in the human theater of Hobbes and Kim. All we needed were some regional props—off-limits bars, short trips to Seoul or Incheon, drugs, booze, exchange of currency. No reminders of what had been. How it had been taken away. How nothing seemed to be the only future.

But Kim told me once, on a wet afternoon in a Seoul hotel, how she came. That was the way she said it: Would you like to hear how I came? I said yes, but also how were you a little girl? She shook her head as if I had insulted her. I probably had.

She came via a small village northeast of Seoul called Kwan-chae. Her given name was Ahnjong, but she stopped using it long ago. By the time she wound up in Suchow, she had gone by Annie for a while, but it started making her feel depressed. She became just Kim or Miss Kim. It was my asking why "Annie" made her depressed that launched her into sharing her history. And the real answer. Bits and pieces over a couple of weeks, stinko and sober, laughing and crying. Mostly the latter. Because the one she loved should know.

And thus did I learn.

*

Her father, Kim Sung-Jo, was a brick maker, churning a daily mixture of clay and water, stirring it with large ladles until it was smooth, ready to harden, then scooping a wet mass from the iron pot and pouring it into brick forms. When the mixture stabilized, Mr. Kim and his partner removed the forms, leaving the brick blocks on the ground to dry in the sun and wind. For two days, the bricks were soft enough to break with bare hands.

We did that once, Sansoe and I. We came across a brick yard in the country on a long hike from the ville, the bricks stretched row on row in the moonlight, waiting for the sun to come and give them strength. We knew they weren't hard yet and thought it would be fun to karate them. Ha! Whack! Squish! they went under our hands, destroying in five minutes an hour's work. We went back the next day, feeling contrite, and wanted to pay damages, but it was too embarrassing even to do that, so we just strolled by as the brick-maker grumbled and swept up our mess, then mixed and poured more. Sansoe stopped and put some MPC under a brick so it would be easily found. We didn't even know the man's name.

Mr. Kim's bricks, safe from GI vandals, hardened like rocks. Then he sold them to the other people in his village, who used them to build small houses, sheds, walls. There was no wood because the Japanese had cut the trees in the 1930s when they occupied the Hermit Kingdom, adding to the history of intruders who left it bare, cold, and poor.

My Kim said the family's house was small, with a tiled roof. A wall enclosed the courtyard, and the house completed the other three sides of the rectangle. In the rooms, everything had a place and was used when needed and put away when not. The tidiness had a function. Even the few square feet provided enough space for Mr. Kim, his wife, and the five children.

The courtyard, also clean and respected, included a well, surrounded by large earthenware crocks used to store kimchi, rice and fish. On sunny days and warm evenings, the family sat in the courtyard, talking and working.

They were in the courtyard on the day soldiers came in, ordered them to stand. An officer, a red star on each collar of his coat, told Mr. Kim they were taking his supply of bricks, that it was a national emergency. It was 1950.

"Is there a war again?" Mr. Kim asked. He remembered the Japanese occupation, the cruelty, the world war that surrounded it. But it was different now. All in Korea now. North and South now.

"There is always a war here," the officer said. He had a northern accent.

Months later, another truck of soldiers came. They had different uniforms, and their captain had a southern accent. They loaded bricks and left. They told Mr. Kim to make more.

It will be all right, he told his wife. We will survive this, too. In a week, when more bricks were stacked in the sun, the truck came again. From the ROK. It took the bricks, and the soldiers took Mr. Kim.

Mrs. Kim waited a month for her husband and then began to pack the wood and carved-bone table and plates and food on the ox cart. She had relatives in Busan. Mr. Kim would know.

But as she packed and wept to herself during the days, every night she felt the earth shake from explosions in the mountains around the village. More soldiers came through, some on foot, some in trucks, quickly, tearing the oxcart roads to shreds. The very young children—Ahnjong (my Kim) was only three—stayed inside all the time. Their mother worked harder, strapping and tying her possessions on the cart.

And then the shells came into the village. Mrs. Kim had just roped the old clock onto the last space on the top of the cart when the first explosion fell nearby. She watched, unable to move, as more and more of the screaming shells pulverized the earth around Kwan-Chae, Houses crumbled, metal zipped through the air. She could see her neighbors running, falling in ditches.

She hurried into her house. The children were crying, watching from the small window. Smoke and dust made the sky brown. Sulphur and carbon choked anything that breathed. They huddled in the bedroom, straw mattresses as the only defense. Ping, ping. Shrapnel sliced

101

into the walls, ricocheted off tile and thudded into the cart outside. Then there was a deafening noise and the sliding doors to the bedroom blew inward in splinters in a shower of dirt and debris,

Mrs. Kim shouted for her children, reached for them under the mattresses. They were all there, All near her. She sighed and moaned, and the explosions continued, Then her hand, wiping the grime from the children's faces, found a small hole in the forehead of the oldest, Sung-mun. She lifted him in her arms. It is only a small hole, a small hole, she thought, but when she touched the back of his head she screamed and cried. Her children shivered and clung to each other. Another explosion, a wall collapsed. A metal sliver pierced her leg. The smallest son, Hi-su, only four, climbed out from the mattresses to look at his mother and in a rush of air and dust and noise he fell, clutching his stomach and whimpering only for a second.

It continued for a half-hour, explosions and choking and the cries of the wounded and dying. Through the hole where the bedroom wall had been, Mrs. Kim stared blankly as soldiers ran by, firing and falling down. Then giant machines. She didn't know the name for tanks. They clanked down the hills. When they paused, flames would shoot out of a long barrel on the front.

Then thick black smoke. Then more explosions. Mrs. Kim passed out, bleeding and holding two daughters and a last son, who cried and watched the war game. That afternoon, other soldiers pulled them from the rubble. The dead remained.

Mrs. Kim and her surviving children made their way to a refugee camp farther south. From there they went to Busan, staying with their relatives until the fighting shifted elsewhere. After that, the family moved to Seoul, where Mrs. Kim found work in a textile plant, still surviving even though the see-saw of troops went back and forth.

She worked ten hours, six days a week, keeping the family alive, dreaming at night of a stranger, a stranger with news of her husband. When the war stopped, Ahnjong and her sister, Ha Jun, went to schools, on and off. Ahnjong left when she was fourteen. The last brother, Lin Wan, got various jobs that came and went. Then he got drafted. He was sent with a Korean Expeditionary Force to Vietnam. One day a stranger came to the door. Very somber. He was an officer in the ROK Army with news.

25

We will survive, her father had said. Ahnjong, the oldest now, had to find work. At first it was mostly as a maid or clean-up girl. Finally, her mom found her a safe job in a teahouse. It was okay, but she missed school. And the uniform: Simple black skirt and white blouse. No one could tell which girls were well-off or which were poor. And she could read, thanks to her dad and mom. She had worn her books tied in a strap slung across her back, same as all the other girls. Her life had been plain but predictable. She rose before sun-up. She made breakfast for her pretty sister, two grades behind.

But not all the other girls had to say goodbye to their mother six days a week as she went to the factory to weave cloth for shirts and suits that American workers said put them out of work. Nor were all the other girls without fathers. Most were daughters of men who survived the war and then filled the country's labor vacuum, went to a university to improve their social ranking. Men who had families and even houses.

Still, every day, Annie and Ha Jun and their mother had reaped what their father had said, that, they would survive. Endure.

And then it all changed. Within a year, Ahnjong was a hostess. Everyone called her Annie. She looked older when she wore the dresses the tearoom provided and welcomed the customers when the bamboo door opened with a smile and the "annyeong-hashimnikka," greeting before taking them to quiet tables. The customers would order pots of tea and small cakes and spend an hour sheltered from the pollution and crowds of the city.

When there were no new customers, Annie sat alone on a wooden stool, looking at the green vines in the courtyard fountain, thinking of the girls in the Japanese magazines. They wore new clothes and smiled above advertisements for soft drinks. Men looked at them, admired them, longed for them. Annie touched the glossy pages, smoothed her fingers over what she saw there, and rubbed her shoe against the floor.

Day after day, the door would open, briefly revealing the light and dust and honking horns outside, and often enough the faces of lovers sneaking in a tryst in the afternoon. "Annyeong-hashimnikka," Kim would smile, and put the magazine back on the table. The images sunk in as the months passed, but before long, what she was really doing was anything possible to keep her from constantly thinking of Ha Jun, who had died of tuberculosis, which was going around at school. In time, Mrs. Kim was gone. Factory accident from a machine damaged in the war. And then Annie was a casualty, too.

26

Kim's teahouse, when she had been Annie, was a tiny oasis from noise and bustle near the East Gate. Now, almost twenty years later, it was surrounded by hundreds of shops and thousands of shoppers as Seoul and the economy rebounded. I tried to find it once when I went to Seoul with Cpl. Yu but couldn't. Maybe it was gone. Maybe it was something else now, like Kim.

The city also was full of air pollution. And getting worse, according to the buzz. It seemed like half the people we passed were wearing masks. I had first noticed the masks on A-frame carriers and cart-pullers, but really, they'd be on the faces of just about anyone, from bustling businessmen to casual shoppers and even schoolchildren.

"Good way to fight the smog. Maybe they could wear them in LA."

"What you mean, 'smog'?"

"You know, this dirty stuff in the air."

"Oh yes, smog." He smiled. "You think these for smog?"

"They're not? I mean what else could they wear them for? They can't all work at the hospitals."

"Look out," he warned and pulled me to one side. A small kimchi cab fighting its way up the street inched along toward us, beeping its horn and racing its engine. People banged on its doors when it annoyed them.

"Those masks for TB. Everybody supposed to get shots."

The cab grazed my shin. I kicked the rear bumper as it crept away.

Cpl. Yu shot me a look. The point of the trip was to introduce me to some regular Korean women, and I was already doing the Ugly American. He knew about Kim and disapproved, not only because I was consorting with business girls, but also because he wanted me to get a better idea of what young Korean women were really like. Women who did not work for money from GIs. Who went to schools, and colleges, and had real jobs and went to restaurants where they were not automatically pegged as yobos. He had scolded me many times about my habits of just seeing his country through the ville, but as a KATUSA corporal he knew he had to be careful around American officers, even those who were friends.

A KATUSA was a ROK Army soldier being trained to work for the Americans. KATUSA stands for Korean Attached to U.S. Army. It was an alliance program based on simple logic. The more Koreans, the fewer Americans. Col. Samuels called it kimchi NATO and said he didn't like the way the cadets were so harshly disciplined.

The two girls were very nice—almost disorienting to me. The kind I would ask out on a date in a second. They even spoke English, to my zero Korean. But I wasn't that person now. As we walked along toward a park after lunch, the girls ahead of us, I quietly asked Cpl. Yu if he had slept with one of them. Guy talk, I thought. He went red-faced and I could almost hear his teeth grinding. He said he wanted to marry her but couldn't until he got out of the Korean Army because his pay was too low. He hoped she would wait.

I liked him a lot. And he had gone out of his way to bring me to the "real" Korea, as he put it. I knew I should be humbled, and I was. And it was a wonderful day—my only one in Korea that would ever be like that. Making new, real friends against all odds. And in return I was acting like just another GI—kicking cabs, cursing, but most of all insulting his secret girlfriend.

Never after that day did Cpl. Yu offer his friendship in the same way, and never again did he introduce me to anyone close to him, female or male, even KATUSAs.

*

And so back to the yobos. I tried to ask myself why. Why did it turn out this way for both sides—the GIs and the women. Kim had told me her life story, but as for why-am-I-a-yobo, the details remained vague. At first, I had thought they should explain, be straight about what they were doing, how they got there. But it did not need to be said. The silence, the evasion, the lying, was truth enough.

Nor did GIs have to say it to know a yobo was not a whore, not a whore/yobo. Of course we paid them, of course they lured us, fought for us, laughed at us, and took our money. But they were not hookers, man-eaters. We didn't even use those words. We called them yobos, sometimes chicks and mamas. Called them baby when we curled together. The older guys called them "mouse" or "mice." I never did because I just didn't like the way it sounded.

As if it mattered. As fucking if.

Sansoe said having a yobo was like having a date with somebody and instead of bullshitting all night over dinner and a movie, you just paid them straightaway for sex. Arnie said the whole "people exchange system" was completely fucked up and predatory even if we did get horny with nothing else to do. But of course, he was married and happy to be. Not that he didn't have a point.

I always gave them ten dollars, even though the old lifers said I was a fool to pay over five, that you could get it for three MPC up North, that back in the war you could get it for a candy bar. Maybe that's why I thought they were special, Travis suggested, because I never had to fight them about price.

But even with my own Kim, though there was sex, there was more. Right from the start. Always the unspoken possibility. It was, in its lingering, alienated way, a kind of love. Love, even just the thought of it, came easily to young men in those circumstances.

That was why the airport at Kimpo was so insanely, desperately sad and fantastically exhilarating at each flight. It became a closed circle of the senses, where innocence and guilt could no longer be separated and kept safe.

The yobos waved and cried and held their GIs at the final wire mesh runway barrier. More than the men, they held onto the unspoken possibility—the American Dream. It was in their slender arms, had embraced them late at night and called them darling, and now—so horribly, incredibly, mercilessly—the American Dream, even a drunk ugly GI, was stepping up the ramp and into the Red Tail door.

The yobos had tried so hard. They dressed in Western clothes: hot pants, tight slacks, tie-back halters. Stuffed their bras with tissue, called themselves Nancy and Susie and Candy, painted their eyes to make them round. Died their hair blond or red.

But after one too many goodbyes, one too many failed I-love-yous, they began to see. You could pick them out with their cosmetic complexions and paste-on smiles. And you went for the fresher ones. But not to worry about those left behind. They could still find business. There was an endless supply of GIs, all kinds, fresh or grizzled. And a blow job didn't require a beautiful mouth. And still went for a couple of bucks in hard times.

None of this human bondage would ever change. It was the endless fuel of the after-market of war.

27

I had been in Korea a little more than half my thirteen-month tour, summer just coming along. One morning on the way to work I ran into Travis near the KATUSA school. He saluted for a laugh and said he'd walk with me as far as HQ. It was good to see him, and it occurred to me he hadn't been around much lately. I didn't want to pry.

We stopped at hearing angry yelling and saw that it was coming from a ROK sergeant in front of a small morning formation administering corporal punishment in the form of a fist to the stomach to a KATUSA cadet.

We watched the cadet drop to his knees, then more yelling as he struggled to stand as erect as possible. A ROK colonel showed up, talked to the sergeant, saw Travis and me, said something to the cadet we couldn't hear and wouldn't understand, and dismissed the formation.

We decided to check in to our own offices and then meet over at the White Elephant. We got to my battalion headquarters just as Cpl. Yu came up. He lived in a KATUSA barracks.

"What was that all about?" Travis asked.

"Oh, you saw?

"We saw."

"He was in big trouble. Not come to formation last two days."

"You guys play pretty rough," I said.

"He was in big trouble."

"Whatever," Travis said, and headed on to his own office.

"Be careful," I told Yu.

He looked at me, then off into the distance. "Yes sir. I having to report to colonel most skochie. He is go to Yongsan today." He saluted me, unnecessarily, and went into our office building. I'd seen this polite shut-down before. The KATUSAs never said anything that might sound bad about their unit.

I made it to the O Club in about a half hour. Nobody really cared if you did the coffee sham as long as nothing was going on. For some reason, I had expected Travis to make an issue of the ROK discipline, but he didn't. I mean such corporal thuggery would've been part of his Yankee creed. I mean Americans would never do that to each other. Especially officers. We were the good guys.

Instead, Travis commented on the weather and when we'd change into summer uniforms and then seemed to kind of drift off and then seemed to come back into focus and asked me if I was doing anything remotely interesting at my "shop." A word I'd never heard him use. He said at his shop it was endless boredom.

I let it go. Maybe he just needed more coffee. He looked at me, and at Miss Lee, and then out the dining room windows. More drifting off. So, I thought I'd move the conversation. What popped into my head was the business with the food and the mess sergeant. It had been eating on me, and I actually put it that way just to see if Travis would groan, which he did.

So, I gave him the short version of a long mess. Using another food reference, also met with a groan. It started back in March, I told him, when I wanted to send leftover food from the mess to the orphanages scattered around us. They were the kids, mostly the outcast mixed-race (Korean and American) ones in the dirt playpens you could always see when you drove by. The battalion mess sergeant, an E7, close to retirement and bitter as hell, let me know in vivid language that I was a fool and that it was against regulations. Black market and all.

As it happened, though, the sergeant shortly thereafter was arrested and put in the stockade by the CID for selling about five thousand pounds of steak to Korean restaurants. I got involved because I had to find his replacement. Also, because his yobo had come around to headquarters looking for "Big E" (Eddie) and I had to tell her. I could hear crying and cursing in pretty good English once she was outside the office, heading for the gate. Not so much about Big E, but because she knew plans to get to the States with him were gone.

I recounted the story to Travis, and he was oddly quiet. Miss Lee brought more coffee.

"Something on your mind?" I finally asked.

He drank all his coffee, hot as it was, without flinching. Then put his cup down, stared at me. "What do you think will happen to all this, Hobbes? I mean if we pull out, what'll these people do?"

"No idea." I thought at first, he was starting some kind of joke, but I could see otherwise in his eyes.

"That's what I mean, man. No fucking idea. Nobody has any fucking idea. I mean the ville, the town, the command, the whole damn place. We act like it'll be here forever." He paused. "And you know, some guys actually want to be here forever."

I tried a smile. "For sure not you and me."

"No, seriously. That mama-san you just told me about. Her guy gets busted, she's shit out of luck."

"Come on. When was she ever shit in luck?"

"Fuck." Miss Lee saw that he'd gulped the last cup, poured him another. I noticed he put three spoonsful of sugar in his cup. He usually drank it black.

I leaned in, lowering my voice. "You got a new yobo in the ville now?"

"Why? Why do you ask?"

"You've been a vapor man lately."

"We'll go into it some other time if you don't mind." He sounded like a lawyer.

"Sure, man."

A few minutes more silence. The dining room was empty, and we were going to have to move on.

"How's Kim?" he said, looking down at his cup.

"She's fine."

"You going to take her home?"

"Sure," I laughed. "You bet."

"We'll see."

"You think I'm in over my head, don't you?"

Travis's expression hardened. "We're all in over our heads, Hobbes. Take my word for it."

I finished my coffee. "Sounds ominous."

His eyes flashed. The intensity made me realize they were actually dull.

"Are you stoned?"

His smile was almost aggressive. "What's the matter? Too early in the day for you?"

"No. It's never too early. Except, you know, when you're supposed to be at work."

He looked at his watch. "So, I'd better get back." He stood, threw down some MPC. "See you later."

"Later." I stayed at the table, watched him leave. I had some thoughts. Not about him. About me. For some reason I must have smiled to myself.

"What's so funny?" Miss Lee said, picking up the cups and the tip.

"You think our Lieutenant Travis has changed?" I knew he had gone home with her once or twice.

"Everybody change. Everybody change." She looked off toward the door. "Me, maybe too."

28

Before going back to the battalion office, I detoured to the men's room and then the newsstand in the hall leading to the BOQ stairwell and picked up a *Stars and Stripes*. I paused to check out the headlines. The news from Vietnam was as usual. Incomprehensible. It didn't seem so far away anymore, but far enough.

Halfway down the page, I heard the high whine of the compound siren. I glanced at my watch. A little after eight. Odd time for a siren. The whine died, in the annoying theatrical way it always did. Then started again.

I hurried toward the front door to get over to battalion, but stopped when a small gaggle of majors and colonels were emerging from the White Elephant meeting room, more often a private party room, at the far end of the dining area. Caught my breath because I wondered if they'd noticed Travis and me loafing, but I stopped thinking about that when Col. Arthur Bridges, the compound commander said to be in line for general, emerged, clutching what looked like a telegraph print-out. One of his staff, a major, was right beside him, talking in a low voice and breathing hard. Col. Bridges waited for the siren to stop.

"Gentlemen, this may be it," he said, holding up the papers, as the officers circled around him. "Report immediately to your duty station. I'll be in touch with 8th Army if that's possible, so stay close to your comms. I'll get all this to you straightaway."

The officers looked at each other seriously, although several half-smiled as if to discount whatever was up as yet another useless drill. An invasion was absolutely out of the question. Still, the red alert siren had sounded. Still, you never knew.

114

Miss Lee leaned impassively against the coffee machine near the bar. I think her only concern was whether anyone had left tips from the meeting. In the back, kitchen fans droned.

The officers crowded each other toward the front foyer, pausing to let Col. Bridges and his aide get out first. Several in Class A's instead of fatigues had to stop to pick up their "covers," mostly saucer hats, on the cloakroom shelf. Which reminded me I had left mine there several days ago after a meeting.

So, I grabbed it to take with me back to my office and felt lucky it hadn't been stolen. "That's not yours, that's a major's," a strac captain I'd never seen before barked at me on his way out. Like me, he'd waited his turn to leave. "Sorry, sir," I said, and examined the front of the hat. He was right. I looked on the shelf and couldn't see mine. I was putting the mistake back until I noticed the name written on the inner band: Maj. Matson. I hadn't seen him, and time was flying, so I tucked it under my arm and headed out. I could give it to the Flamer, which is what we called him, back at HQ. He'd probably ask if I'd stolen it.

A string of officers were heading across the field toward the foot-bridge that led to the rest of the compound, so I double-timed all the way to battalion. I still didn't see Matson, but I hoped he was back in the Club looking for his hat.

I hit the HQ office ahead of anyone else, and then another idea just hit me. I threw the hat into the bottom of a corner trashcan, sprinkled some throwaway papers on top.

Within minutes, Maj. Matson burst through the door breathing heavily. His face was beet red. Partly from being angry and embarrassed he'd lost his cover, but also because he was so far from being in shape that he could barely make a long walk without getting exhausted. It would probably cost him a promotion again. I stood up and greeted him. He looked me over, then my fatigue cap on my desk. I realized that he hadn't seen me at the Club.

"Lieutenant, some sorry horseshit bastard slickied my hat back in the Club. Call supply and get me a new one right away."

"Yessir."

He eyed me closely, then strode towards his office, next to the colonel's, who for some reason, perhaps pity, hadn't had him transferred.

In less than a minute, Col. Samuels rushed in, flustered and drowsy from what must have been another bad night. He looked at me, Sgt. Frye, and Cpl. Yu, who'd also arrived. We looked back at him. We knew none of us knew anything.

"Coffee, sir?" I ventured.

"Not now, dammit."

"Yessir."

The colonel stood alone in the center of the room, looked toward the small row of inner offices, then called out. "Major, you got anything yet?"

"No, sir," the Flamer answered, emerging.

"You, lieutenant?"

"No, sir."

The colonel rubbed his eyes. "Somebody," he began slowly, then forcefully, "find out!"

Cpl. Yu, standing at attention near his metal chair by the water cooler, raised his hand. "Sir, I have hear rumors."

The colonel let out a deep breath, looking at the Flamer and me icily. He turned to Yu. "Well, corporal? At least somebody knows some damn thing."

"Sir. Mr. Lee, the carpenter, came from the village just now and he say people there say North Koreans near Incheon and headed to Seoul. He say they have kill some people already."

We looked at each other.

"How many does Mr. Lee think there are?"

Cpl. Yu asked for permission to go outside, where Mr. Lee was repairing a window. The colonel waved his hand as a sign of permission.

Cpl. Yu came back in quickly. "Mr. Lee think about one hundred. Or maybe five hundred. He not know for sure."

The colonel nodded, then seemed lost in thought. Better than lost in battle. I knew the colonel's thoughts. If this is the real deal, then okay. Vaguely, guiltily, it would be good to be there. In battle. For a career soldier to be there. For everyone else? That was the guilt part. But still. It might be nothing.

Sgt. Frye was not conflicted at all. "Son of a bitch," he grimaced, crunching on the cigar that he couldn't smoke because the colonel didn't allow it in HQ. "Wouldn't you know it? Fourteen days 'til I go home, and they start the fucking war again."

The colonel smiled at him slightly, turned to Cpl. Yu. "Thank you, corporal." Then, to the Flamer. "Major, pin this down, will you?"

"Yessir. Sir, okay if I change into fatigues? I got a pair here."

The colonel seemed to try to figure out why he wasn't in fatigues in the first place, but let it go.

"Just make it fast."

"Sir, where's the XO? Or Snelling?"

"Major Antone is up at compound. Captain Snelling had some kind of doctor thing. But I'm sure they'll be here soon. Just move on."

He did, and we could hear the Flamer cursing inside his office,

For an hour, no one could find out anything other than what Cpl. Yu heard from Mr. Lee, who patiently worked on the window damage. A month or two ago, we had paid Mr. Lee $10 U.S. to put tile in a headquarters office annex. It took him three days. Sansoe thought he should get a lot more money, but Maj. Matson laughed, "Fuck him, it's good money for a gook."

Still waiting for orders, the colonel had us go down to the armory and draw our weapons. The armorer, Sergeant First Class Slayton, was *toc sahn*, another slang that more or less meant "too much," not happy about it. "Fucking waste of time," he said, handing me an M-16. "Those fuckers ain't gonna attack. And don't get that dirty, either lieutenant. I just cleaned all these goddam things. Now move along, damn it. Shit, I only got three guys on duty here this morning to help the whole goddam battalion."

I stepped aside instinctively to let the line move along. Fortunately for the sergeant, our battalion was really just an enhanced HQ company, thanks to Army downsizing. Even so, I should have reprimanded him. Right.

Battalion officers quickly spread through the various barracks and office areas, ferreting out troops and making sure they had or were getting weapons and web belts with M-16 clips, canteens, first aid kits. Then we made the men stand in loose formation outside the barracks waiting for the orders.

I went back to headquarters to help with phone calls and messengers. I began to answer inquiries gruffly. "We'll tell you when we know!"

Staff Sgt. Trevor Davis, NCOIC of the commo shack, ran into the office after an hour with an "official" report. It was from 8th Army top shelf and said 120 North Koreans had landed near Incheon and were coming our way on buses commandeered by killing the passengers on board.

Col. Samuels read it slowly, twice. "This is it. Major, have the battalion form a defensive perimeter. Lieutenant, stay with me to handle comms. Okay, let's move it."

Within minutes we received further orders from Col. Bridges at compound command. He assigned our battalion a sector and instructed us to "hold" it. There was a succession of orders, questions, SOPs.

Capt. Snelling, the S3 (Operations), a Vietnam vet and along with Arnie one of the handful of Black officers on the compound, showed up and said he'd cancelled his appointment. He immediately started rounding up all our secret documents to burn them in the special barrel he had requisitioned two months ago but hadn't had a chance to use yet. Company commanders argued. Sergeants bitched. The EMs mostly laughed.

I walked past the armory again and overheard Capt. James, from financial, argue with SFC Slayton, who didn't want to issue grenade launchers for the occasion because they were especially hard to clean and re-pack. "What do you expect, a bunch of goddamned clerks to do? Fucking staple them to death?" the captain said, but Slayton wouldn't budge.

For his part, Maj. Matson was barking orders at Spec. 4 Dubose, his clerk/driver, to stay ready although no one knew where anyone would be going. Or why.

Most of the EMs were milling around waiting to build sandbag bunkers lining what Maj. Antone, just back from his errand at compound HQ for the colonel, called "our defensive perimeter." Sansoe dubbed it our Invisible Shield.

The shield was rotten. The sandbags in storage back of the motor pool had disintegrated from disuse, their contents busting open to spread on the ground like tiny Saharas. Still, the EMs carried around what bags held together so they could crouch behind them, wiping grit from their eyes when the wind blew.

Luckily, it wasn't winter.

Most of the "perimeter" faced the Incheon secondary road, across which was Suchow. The M-60 machine gun clerks, who in normal duty posted notations on 201 personnel files, plotted fire zones on the bars and hootches. Or pretended to.

Few of the enlisted men believed anything would happen. "Even if they attack, what difference does it make?" a Spec. 4 said to his buddies.

Sansoe felt the same. "If there's only a hundred of them, it's no big deal. The fucking Air Force will zap them. If it's more than that, they'll bring the infantry down from the Z. So why go through all this shit?"

We waited two hours. The excitement died. If it comes, it comes. But it didn't.

The colonel paced from one section of our redoubt to another, looking at the sky, the mountains, the Incheon road. He wasn't in the compound. He was in Virginia. Or West Point, Sacrificing, always sacrificing, to save his country. To have a part. To not have been forsaken by legend and history.

I walked with him most of the time because that was the adjutant's job, but he seemed to barely know or care. There were no orders to give, decisions to make. No updated intel beyond Mr. Lee.

What the colonel saw: Fourteen men from the DPU sailing paper airplanes from stacks of orders they had bundled to augment the sandbags. I told Sgt. Swan, the new NCOIC, to make them stop. The colonel didn't say anything. Just simmered as they picked up the mess.

But the sarcasm was spreading. On the far side of the perimeter, PFC McCarty and Spec. 4 Gunter sat alone at a bunker, stoned, building sandcastles from broken bags. I saw it before the colonel had time to glare at me. Knock it off, I told them.

When the alert had begun, Col. Samuels swore vehemently at "whoever was responsible for our poor defenses." By late morning, except to ask the radio operator if there was any news, he only mumbled, "Jesus, get me through the month," which was a reference to when his tour ended and he was going home.

About 12:30, Col. Samuels said I could take a break. He was going to his office and see if he could get a call through to his wife.

I found a place in the shade of a Quonset hut and sat down, leaned back against some stray sandbags, found myself looking up into the sky, into the high yellow sun, and the clouds, and the nothing.

And then I saw them.

Hanging, waving from old tangerine buses, led by a convertible kimchi cab with posters taped on the doors and flags whipping around the radio antenna. From the bus windows, the North Koreans waved and grinned. Have some of this joint, one said. PFC Gunter took it. We gathered around the buses, smiling and laughing, taking photos. The colonel showed up, singing some old WWII song, and showed a North Korean officer a picture of his wife with a North Korean colonel. Around the buses we danced and then girls from the rice fields joined us. We followed them to a small lake. They're not working girls but girls from a place in Kim's past and so we just swam and danced and splashed and laughed as we try to talk to each other. Soon we all basked in the sun on our ponchos, rifles and canteen belts strewn on the shore. Then came a high whistle in the wind. And the napalm. We melted in the lake...

I blinked. Squinted from the sun. I was back in real time.

Col. Samuels was standing in front of me.

"Sorry to disturb your dream or whatever the fuck, lieutenant. But I think Sgt. Davis is looking for us. So, I've been looking for you." The sneer on his face was lethal. "Perhaps you could take a minute."

I stood at attention as best I could. "Sorry, sir. Of course. I'll go find him." I took off in the direction he was pointing, spotted the sergeant quickly, and brought him back.

"Sir," he said, saluting the colonel and holding up some papers—a message transmission. "I got the word."

The word, from Staff Sgt. Davis, was: "It's over."

"Over?" the colonel said.

"Yessir."

"OVER?"

"Yessir." The sergeant looked at me.

"What is over? What the hell ever happened?" the colonel said. Growled, more like.

Sgt. Davis almost flinched. "Oh, yessir. I mean I guess I thought you already knew. I was just bringing it in writing so you'd have it—"

"—Just read me the goddamn message, sergeant. I don't have my glasses."

Sgt. Davis looked at me again. I nodded.

"Yessir. Of course, sir. You want me to just read it now, like it's typed out?"

"Good lord, sergeant."

"Yessir."

Sgt. Davis held up the two-page message so he could see in the sun's glare.

"Yessir. Well, sir, apart from the heading, it says, uh, it's from G2 in Yongsan and it's addressed to all installation and division commanders and battalion level COs."

"Go on, go on."

"Yessir. It says: 'Alert Red Fox III cancelled. Repeat Alert Red Fox III cancelled. Appropriate commanders may inform units there has been no repeat no invasion from DPRK. Fighting caused by what believed 36 repeat 36 North Korean nationals. All killed at approx 1200 hours in attempted assault on provincial police station on outskirts of Seoul. ROK and KATUSA reinforcements quickly flown in overwhelmed attackers. Infiltrators landed via trawler near Incheon, commandeered two buses. Infiltrators took back roads bypassing several Incheon area compounds.'" SFC Davis paused to turn to the second page of the message.

"'ROK commander informs all infiltrators on Bus No. 1 killed in fire fight. All killed on Bus No. 2 believed from own grenades. ROK Army and our G2 believe this an isolated harassment and does not foreshadow general operations from North, which is expected to deny incident. No observed DPRK troop movements elsewhere and no incidents reported along DMZ. All units may resume normal operations. End of message.'" Sgt. Davis stopped, as if surprised.

"Oh, that's it, sir." He handed the document to the colonel.

Not quite a false alarm after all.

Col. Samuels thanked Sgt. Davis, who saluted and said he would be going back to the commo shack. The colonel looked at me, not exactly in strac mode, with my M-16 hanging uselessly on one shoulder. He started walking and I followed as he surveyed the collapsing sandbags and the windblown castles and the clerks napping in the sun in their ridiculous bunkers. No fighting now, no adrenaline rush of commanding men toward death, no nihilistic fervor of battle—what career officers were for.

The Flamer was coming our way, striding importantly. "Tell the men to stack arms and get back to their jobs," the colonel said, curtly. Then he walked back toward headquarters, almost tripping over a half-empty sandbag.

The Flamer and the XO and I supervised the return to normal. Capt. Snelling re-gathered the documents he was prepared to burn. We bustled here and there, making sure arms were turned in and troops were dismantling the sandbag bunkers. Which was actually kind of amusing to watch but no way I was going to be caught smirking. We told everyone to take the rest of the day off but stay on compound.

The XO had Spec. Dubose make a list of every bunker that needed new sandbags. Basically, all of them. Capt. Snelling and Sgt. Sawyer were poking in the ashes of the new security burner, trying to recover secrets that no longer needed to be destroyed. SFC Slayton had thrown open the armory and told everyone to just put their weapons wherever they goddam wanted. He sat behind his desk with a bottle of Merry Wedding and said, "I could've fucking told you so." I slipped my rifle into slot 245.

By 4 p.m., we were finished and returned to headquarters to close up shop and presumably head for what could be a very strange happy hour.

Mr. Pak, the houseboy for the office, was emptying the office trash into a Dempsey Dumpster outside. Too late, I saw the Flamer's "missing" hat catch a sudden breeze and go sailing from the bottom of a trash basket to the top of the garbage pile in the dumpster.

I glanced stealthily at the Flamer. He didn't see it. Mr. Pak did, though, and started to say something. I shook my head sternly and put a finger to my lips. Mr. Pak shrugged and covered the saucer with waste papers.

29

I hold her in the night, but we have argued. Just last night.

Sell your goddam TVs and radios and tape decks, I had said, scornfully and with more than a hint of superiority. Fucking gook cunt. I had said something like that. But don't go around fucking guys behind my back. You're supposed to be my yobo. I said that, too. But we let it pass and made soothing caresses. "No, no, Hobbes-san, you no worry. My old yobo he okay. You think I give you something?" I didn't answer. She pushed me away and told me to go back to the BOQ. I did.

But it doesn't matter, not now. What matters is how often this happens, and we talk about it as we lie naked in bed, unable to sleep. My fingers slide slowly along her body.

"You no worry," says she and rolls on top of me, sits up and puts me inside her. We heave and press against each other on the soft bed. "Come in me, come in me," she says.

After that, she says she won't see her old yobo anymore, not even to sell something. I am not worried about that now. I have her. Or do I? "Why did you see him in the first place?"

"Sshh, yobo, you no start this again. You hold me and no talk, okay?" I pinch her ass gently. I am only mocking when I ask, "Wasn't I good enough or do you want to fuck every GI in Korea?"

She stops smiling and looks at me. Angrily. I could say I am sorry in that split-second, but don't. She rolls away and sits up in the bed, flinging the covers to the floor.

"You, you GI bastard. I love you, yobo. I love you. Not him. Not no one else. I love you. But you no see that."

"Kim," I begin.

She slaps me in the face.

"Quiet you and listen me. Maybe I go butterfly because I know you no love me and most skoch go stateside no see me no more. You do that why I have to be true blue now? You gonna take me with you stateside? Hell no. You fuckee me lots here then go for good. So why hell I not butterfly? You gonna love me? Maybe you love me, I no butterfly. Maybe you no love me, I go stay with my old yobo all time. That maybe better choice? Huh?"

I slump on a pillow against the wall.

She crouches toward me, her long hair shaking over her breasts. "You know this, Hobbes-san? Maybe I hope you get clap. You know that? And it not be from me either, my yobo-butterfly-yobo. You better check out other Kim again, smart GI bastard!"

She sits back, her buttocks resting on her heels, cradling her knees. "You think I so dirty! Maybe clap make you remember me." She shudders. I think she is crying but she doesn't look at me.

I look at her, wanting to love her.

I love her.

"I'm sorry, Please don't be mad. I just, I just don't know." My voice trails away.

"Yes you do." She rocks back and forth in that curled-up position. I have to look away.

A week later, I am standing in line at the dispensary. The medic gives me a slide and I go into the latrine. I hear the groans of others as they struggle to produce a sample. Just put your palms against the wall, shut your eyes, and work it out, I want to yell. And feel guilty. Guilty as hell.

"Everybody gets that shit," Nick says.

I am recounting the incident at the Blue Dragon.

"Your sweetie give it to you?" Sansoe asks.

"Probably. Or maybe somebody else."

"You were telling us about the virtues of keeping a yobo?"

"Fuck you, Sansoe."

"Not till you're well, big fella."

"I thought this was supposed to be an enlisted man's disease," I say. "Maybe she fucked a Spec. 4."

30

It could lull you right out of fucking existence. The time drag flowed like the string on a loose kite. Drift with the breeze, roll with the *makgeolli*, once I got a taste for rice wine. In and out, in and out.

"All we do is fuck. And drink," Nick complained to Coletti and me as we joked with Sammy in the Blue Dragon. "I mean, except you, Hobbes. How much longer you have to be celibate? Don't try to fudge now, just makes it worse. Same with your yobo."

"Not long, we know it. And fuck you with a ball bat."

After Sammy stopped laughing, he took a picture of the three of us and went off looking for more customers. We'd get the prints later tonight or the next night.

"Nothing else to do," Coletti said. "At least for you guys. I mean you're not trying to get anything constructive out of it at all."

Nick groaned. "If you didn't run this bar, I'd have nothing to do with you."

"Maybe I'll sell it."

"Ahh, fuck it. I'd run into you all the time anyway. Might as well try to get along."

"One of the dilemmas of modern man."

"Hey," I interrupted. "Isn't that Travis over there?" We looked across the crowded dance floor. He spotted us, too.

"Haven't seen him around much," Nick said.

"Yeah, I know."

Coletti nodded.

Travis glided up. His eyes had that false fire, blazing but dilated. Coletti gave him an obvious once-over. Travis threw him the finger.

"Yeah, I see you giving me the look. But fuck that. Jesus, am I glad I found you. Nobody would have believed me. Come on. You won't believe this fucker in the alley." Without waiting, Travis turned and made his way out the back exit. He was waiting when we got outside. He waved repeatedly. "Come on. You won't believe it."

"Believe what?" Nick said when we caught up.

"See for yourself."

Just ahead of us in an adjacent alley, a crowd had formed in front of a late-night food cart. A string of bright white bulbs stretched overhead. A middle-aged man was standing on some empty crates, weaving deliriously from side to side, waving his arms and talking rapidly in Korean.

"That's him," Travis said.

Coletti tried for a better view. "What's the deal? What's going on?"

"Watch."

The man bent down, opened one of the crates and pulled out a snake at least three feet long. Its tail writhed in a slow arc. The man waved the snake before the crowd and started ranting. Then he grabbed the snake's head in his right hand, and the tail in his left, and hoisted it high over his head. He shook it like a slimy rope and after screaming something, stretched the snake tight. He brought it to his lips and with a quick snap, bit it in half.

The severed ends twisted and twitched, spraying blood on the man and spectators in the front row. He chewed ravenously and swallowed as much as he could, the rest falling out of his mouth. Then he smiled, sort of, while blood and clotted white tissue dribbled down his chin and cheeks. He spit something out, tilted his head to scream, "Aieee!"

The crowd, half Americans, half Koreans, cheered and applauded. "Hey mothafucka, do that again!" A few others yelled in Korean.

"Did you see that shit?" Travis said. "Can you believe that?"

"What the hell is this?" Nick looked at his shirt to see if it caught any snake blood.

"No fucking idea. I just saw him doing it when I was looking for a chick. I just about dropped my cookies. I got so excited I forgot about everything." He looked around. "Now I don't see her. Anyway, I had to get you guys or no one would have believed me."

"I still don't believe it," I said. "Is this an act or what?"

"Search me, man."

"Maybe he's a religious freak," a GI standing near us said. "Some tripped-out evangelist or missionary or something."

"Yeah, maybe," Nick said.

Coletti shook his head. "He's whacked the hell out on speed or acid."

More people had come now, even though it was nearly curfew. But the man stayed on the crates, mesmerized, gesturing in the harsh light. GIs taunted him and egged him on. "Another snake, Another snake." Koreans chanted something, but we didn't know what.

The man threw down the snake halves, rubbed his face violently and seemed to shudder. He began pumping his legs, running in place, bowing his head and waving his arms over his head. When someone spoke to him, he screamed horribly and seemed to curse at them. At times, the light would fall across his eyes, and they would flash with madness, He could have burst apart.

He bent down again and pulled another snake from another crate.

In the same routine, he grasped it at each end and waved it over his head, then, pulling it tight, bit the middle clean. This time a woman screamed and her husband helped her away.

The man was gyrating now, babbling sounds that came from no language. He danced and twirled the wriggling snake ends more frantically than before. I told Coletti they looked like bleeding thunderbolts. He didn't appreciate the simile.

Suddenly a loud crack sounded, and the man collapsed.

"What the hell?" Nick shouted. We all turned towards the sound.

"It was a fucking shot is what," said the GI next to us. Four Korean policemen were moving through the crowd.

"Let's get the hell out of here," Nick said.

"No, wait, what is it?" I wanted to know.

"Forget it," Coletti said. "Let's go."

The crowd was dispersing rapidly.

As it parted, I caught a glimpse of the snake-eater's body limp across the crates, now just a jumble. His head was hanging upside down, facing us. His chest was dark red and blood was streaming over his lips, across his eyes. His hands had closed in a death grip on the snake ends, still, twitching. A policeman with an M-16 slung on his shoulder bent down to see that the man was dead. He looked back in our direction, a warning to leave.

We were already hurrying away when I realized Travis wasn't with us. He was still looking at the body. I told Nick and Coletti to go on and I went back, grabbed Travis's arm and pulled him along. He seemed to wake up and fall into place with me. Nick went back to the compound, and I decided that was a good idea and made sure Travis was with me. Coletti went to the Blue Dragon. He would be safe there.

But before we got to the gate, Travis slowed to a stop. He said he wanted to go back to the ville to find that girl. Which was probably the new yobo that he wasn't telling anyone about. I couldn't stop him, so I followed him until he went into the Acid Bar. The rest of the night was up to him. But curfew was in a half-hour. So now that I was out in the ville anyway, I went to find Kim. Then I remembered our clap quarantine and turned back to the BOQ. Still another no-fuckee week to be safe from what some GI gave her that she gave me. But I wasn't mad anymore. I knew why but I wasn't going to admit it.

The next day, that night was the big gossip. Did you hear about the police shooting that crazy guy in the ville, the fucker biting snakes? They said he had flipped out when his wife got killed by a Marine up in Seoul who had given her some bad speed and then the guy got some bad shit of his own and had been going on four days freaked out without sleep when he was trying to get back to Incheon but got off on the wrong stop in Suchow.

Of course, we had no way of knowing if that was true or how he got the snakes or if it was just some of the usual made-up shit we lived with and that fucked up our conception of where we were. All we knew for sure was the guy was out of his mind and the cops killed him with one shot.

31

Travis disapproved of Coletti, perhaps more than the reverse. He drank with him, and Coletti got a few things for him, but by now everyone knew that Travis considered himself different than all of us. I remember what he said one night when I was musing about Kim. I said I wondered if I could marry her. His exact reply was: "A guy like you probably would marry her."

Nonetheless, Travis hung around Coletti in a peripheral way. I never figured it out. Coletti was a convenient myth, the amorality of success. Travis was untouchable, beyond our filth and decadence.

I was in the O Club, drinking as usual, but also celebrating because five nurses from Seoul were TDY at the compound and had to stay overnight. Real round-eyes. The few nurses left at the Evac hospital were spoken for, either by marriage or boyfriends, always officers, and basically off-limits. Other than for staff meetings or small, exclusive, intra-evac parties, they never even came to the O Club. Mostly we'd see them at the PX, where everyone could say hello and keep on shopping. The only one of my friends that saw them much at all was Nick, because he was a dentist. But he didn't mingle with them and told us they were pretty stuck-up anyway.

"Who wants to fuck around with round-eyes, even the donut dollies, and go through all the old bullshit when you can just find a good-looking yobo?" Nick said. We had been buying drinks for these TDY nurses—elbowing past each other to talk to them. Just talk to them. Nick stuck to himself at the bar.

As we downed more alcohol, we tried a sort of a game to get

131

these visitors to go back to our rooms with us, which of course they wouldn't, as Nick also told us, since we weren't doctors or pilots. Even a mere dentist was low value. So, giving up the pursuit, we downshifted into melancholy harangues with each other about girls in the World. If someone came into the club with a yobo, the nurses would smile. That's a cute one, they would say. You almost had to see it to believe it.

It got to be about 10 p.m., I remember because I had just asked what time it was, wondering if I should try to find Kim. Who would give me hell if she knew I had been part of the rope-a-round-eye idiocy. She told me she would be "working" that night until late. Not sex. Something else, like TVs. I believed her and didn't press.

A thin NCO in a half-open field jacket rushed into the bar. Arnie, who was with us, recognized him and beckoned. "Hey Sergeant Lutz, over here."

"Captain Pearson!" The sergeant tried to catch his breath. "I came to tell you. The hospital's on fire, just started, and it's already kicking ass. Firefighters are coming, but I can't find our CO or really anybody. I thought you should know. So, I just came over here, sir."

Arnie broke away from our group and went to the window facing toward the hospital. Flames for sure, although mostly just smoke, like some kind of routine burning. I could see why no one had taken notice. A sudden red-and-orange plume shot into the sky. Arnie drained his scotch, looked at me and Nick. "Let that rotten motherfucker burn. But damn. Not like this." The sergeant looked at him, then the rest of us. "It's going up real fast, sir." He saluted Arnie and hurried out, mumbling something.

Nobody wanted to leave a bar full of round-eyes, but we had to. Some officers who knew the nurses huddled them up, told them what was happening, and escorted them out through the foyer. Arnie intercepted them briefly and they went the way he pointed. Then Arnie went straight on towards the fire. Nick and I caught up with him en route. He said one of the nurses would call Yongsan medical in Seoul, figuring they probably hadn't heard yet.

"They were gonna tear it down at some point anyway. It's a

goddamn danger," Arnie said as we walked fast across the open fields toward a small hill about 500 meters on. The fire, and the smoke, now lit up the hospital's profile against the night sky.

"Shit, I hope nobody was in there," I said.

"I'm pretty sure everybody could get out in plenty of time," Arnie said. "I mean I hope to hell so."

About halfway there, I saw Travis jogging toward us. "Holy shit," he said, "you know anything?"

"Going to," Arnie said, hurrying the pace. He didn't want to run because he wanted to have some time to process what he was seeing.

I asked Travis where he'd been, but he just kept looking at the flames. As we got closer, I could see that that weird mix in his eyes again, and maybe a little glassy. He appeared very cool, though, in the sense of no concern with anything.

"I was in my room," he finally said, "just about to go out for a while. And then that new guy Wilson ran through the BOQ yelling about the fire. Pretty much all of us started peeling out to go over there."

Closer we got, the less I could really figure out how bad the whole picture was. Real bad was my guess. The building was old, another left-over from the Japanese occupation. It stopped being a hospital in the spring when what was left of the Evac staff relocated to Seoul. A replacement building was on the schedule, but construction hadn't started. We still called it the old hospital, but it had become temp quarters for lower enlisted ranks, mostly from Arnie's unit on the compound, and also some from Travis's. Some kind of small Quonset clinic still operated, mostly for minor injuries and scrips, but it was going to close down, too. I'd walked by it many times, but only gone inside once.

We slowed down as we closed in on the chaos. People running around everywhere. Firefighters arriving fast as they could. For some reason, Travis grabbed my elbow, so I'd stop and look at him.

"I got to tell you, man. I said I would the other day."

"Tell me what?"

"It's great shit. Great shit."

He was smiling. His face looked like gelatin.

"Where did you get it?"

"Guess."

"Coletti."

He nodded and shrugged.

"Fuck man, you've been weird, you know?"

I was glad Arnie and Nick were too far ahead to hear us.

"Tremendous stuff. I mean it's got drawbacks, but I can get out of using it whenever I want. Goddam it Hobbesie, don't give me that look. I'm not a junkie. It's just good shit."

"Hey, you know there's a fucking fire about a block in front of us."

"I see it. But you know, I just wanted to let you know. And how good I feel. So have Coletti get you some. Not much worse than opium. Or you can get it from K—." He cut himself short. From the far side of the building something exploded and shot a flash of flame into the sky.

I stepped in front of him, almost nose to nose.

"Or Kim? Is that what you said?"

"Well, yeah, but—"

"Jesus fuck."

"I mean just a little here and there. I mean she does a little on the side for Coletti. Not a lot. I thought you knew."

I looked at the fire again, started to say something but what was the point? And by the way if we didn't move, we were going to get barbecued. I walked on ahead to get a better look at the fire.

"It'll be cool," I heard him yell, but I didn't turn to look back.

He caught up with me anyway. It seemed like everyone was trying to get closer to whatever what happening. It was like a fireworks celebration, all fucked up.

"Your attitude is insulting. You have no goddam right," Travis said, shuffling from leg to leg as if nervous, or agitated.

"What? Come on, let's go see if we can find out something from Arnie, or help him. And goddam, it's hot."

He spat. "You're looking at me like I was a freak."

"Well?"

"Hell." He looked around and swallowed, then spit again, maybe from the ash that was starting to kick up. "Hell," he repeated. I gave him a quick look. He followed me again.

We passed young soldiers in various stages of undress, holding or watching over boxes and duffels filled with their stereos, cameras, PACEX catalogues. Their letters from home. Their dope. From Coletti? From Kim? From now on I'd never *not* think that those two could be their sources.

Firefighters, mostly Koreans hired by the Army, were doing their jobs, helped by Army equipment, including pump engines and big water trucks. U.S. always had the supplies. Koreans always had the humans. Equally dispensable to the brass.

"What a waste of time. That whole place is a fucking slum nobody ever ought to have to live in," I heard a kid grumble. He was maybe a PFC, in shorts and T-shirt and Korean sandals. He was right. The firefighters could risk their lives and work like crazy, but it was a useless cause. And a dangerous one. Not only was it made of wood, and covered a big area, its three main wings, each with multiple floors and rooms and ersatz hootches, were completely connected. Good for a hospital, but as a half-ass barracks, it was a firetrap.

To make worse even worse, the inner asbestos panels that had made the building plausibly safe when it was a hospital were gone. The Evac ripped them off and took them to Seoul along with the rest of their equipment, despite the objections of Mr. Wilson, the eccentric civilian safety officer sent down from Seoul. He demanded that engineers lessen the danger by disconnecting the wings from each other and installing fireproof barrier walls.

The commander of the engineer battalion said that was too expensive for a building that would be torn down. Instead, he said, the engineers would construct plywood partitions with asbestos mats nailed on to act as a "temporary measure." So that's what they did. Mr. Wilson said it was completely worthless and found himself transferred to Busan.

Travis once said all it would take was one space heater knocked down during a brawl to set the whole place on fire. He said he only hoped he could get out of Korea before the damn thing went up because he would somehow get blamed for it.

We later learned that the fire in fact did start when two quarreling junior NCOs crashed into a shelf full of scented candles used to camouflage the smell of pot, and one of the rooms turned into a furnace in minutes. It quickly fed on wooden beds, cabinets, mattresses, and footlockers. By the time flames hit the plywood-asbestos mat barrier, they had enough air and fuel to explode into a new wing and so on.

Former tenants and their friends continued to watch from the hillside, some with their yobos. Travis said it looked like they were at a drive-in movie. In this one, the main attraction was making them homeless. All they could do was get wasted, take pictures with their Japanese cameras—shit, I forgot mine—and routinely chant the GI curse: "Fuck the Army. Fuck the Army."

It was easy to find Arnie. He was more or less in temporary command, making sure the soldiers in his company were accounted for, and checking in with the other officers from across the compound who had shown up. I asked Arnie if we could help, and he said not really but thanks. I got Travis's attention and told him we should just go back to the White Elephant, or at least on the hilltop with the others, and stay out of the way of the firefighters.

Travis nodded, but he had a certain look. Maybe he really did think he'd get blamed for it somehow. Someone sure as hell was going to be. Junior officers were always the go-to scapegoats. That was the Army way.

If he wasn't thinking that he was thinking something worse. I could see his mind reshape his entire head. Inside, it was a good bet that the smack that was so smooth to smoke that Travis didn't even need a needle was galloping around in his brain. It could talk, and it was saying: *You, junkie. Yes you! Ivy League Wonder—yeah, you, junkie. You are a junkie, are you not? Or do you think you have it under control, eh? Or do you have the other thing—the Fear? What you gonna send home to momma, boy? A green bag of sick meat? Why'd you do it? Smoke the shit*

you didn't have to? Say man—Mr. meat man—hit on this, mother fucker.
What a ride, huh? Mother? Fuck her.

"Where's the goddam duty officer?" Travis said, coming back into real time. "Son of a bitch was supposed to be on duty."

"Who the fuck knows? Maybe he snuck up to Seoul for the weekend. Let's get out of here."

Travis looked at me angrily.

"Nobody's got hurt," I said. "It's the firefighter's problem. Fuck it, man."

He saw some enlisted guys he knew.

"Hey, you hear if anybody left in your hootch?"

"No, sir," one answered, like he gave a shit.

Travis nodded.

"You act like a goddam mother hen," I told him.

A terrific explosion suddenly pushed flames high into the air. It came from the second wing of buildings, on the other side from us. Ashes and glowing cinders rained down.

"Jesus shit! I've got to get back over there."

I tried to grab Travis's arm. "Let the firefighters do it."

He broke away.

"It's their job, Travis, for Christ's sake!"

He disappeared in the smoke. I stopped. I sure as hell wasn't going closer. That whole wing was about to collapse. Who knows what else might blow up.

But shit. He was totally fucked up. I ran after him.

The heat was daunting. The remains of half the wing were burning fiercely. Three Korean firefighters were standing near one of the jerry-rigged hootches, also full of flames. Then I could see Travis and two other Korean firefighters heading for another part of the wing, not yet immersed in the burn. I started for them, but an Army fireman, a young buck sergeant, motioned for me to stop.

"What the hell are they doing?" I asked.

The sergeant adjusted his black metal helmet. "Hell, that lieutenant thinks he can close off what's left of that wing and bottle the thing up. Crazy son of a bitch. I told him. I told him no way in hell, that it was a waste of time and dangerous. Besides, we got it sealed off and it won't get no farther anyway." He wiped grime from his face. "But, seriously, that louie thinks he's gonna save something. You know him?"

We were screaming at each other to hear.

"I do."

"Can you get him to back off?"

"Not so far."

The sergeant looked at me. He couldn't have been more than his late twenties. "He's gonna get my men killed, too. I mean goddamn it."

"Tell me something I don't know."

The smoke parted and we could see Travis and two Korean civilian firefighters move toward the building.

"Maybe they're looking for a body," I said to the sergeant.

"Nobody's in there. We already did a check." He looked at his watch. "They got about ten minutes, I figure, before that one gets out of control, too. After that we drag 'em out if we have to brain 'em with a fire ax." He walked off to reach two other Army firefighters and order them not to enter the building for any reason.

"Travis, get your ass out here!"

By then I could hear him, and then see him and the Koreans chopping and yelling and moving cabinets or something, who knows what. Trying to shore up a barrier, maybe.

He saw me, waved. "Hobbes! Give us a hand, will you? We're almost through."

"Is somebody dead in there?"

With a roaring crash, another fireball burst out, smaller, but rushing completely over Travis and the Koreans and knocking them down.

I started toward them. The sergeant saw and blocked me again. Two other Army firefighters came up and did the same. "But look, they're burning up!" I yelled, as if it wasn't obvious.

The sergeant tried to take a few steps but stopped himself. Then turned toward me. "It's the dispensary. Oh, fucking hell. I forgot they still had one."

I think all four of us cursed simultaneously. The dispensary, close to the Quonset clinic, had been fitted out with tin and metal walls, iron bars on the windows, so GI junkies or slicky boys couldn't steal drugs. I couldn't put my head around what Travis might have been thinking. It was his job to save medical supplies for his unit. Nothing made any sense. Whatever it was, time was up. What was left of the dispensary was now an oven.

We could hear screaming and could see Travis and the Koreans already on fire but trapped. Nor could we get past the flames. One set of the iron window bars had fallen into the mix, hitting one of the Koreans, who fell under it, not moving.

The Army firefighters had found a way around the worst and were trying to push in as far as they could. They let me come with them, but we couldn't pull anyone out. We could hear Travis. "Help us! Help us, for god's sake!" But then nothing. It was beyond anguish to be unable to reach them.

Then the weight of another set of iron bars dropping into the fire and smoke pushed a pile of glowing debris into a sudden slide, which had the effect of pushing Travis and the Koreans out to the edge of the dispensary's fallen wall, just far enough for the Army firefighters to finally reach them. In seconds, Travis and the other two were spread out on the ground a safe distance away. I was helping them untangle, and pulled a piece of broken, red-hot tin from the thigh of the unconscious Korean felled by the iron bars before it reignited his clothes. I burned my own hands in the process. But the Korean wasn't unconscious. He was dead.

Travis and the other Korean lay still. They were third-degree all over. I had never seen humans burned like that. So, I couldn't believe Travis, now coughing and wheezing, was trying to get to his feet. I didn't let him. He didn't even know he barely had feet. He looked at me, could see who I was. "Just wait here a minute," he said, and repeated.

Every part of him seemed to be black and bleeding. His hair was burned away, most of an ear. The compound fire captain appeared, talked to the NCO, and yelled out for someone to bring a medic. The sergeant said he'd already done that.

Travis tried to get up again but could only sit. We let him. He laughed, looking at what was left of his fatigues. "I'm next! I'm next," he said.

Another fireball, smaller than the last, erupted. Travis flinched, and the firefighters moved him and the surviving Korean farther back.

"I'm next, I'm next," Travis continued, no longer able to sit. All I could do was watch and try to somehow communicate, but he just kept saying, "I'm next."

Two medics showed up fairly quickly and began treatment but had to wait for the ambulance to arrive with oxygen and other equipment.

The medics checked the dead Korean just as procedure. He had no face, barely a head. I didn't want to ever think of how he looked again, although I have.

Meanwhile another water truck showed up and extinguished the worst of the fire. All the wings had now collapsed. Little was left but smoke and cinders.

Travis began shaking violently. I think he was looking at me as if he could see anything. He coughed again, like his lungs were raw, and then yelled, as best he could, "Next, next." The medic asked if I knew what he meant and I said no.

Then his head dropped back onto the scorched grass. The medics checked to see if he was breathing. He wasn't. They tried resuscitation. Nothing. They tried for a pulse. Nothing.

It was too much to cry. A doctor who had been helping with minor injuries on the other side of the building rubble showed up. I'd seen him in the Elephant a few times and I appreciated his look of sympathy, but nothing he could do.

In place of tears, I had anger. At what? At whom?

Travis looked so lonely. It was so wrong.

Soldiers pulled up in a Jeep with stretchers for carrying away the dead, and then the ambulance showed up for the surviving Korean, who later died in a coma.

I asked where they would take Travis. The only place there was. The morgue.

There would be reports. Questions from the MPs. Letters to his mother. Many, many drinks in the O Club. In the ville. Alone in my room.

I didn't go back to the BOQ. I walked to the hillside and sat. I could make out the dying embers from the fire that never should have happened.

I was surprised, but thankful, when Arnie came by later, exhausted, covered in soot, smelling of smoke. Same as me. He sat down. He knew about Travis and the Koreans. Turned out they were the only casualties. He said the fire captain said it was under control, and they could sift through whatever was left tomorrow. He said he'd been with other compound officers from the time we'd first gotten over to the fire, and he had to be at an after-action meeting at 0600.

Like me, Arnie wasn't going back to his room. Sleep was out of the question. And so we sat. Looked up at the stars. But mostly at the smoking remains. Arnie said they indeed might transfer him to Vietnam, "but not the way I wanted." Just before dawn, he stood, said he was going to grab a shower before the meeting, that the smell was starting to make him want to throw up. He left with a pat on my shoulder and a "Damn."

After a while on my own, I noticed my own stench too. And I was shivering, though it wasn't cold.

I couldn't stop seeing Travis.

I cried. Just to myself. But with real tears. Fuck it. When I dabbed my eyes, I noticed my hands were blistered.

32

The Red Tail carried First Lieutenant Howard Scott Travis to Connecticut. On his coffin was a medal for bravery. It had been Col. Bridges's idea. If Travis had lived, he probably would have been reprimanded. Court-martialed, maybe. I wasn't going to think about that. Some guys made jokes about the medal. Travis's mother wired something about appreciating it. Nick said if the family was comforted by the award, it was none of our business. There was a small item in the *Korea Times*, with a picture of the blackened bones of the old hospital.

None of my friends but me saw Travis die. Sansoe had been watching the spectacle a safe distance away, on a roof in the ville, with a bar girl. Nick was with one of the round-eye nurses, who decided a dentist was okay. Coletti had been in the Blue Dragon and walked out on the street once to have a look. I asked him flat-out if he had any connection to Travis's interest in the dispensary. He got so mad I believed his answer. "Fuck no, you asshole." We left it that our New England fallen Brahmin was trying to fight the fire. We left it that a friend is a friend.

No one saw the coffin off at the airport. Nor was there any official ceremony. Instead, his friends caught a taxi and walked up a nearby mountain foothill the morning after the Red Tail left and toasted Travis with tequila.

"You dumb asshole," Nick said, not really fooling anybody. "You only had a few months."

"Could've picked a better reason for dying," I said.

Sansoe smashed an empty bottle against a rock. "He really did have a yobo, right? Miss Wu, right?"

I nodded.

"Somebody will have to tell her."

There was a silence: sinister, malevolent, aggressive. The wind rushed over us in endless small bursts.

We had to walk the three miles back to the gate, drunk, because the kimchi cab driver who dropped us off never came back.

II

Hobbes

(The Fear)

33

We wanted to know what was happening in the World. "What's it like now in the World?"

Or "Man, when I get back to the World, I'm gonna get me some real cheeseburgers."

Or "What's the matter, you fuckers think you're in the World?"

The World. It wasn't easy to take in that GI slang.

Not like yobo, or skochie, or mos skosh, or stinko, or toc sahn, or oop-soh, or number 10, or the other Army/pidgin English-Korean that nobody really knew how to pronounce, let alone spell, other than to just repeat what you heard or read. Vietnam had the same muddled mini-language, and probably every U.S. military base around the globe, of which there were many. Too damn many.

"The World" was a reference in most of them. It was a concept—broad, vague, and sacrosanct. It was completely international because it implied being away. Like speaking of yourself in the past tense. It implied that wherever you were was not as real, or authentic, or great, or powerful, or comfortable, or in any way equal to the place you were from. Which also meant that other rules applied outside the World. From killing to sex.

I couldn't say "the World" freely for weeks. Later it seemed normal. The World was where we had been and where we would go and wanted to be. It was suspended reality. There was not a comparable term for Korea. It was not "anti-World" or "un-World." Korea was only Korea. Sometimes fucking Korea, with towns called zip-city and people called gooks, sometimes simply The Pit, or Hell, or the Asshole (Armpit) of

147

the Universe. Once again, same kind of language at every Army base in existence.

The Japanese had a much better name for Korea: Chosun, or originally Joseon. In Seoul there was a hotel by that name. For Westerners and other rich. The Chosun Hotel. Of course, the Japs had treated Korea as badly as anyone, probably worse.

But there was only one World. An unfulfilled dream, a quick hop across the cloudless ocean, two stars to the right. Back there, back home, we might have said, of our own land: "This fucking country" or "this place sucks," and had a library of racist epithets as extensive as anywhere. But away, the U.S. was the World. It assumed easy reverence.

The Army, the KAMUP training, told us to forget the World—you are no longer of it. They didn't mean forget. They meant suppress, put in the back of your mind. Pay attention to *this* now. Not *that*. Soldiers have no past. And what they do have can motivate them to sacrifice their own lives for the slightest sliver of what we called the American Dream.

Some forgot everything. And they were the worst. Freaked right out. Gone from the World, they had no new rules, no old burdens. Most of all, they could suddenly exist in the clouds of good sex, easy dope, no one caring. Detached, 7,000 traceless miles from some version of actual home. Time was carved from their lives and had to be filled. Besides, it wasn't the World. What did it matter?

See the yellow pus ooze from the penis. It is not terrible. Only funny now. You fucked up. So what? Who will know?

Fall drunk on a broken sidewalk. Stumble over a whore sucking off the captain. Laugh, laugh. What else to do?

Count the days with whore's names. Friday Miss Kim. Do I dare eat a peach? Tuesday Miss Lee. A goddam peach, that guy wonders? Why wonder? Eat the fucking peach. Kim, Lee, Yu. All varieties. It is something to consume.

All this we have here, suspended from the World. It can be all we want. Your big chance, Capt. Plato said. Enjoy your freedom—you can call it that. It is as close as you'll know, little WASP. Or Black or brown guys, for that matter. As long as they were from the World.

But in fleeting hours we wasted it. It was a prison, and the sentence could not pass too quickly until we returned to our warm shroud, our World, that safe place from which we could again look out.

From where we could know the sun was shining on us, too. While somewhere else, on the other side of planet, what-the-fuck, people in bamboo houses scurried pointlessly, often blood-drenched, in the dark, and remained secretly in our heads. Forever.

34

I became restless as my year rolled on. More time in the Club for happy hour, more useless trips to the mail room for letters that weren't there. Embarrassed at their absence, I would walk back to the Elephant, turn up my Japanese stereo, write my own missives, throw them away. Think of Kim, her sisters of the night in the ville. What was it in those melting smiles that I had never seen from Beth, from anyone? How to tell them I knew so little?

One round-eye from college days, Sally, said I was a marshmallow. Grow up, she said, as her justification for breaking up. Leaving me holding my three-ring binder and lord knows what kind of expression on my face on the library steps. I would like to see her now, to tell her.

I took the Korean exposure and felt the Fear. Travis took it but died in his junkie fire. Later, Kim said Travis had told a yobo he had found a way to get downers from the old hospital dispensary. She said maybe that was why Travis went in. If it was even true. But I said no, it was something else.

We were sitting in our hootch, on a new braided rug she'd brought in one night a week ago. I didn't ask where it came from.

"Did you give Travis smack?"

"My friend did."

I closed my eyes. "But you sell that shit?"

"A little."

"From Coletti?"

"Yobo, why you want to know?"

I tried to stare a coldness into her. "Because he was so fucked up, he didn't know what he was doing that night."

Kim's features were blank in that shield of business girl indifference. "I sorry, yobo. But Travis-san, he one who ask."

We carried the discussion some words further, but it led nowhere. "Promise me you'll stop doing that. Sell fucking whatever stolen PX shit you want, but don't do dope. I mean I thought it was already that way. So, I'm asking again. Don't have it. Don't sell it. Okay?"

"Okay."

It was impossible to reconcile the death. If Travis had been into other things, got himself hooked, I didn't want to know. Nor did anybody else. The art of not brooding, of letting the dead bury the dead, was in a high state of mastery in or around the Army or any other military service. And definitely in the ville.

Travis had told me I had no right to ask about what he did or didn't do. That it was his business. And what the fuck was wrong with me?

*

"He didn't get it from me anyway," Coletti said when I pressed him several weeks later. The annoyance that I'd brought it up again was clear in his tone.

"He said he did."

"That was just once. He said he wanted to try it and asked me to tell him where he could hook up. You know, hell, I'm no goddam pusher, Hobbes. If I get a little stuff now and then on some trades, okay, but shit . . ." He looked away.

"But you got him started."

His eyes snapped toward me. "What the hell should I do? He wasn't a junkie." His jawbones showing in his cheeks. "Not yet. I wouldn't have let it come to that. Come on, you don't mouth off when I get dope for you."

"That's different."

"Bullshit."

"You know it is. And both times I asked you, it was just pot."

"He knew what he was doing. You can't blame me for that. Jesus, man."

"It's not the same as pot. As radios and TVs and PX five-finger discounts."

"Fuck you, Hobbes."

"You want me to pretend that time in the alley didn't happen? All those times?"

Coletti's face now dark red. "I don't have to explain this to you."

It was getting close to fists. To avoid, he stuck his hands into the edges of his trousers like a little boy. His head tilted, a heavy breath from deep in his chest up through his nose and clenched lips. His eyes asked for an exit, a solution. I had nothing but silence.

*

Later, in bed with Kim. I closed my eyes. I saw Travis crisp and roasting on the ground. I could hear "I'm next" over and over. I felt myself reeling with my own poisons.

The only thing I could feel now, with Kim, was her ecstasy beneath me, and mine on top. I had completely forgotten we were fucking, or that I was with her, or in the hootch, or anywhere at all. I rolled over onto my back. She was in her own movie, eyes closed. And I was in mine.

Roll film: I'm in the alley behind the hootch. A slicky boy passes and bumps me. My first thought—my first thought—is to strike out with a long razor and rip his throat as he walks and then laugh while he sinks to his knees, gurgling. Fuck it. I don't like Travis anyway.

Roll Film (cont.): And then I am back with Coletti. He won't leave my brain.

"Are you using Kim? Is she your street delivery girl?"

"No. Didn't I just say that?"

"Yeah."

"I'm sorry it happened, Hobbes. I really am. But it wasn't my fault."

"Whirlpool ethics."

"What?"

"It doesn't matter."

"Seems like it does."

"Fuck it. Just fuck it."

"Want a drink?"

"Sure."

End film: Fini.

Credits. There are none.

Back with Kim again. In our bed. I didn't know my mind could do that so often, escape like that. Travel outside my body unattached. No drugs. And return.

Her face was all I needed to bring me back to reality. Such as it was.

What her movie was, how her eyes saw it, where it had gone, I had no idea.

But I would rather watch her screenings than mine. Then. Now.

35

Travis still weighed on my mind, and Kim, and this: Even if I went home, to the World, would I find it? I looked at myself in the cracked BOQ mirror. My eyes were still clear and blue and round. Most of all round. As if that were even a biological category. My canines showed, and my half-broken incisor. I wouldn't exactly have called myself career oriented. Or even clean-cut. If that is what someone else called me, they would have to say: Past expiration date.

I didn't know people's bodies smoked like that after a fire or smelled like that. But it was perfectly obvious. Science rules. Fuck Travis. We all knew he was a prick.

It was warm outside, and I pried my window open and looked out at the compound. An MP Jeep droned around the perimeter road. Off-duty soldiers headed for the craft shops and the ville. A colonel stepped out from the field-grade hootches, looked at the sky, and went back inside. I rolled back onto my bed and stared at a crack in the ceiling.

The week before Travis died, or maybe it was two weeks, I had escorted Master Sgt. Nolan's body to Busan. He was 52, overweight, smoker. He died the same day he landed in Korea, of a heart attack in the replacement center. I had to supervise his exit. His body went to Busan because he was married to a Korean and that wish was in his will, in his duffel bag. Which struck me as a strange thing for him to bring. His wife would now be a War Bride. PX privileges.

At least that was the way my bosses in Yongsan ruled it over the phone when I called for instructions. When Sansoe and I checked Nolan's belongings to make sure nothing embarrassing reached his family, we had found black-and-white snapshots of two different women. Yongsan said we should throw them away because we didn't know which, if either, was the wife. And make our best guess on the one to get his belongings and body. Worst case scenario we'd have to apologize and re-route everything to the other woman. We picked the one whose photo he had written, "All my love, Chester." It wasn't necessarily funny.

36

"Hobbes-san?"

"Uhh?" I pulled the down-filled quilt over my head.

"You awake?"

"What do you think?" I pulled the quilt back to look at her. She was a goddam treasure.

"I think you awake in eyes but not down here. Something I think still asleep here."

"Do you ever want to do anything else?"

"Maybe some things." She purred and slid down under the quilt, kissing my chest and stomach along the way. She held me tightly when we had finished.

"Aren't you sleepy?"

"I no sleep yet," she whispered.

Melding bodies in the bed, we kept the morning chill away. I turned on my side to hold her and see her. Her eyes glistened. She pressed against me harder.

"Yobo?"

"Yes."

She paused. "Yobo?"

I kissed her lightly,

"Yobo?"

"I'm here, Kim."

Her lips touched my ear. "I love you."

I kissed her. She was saying that to me all the time now.

But I didn't speak.

"I make you happy, Hobbes-san?"

"Very happy."

"You like make love me?"

"Of course I do. Very much."

"Good."

"Yes, good."

She traced her forefinger behind my ear. "Hobbes?"

"Yes."

"You no love me?" She asked as if it didn't matter. Another kiss.

"In some ways." But inside my head, I said: This is your yobo, Hobbes. Your whore. That's all it is. Army ruling. Don't forget.

"I love *you*, my yobo, yobo,"

"I know you do."

She rolled onto her back, out of my arms. I slid closer.

"You think I just whore."

"No, no. That's not it." I held her breast lightly.

She pulled away. "That it. I know. I know how GI think."

"I'm not a GI."

"What, then, GI officer?"

"I mean I don't think you're a whore."

My brain, another secret transmission just to me: But you just said you did.

Kim: "Why you no love me then?"

Me: "I didn't say I didn't love you, did I?"

Let the Brain speak.

Brain: *Do you?*

Kim: "Then do you?"

Brain: *Tell her, asshole.*

Kim: "Then do you?"

Brain: *This is my whore.*

Kim: "Then do you?"

Brain: *Kim is a whore.*

Kim: "Then do you?"

Brain: Kim is a whore who loves me.

157

Kim: "Then do you?"

Brain: *Why does she still bother?*

Kim turned away. She was crying softly into her pillow, not wanting to show it.

Could this have happened? Could I have done this Silence?

Then do I love her? Of course. But not enough. My brain can't handle it. There are other things. She is my whore, and she is not perfect. Better to have love from Beth, who should be perfect. Not love from my whore, who fucks me and says I love you and who will leave everything for me. Risk everything for me. For whom I can do so much. For whom I can give new life. One she deserves.

Of course, I should love her.

When I parted my lips to tell her, the words stuck. In my throat, with the juices of hers.

I wanted my head to explode.

37

I thought, well, hell, maybe I could give self-medication another shot myself. Maybe it would kill the disease that blocked my love. I knew a place deep in the Suchow alleys where you could get it at a vegetable stand. Smack. Or opium. The mama-san who would sell either to you so easily she probably had a pay-off deal with the cops.

On the way, I thought I saw Kim. I had a paranoid flash. It was night and it might not have been her. I could have easily called out and caught up. Instead, I trailed at a distance, just to see where she was going.

But she turned up a small side street and I lost sight. I thought I knew a way to find her again. But in less than a minute, I was lost in the alley maze. I saw a familiar sewer footbridge, crossed it and turned back toward what I thought was the main street. But I'd headed for it the wrong way, into Panther Detour.

A mostly Black part of the ville's off-limits clubs, it ran behind Sam's Place, the Homestead, the Purple Cow, Buffalo Gap, Soul City, all the main bars. It wasn't a club. More like an ill-defined intersection of paths, a gathering area where mostly the big city Blacks hung out, gambled, traded info, found whores. It was similar to a lot of other places in the ville, except the Black GIs made it clear it was their turf, and not to be crossed unless by invitation. Usually that wasn't too hard to get, but it was a rule. White guys, Latin guys, almost anybody else knew the game. Even slicky-boys didn't go into Panther Detour at night, unless to sell dope or food.

Black GIs had their reasons, and it was damn awful they had to. And nobody in the Army brass that could have, ever did anything about it. I had grown up in plenty of racist places (or maybe they all were) in Texas and the South, but in Korea, the tensions matched any of them. It's hard but true to say that most of us, Black or white, tended to self-segregate, whether intentionally or just because that's the way it was. Except for the occasional protests and stupid fights over things like hair styles and beards and unfair promotions and assignments.

I wasn't thinking about that when a Black GI, somebody I vaguely recognized from one of the supply warehouses, stepped from a doorway. He was smaller than I but rammed his elbow into my ribs.

I came out of my Kim paranoia and looked at him.

"I said say you sorry when you hit me, muthafucka," he leered, his breath hot with cigarette smoke. I tried to focus on him. His eyes were hidden behind PX shades. I remember thinking he was sweating.

"I didn't hit you," I said, and started to walk away. He grabbed the sleeve of my shirt.

"Fuck you didn't. Now apologize."

"Fuck you. You hit me."

We were going to "make something of it," I knew. Then I became aware of more than one person blocking my way. I tried to count quickly. The odds were bad. Eight of them, one of me. I felt my stomach sicken with that horrible nausea that you will not come out of this one like you went in.

"I said a-pol-o-gize, cracker."

He kept repeating it, one syllable at a time. His face was directly in mine. I could see his teeth. Don't let anyone hit you from behind, I thought. I heard other voices from farther away. So now this was alley entertainment.

I tried to talk my way out. "Look, I don't want a hassle,"

Before I could finish, someone spit on me and said, "Fuck you, cocksucker!" He pushed me against a wall. A not-yet-broken streetlamp down the alley shone dimly.

The pummeling started. I tried to dodge and somehow get away just as a belt buckle cut into my cheek. Then what seemed a rain of fists rattled my head.

Whump. Whump.

Adrenaline probably shut down the pain. I wanted to laugh. I'd had the same reaction to serious danger since I was a kid and got cramps swimming in a river. I started laughing. The thought of me—me—drowning. It was funny. And then I thought of Travis, repeating "next, next," as he died.

But back to here and now. Each time my head jolted from a hit I could feel my teeth loosen. I wasn't laughing out loud, but in my head. I thought: What kind of inglorious end is this? Beaten to death by a bunch of pissed-off drunks and junkies in an alley I was in because of my own idiocy. And I was a cliché. Lieutenants have a reputation for getting lost. Now I would never find Kim and whatever it was she was selling for Coletti.

Whump. Whump.

I took a couple of swings but didn't hit anybody.

I lost consciousness.

I woke up slumped against the wall. No one was around. Maybe some guys hanging out farther up the alley. I couldn't see or think that far. My face felt sticky. My shirt was bloody.

I felt someone help me to my feet. It was Jackson, a tech sergeant from finance I'd had beers with a couple of times after I'd been appointed as Equal Opportunity Officer from my battalion. I was appointed to everything none of the higher ranking offers wanted to do. Jackson was a good guy, much better than me. Since he was Black, it was obvious we'd been selected to balance things out. Of course, we hadn't run in the same circles. He helped me stand up and walk. I was dizzy and weak, felt stupid.

"You shouldn't have come down here, lieutenant," Jackson said as we headed to the gate. "There's blood all over you. You got your teeth? Jesus."

"Those bastards," I tried to say but my lips were swollen, and my teeth hurt.

He helped me along. He only said one thing.

"You shouldn't have gone there, lieutenant. You shouldn't have gone there. I figured you would know that."

38

When I saw Capt. Plato later, crossing paths on the foot bridge between the mess hall and White Elephant, he asked me about the stitches on my lip. I told him what had happened.

"That should teach you."

I had expected a different reaction. "Teach me what?"

"Teach you to abandon that stupid pursuit."

"What pursuit?"

"That people can be expected to like you."

"When did I say that?"

I stood back, no doubt a puzzle in my expression.

"You don't have to say it. You just do it. You even think getting bumped to first louie means the Army likes you."

"Again, when did I say that?"

"When we celebrated and got shit-faced, it was all over you."

"Bullshit. They had to promote me. I've been in over a year."

"They didn't have to. Not everybody gets past second louie."

"I did my job. At least enough. The colonel liked me okay. It was easier to move me along than explain why they didn't. Shit, Plato, you know all this."

I was glad no one was nearby. I started to move around him. He put up a hand to stop me.

"What you just said—the colonel liked you."

"Yeah?"

"That's what I mean. It's just the machine, man. It can spit you out."

"I don't care."

"Your 'friends' can, too. All of them. Boys and girls."

"Jesus, you got a burr up your ass?"

He flicked my lip with his forefinger.

"Black and white, too, huh?"

"Damn it, Plato. That stings." I swiped at his hand as a caution.

"Well, good." He stepped back, we looked at each other, and then he put his hands on both my shoulders. His expression turned dead serious. "Maybe you'll get real now about where you are."

He dropped his hands but held the look a moment longer. Then he flashed a half-salute, which was really strange coming from him, and walked on past the bridge. "Better not kiss anybody for a while," he called back.

I felt a trickle of blood on my lip. I guess the scab had broken.

39

It took Kim a couple of days to find out about it. We had lapses. Usually not more than a few days. Nobody can stand to see someone every day, we decided. Problem was, the apart times were the ones that caused trouble. You could say we had an open marriage, except we only had the open part.

She knocked on the door to my room at the White Elephant but came rushing through before I could open it. By now the gate guards knew her. They always let her through. "Yobo, yobo, what you do?" She covered my face with kisses and sympathy.

"It's not that bad." Actually, it wasn't. Just a few cuts and bruises.

"What the hell you do?" she asked again, once her inspection determined I was okay.

I shrugged and sat on my bed. She settled next to me.

"You get in fight over other Kim?"

I laughed and took her hand.

"What then? You been butterfly?"

"I was a little drunk and I saw you on the street." I looked down. "I was trying to catch you."

She moved away as if I had given her a bad taste. "So, you following me."

"Sort of, but not really. Anyway, I didn't for long."

"Why you follow me?"

"Look, I'm sorry. It was just an impulse."

"Bullshit."

I didn't expect her to be angry. But she was.

"What's the big deal? I mean what the hell were *you* doing?" I knew how I sounded.

Her stare was Medusa. Her tone was Arctic. "You listen, yobo. I no follow you around all day. You just make sure you no follow me. You understand that? You understand?" She stood, the better to glare down at me. "You my yobo, sure. But no more, you do this. I not business girl, I your yobo, so you not worry, huh? You just better not sneak on me again." She leaned against the corner of my rickety desk. Trembling. Furious. She wiped her eyes quickly. She didn't want me to see.

Rebuttal seemed irrelevant. So many secret areas between us. Always buried. Because, obviously, we were just a GI and his yobo. What was the big deal?

I should have demanded then, exactly then, that she tell me.

Also, irrelevant. She didn't want me to know. It was her secret, at some level hidden from the entire universe, and she was protecting it. From me in particular. At the risk, even, of walking out.

In the few seconds that she glared at me, I connected with her. I don't know how, couldn't prove it, but I felt it and I think she did, too. The way her eyes flowed into mine. For her, whatever she was doing was for the best. And it involved me. Not as an accomplice. As the person into whose eyes she was flowing. That's what was in the secret. And it was none of my business. Could not be.

I stood, reached toward her and she didn't wave me off. I put my arms around her and held, without a word, for what might have been a long time. Just us breathing. Together.

"I don't want to fight," I said.

"No." Barely a whisper.

"Maybe I was jealous. I really did think you might be going to see your old yobo."

She slipped back a half-step. We could see each other in full.

"I'm sorry I made you feel like this. I was drunk. And anyway . . ." I pointed to my face. "I got my comeuppance."

"You come when you got beat up?"

"Comeuppance."

"What that?"

"It means payback."

She smiled. Even as the tears she had suppressed returned. She touched my cheek lightly, as if to draw away the hurt.

"You jealous, yobo? You were, really?"

"I guess."

Her smile was worth the entire confrontation. Going to the edge, knowing it would hold. "Can I kiss you?"

"Try."

40

A week later, it was an orderly, not Kim, who knocked on the door of my room. Because Kim was sleeping next to me. It was barely 0600.

"You better get down to the clinic right away, sir. That new one after the fire. One of the guys in the battalion is hurt bad."

"Who?"

"Not sure. They just told me to come and get you."

"Give me a minute." I groaned and pushed her off me. She knew the drill to leave unnoticed. Wait until after 0800 when everyone is at work. And she'd never wake up before then anyway.

I put on my fatigues, ran downstairs, and got in the Jeep with the orderly.

Inside the clinic a doctor and two medics were giving someone a shot. It was Jackson. His mouth was full of glass and his eye nearly bulged out. He was in shock.

"This your man?" the doctor asked.

"Sergeant Jackson. Of course. What the hell?"

"Don't you idiots ever do anything but fight?" The doctor, one of the few left after the hospital staff left, began pulling slivers of glass from Jackson's tongue with tweezers.

"Weren't you in here yourself a week ago?" he asked, looking me over quickly and noticing the stitches on my cheek. "I think that's my work."

"Yeah, it was me. But nothing like this." It was really bad.

The doctor kept pulling out the slivers while a medic cleaned away blood and dirt. I stood back and watched, fingering the bill of

167

my cap. When the doctor obviously wasn't going to say anything else, I slipped outside.

An MP was at the door.

"Jesus, what happened?" I asked.

"Sonofabitch was a black belt karate. Can you believe it? That guy?" the MP said, shaking his MP head and MP helmet.

"So, what happened?"

"Who are you?"

"I'm from his unit," I said, and turned so he could see the black first louie bar on my collar.

"Oh, yessir. What happened was there was these five guys mouthing off to a girl at the NCO Club, the one out in the ville."

"White guys or Black guys?"

"White guys, except for a Rican."

"Yeah."

"So, your man here comes up on them and I guess plays Sir Galahad and tells them to leave the girl alone, or something like that. Then somebody tries to hit your man. That's when they find out he's a karate ace. Well, from what they said, some other guys who saw it, he was really holding his own, laying those dudes out, when all the sudden he turns and Wham! one of them hits him in the mouth with a beer bottle. So, he falls down and then the two that are able to move come over and try to kick his eyes out. Damn near did, too. But by then the girl has run to the MP station and so we get there and arrest the three he's busted up himself and take him to the dispensary. Yeah, he's a good fighter for a . . . you know, sir."

I gave him a look and told him he could leave if he wanted to. He said he might as well until Jackson could talk more. And anyway, the doc had already called for an ambulance from Yongsan and it was supposed to pick up Jackson in about fifteen minutes.

Jackson wouldn't be talking to anyone for a while. His mouth was wired shut for two weeks and his face stayed swollen so long I can't remember. He lost twenty pounds and four teeth.

It turned out the five assailants and the one witness were off-duty

MPs. Of course, the ville girl couldn't be found. Jackson was charged with disorderly conduct and fined $30 by the compound command. Nothing happened to the MPs.

Sansoe got so mad he punched out an MP down in the ville and the only way we kept him out of trouble was to threaten to lose some MP personnel records, which we did anyway. For their whole fucking platoon.

The MP captain called me in for an explanation. I didn't have to go but I did. I wanted to see his face while I explained that we couldn't figure out how all those records disappeared. A file cabinet must have been lost during an office clean-up.

41

I haven't said much about my Army job. What did I do? (What did you do in the Army, daddy?) I shammed, and, like I told Capt. Plato, did what I could to keep things rolling along without too many bumps. With time, it became possible to completely ignore boring routine and just pick up the green paycheck at the end of the month. I had gotten Coletti his two-year extension. That was one of my biggest tricks. Mostly, though, I knew I was in the wrong time and wrong mind to get a real kick out of the whole war thing, as far as zapping gooks for democracy went.

Another thing I did was protect American soldiers from marrying Korean business girls, working girls, whores, yobos, whatever. I was assigned by the Flamer, who liked to give me extra assignments although I never really understood what his role was in the battalion. "These boys will be boys. They'll go out there and fuck their brains out and think they're in love," he said, like he knew.

That much was true, though. The only way to stop GI marriages was with time. Which is why the Army created the Alien Marriages Office (AMO). The idea was to create so much paperwork that GIs would simply fly home, leaving unwed yobos in the bars, where they belonged. Protecting 18-year-old soldiers, and older, was important. It prevented them, for their own good, from making terrible, life-long mistakes in strange dark beds. And especially to keep them from taking the mistakes home, creating generations of half-breeds, quarter-breeds, octa-whatevers. Of course, leaving them in Korea, where the mixed-race babies, children and adults were treated even worse, was none of our business.

When someone in the battalion, or a few of the other units, wanted to marry a yobo, he had to apply through the AMO, starting with me. I sent the necessary forms to Capt. Wilson at the compound AMO. He almost always sent them back with a red, stenciled stamp: RESUBMIT. Something—a vaccination card, recent photo, government form, would be missing.

Capt. Wilson's boss, Maj. Schwartz up in Yongsan, had been ordered by Brig. Gen. Hawkins of the 8th U.S. Army staff to do everything possible to delay applications, preferably until the soldier had returned home. So, we did. It worked. There was some resistance. Maj. Schwartz returned to his quarters one day and his wife, a round-eye from home, was hysterical because the pet Pekingese had been found on the doorstep, filleted, a small note tied on what had been its collar: "This stays in Korea, too."

I was looking at the application of Spec. 5 Norman Benson. Everything was in order. There was a fake school diploma, fake place of employment, and fake residence for his yobo, whose name was Miss Yu.

I said something about it to Sgt. Frye, my senior office NCO. He said Benson was a career man and he hated to see him fuck up his life marrying a Korean. I noticed Benson was from Mississippi. Nonetheless, I put the 47-page application and supporting documents in a brown courier envelope and addressed it to Capt. Wilson in Seoul.

That same afternoon, while daydreaming and thinking about going home myself, I recalled that picture. It clicked. Yeah, yeah, I knew Miss Yu.

42

"I knew her."

"Who, yobo?"

"Miss Yu."

"You?"

"Yeah, Yu."

"Why you say that? Why you say you know Missy Yu?"

"She's trying to get married."

"Oh."

Outside, it was dark, and I could see nothing through the small hootch window. Kim crawled over my back to look outside, too. But she wanted to see the stars.

"She's marrying a GI. Do you think that's right?"

"What? Getting marry?"

"No. Marrying a GI."

"You mean a Korean marry a GI? Sure, why not, if they love each other."

"Yeah, you're right."

I took a few quiet breaths. "I mean, he's marrying someone I slept with once. As a bar girl."

She turned her head toward me. "You sleep with Missy Yu?"

"Not sleep. Slept."

"Before Kim?"

"A long time ago. When I was young and stupid." I touched her hand. Which was on my cheek. "Before you. Right after I came here. That's why I couldn't remember her, and she used a different name." I shut my eyes to try to see her. "Penny. Yeah." Kim slapped my cheek lightly. "It was a long time ago, I said."

"You like her better than me?"

"Of course not."

I could feel her smile. "You better not."

"That's not what I mean. It's not whether I like her or not. It's that I slept with her."

"You sleep with me."

"I know, I know. But now she's marrying Benson. You know who he is, just a dumb redneck. And I gave his fiancé ten dollars one time."

"But you say that long gone."

"But I did it. I mean I knew his yobo as a whore and now he's going to marry her, or at least wants to. I don't know."

I slid back onto the mattress, rolled over. Kim ran her fingers across my stomach, then held my hand. "I like your tummy. But so why you worry?"

"I don't know. It's like, it's like it was wrong or something. Sort of wrong for him to marry a whore like that. Don't you think so?"

She pulled her hand loose.

"Not if they love each other."

"Kim?"

"Yobo?"

"I'm sorry."

"For what?"

"You know."

"What?"

"What I said."

"What you say?"

"About whores. About GIs."

"Oh."

I kissed her. Eyes so open. Lips so soft.

43

Nights I wasn't with Kim, I only half-wondered where she was. I should have wondered more. We'd agreed she had a right to do her extra business—the kind that didn't involve fucking GIs—to make extra money. But it was only supposed to be delivering black-market goods for Coletti. Not the hard stuff. We had talked it through. We had bonded our love on it.

But in the foul, loud night air, she wound through the alleys. Mama-sans bought the packages of smack, drug-laced cigarettes, bottles of acid for their girls, who then sold it to their GI Johns. Coletti paid her a commission, just as he did on the TV and tape deck deliveries, but on this, he had another link than the local thieves and crooks. For the hard stuff, the supply line came from Lee Hae-Sing, the half-Chinese gang thug.

I didn't know of that connection. Indirect but just as real. I wanted to trust her. So, I tried not to think about it.

"I love you," she would whisper as we slept under the orange quilt. In the carved-bone box from her childhood, hidden under a tile in our hootch and locked, she secretly put the money, first changing it to greenbacks or MPC. Because I didn't know, I couldn't feel her pride, growing with each deposit, nor see it in her smile. She would not let me. She had asked Coletti not to tell me anything, either. Thinking it was in my best interest, he agreed.

As her commissions and experience and stack of cash grew, so did her own deals. Skim a little here. Deliver a little less there. They won't know. She was Coletti's "local girl"—insulation from Lee, who stayed in the shadows. He only arranged things, greased the wheels of commerce. He never saw the ghost-faced recipients. He held out firm while junkie whores begged for credit on loans.

Coletti said that without Lee, half the business girls in the ville would have been wading in rice paddies or stuffing cabbage into giant brown crocks, watching the GIs through the barbed wire. Now they all got some of the action. An entrepreneur can't be too picky, Coletti said. He was just part of the flow of the economy.

Kim was in the flow. After the prescribed deliveries, she was free to have rounds of her own. Her profits doubled. A little for the bribes. Everything else for the airplane ticket.

At night she held me and smiled. Told me she loved me. But didn't tell me what was really going on when it might have made a difference. She had a reason. What no one knows, no one can destroy. Sometime, in her sealed past, she had waved goodbye at Kimpo. In the jet fumes she had breathed the rottenness, and the Fear, and there was nothing she would not do to keep that pain away forever. To be not forgotten. Not left behind. Not lost. To be not without a trace in her own land.

44

Summer brought constant, reliable, sweaty heat, and the smell of kim-chi. The country looked different. Alive. I wanted to shake bad feelings, and hooked up a helicopter ride to Busan to deliver some paperwork that could have just as easily been handled by routine land transport.

The Huey arced sharply over the hills, across the Incheon inlet, and south toward the Busan harbor. We were in the air three hours. Below us, green foothills showed off patches of rice, ringing the mountain-sides in glistening terraces. Beside the fields, villages that knew only the old ways huddled under thatched roofs. Shirtless men trudged through muddy fields behind oxen. Children playing in shallow pools looked up as we sliced the air. Farther south, the mountains grew higher, the foliage luxuriant. Then the terrain dropped into broad river plains, brown and dotted with hamlets and cities.

At Daegu, we dipped down for fuel. The pilot and I got out, stretch-ing our legs, our shirts immediately damp with sweat. Then, for no rea-son, a mountain chill swept the city and it rained hard, then hailed.

We ducked into the airfield waiting room, half-filled with other pilots and passengers. "Goddam Korean weather," cursed a major in a zippered flight suit as he looked out at the storm. "Does this shit all the time now. Monsoon's taking its time, but it's coming. Tears the fucking hell out of our shit."

When it stopped, my pilot and I checked for damage. There was none. We were airborne just behind some of the other grounded chop-pers. Approaching Busan, we followed the highway below as an easy guide. We passed another helicopter, its blades gleaming in the sun.

Busan is ringed by mountains and as we came in through a pass, we hit an air pocket. The Huey dropped fifty feet. My stomach climbed into my mouth and the pilot cursed, but regained control. A second lieutenant met us when we landed, and I gave him the stack of personnel folders I had promised. On the ride home, I fell asleep.

Most of the summer passed about the same way. The monsoon wasn't that bad, I thought, and you could sort of plan for it. On sunny days, after duty, I would return to the White Elephant, peel off my sweat and starch-soaked fatigues, and sprawl on the itchy wool blanket on my bed. Kim sneaked in sometimes because the hootch could get even hotter, but often enough we just crashed over there, wasted enough that we fell asleep anyway.

A fan for my room would have helped. I actually had a goddam fan for three days, a small plastic box with a blade the size of a toy motorboat propeller, but the BOQ building manager took it out while I was at work to give to a doctor.

So bitter, Lieutenant Hobbes, for such a young man.

Fucking doctors.

The PX was usually out of fans, so mostly, we hung out down in the air-conditioned O Club. But there was also the Beach when it didn't rain. It wasn't cooler, or pretentious, not that gravel sprinkled on a tarpaper roof could have any pretentions at all. But at night it got breezes, and during the day we could take the summer sun like Coppertone wanted, in a Tahiti fantasy.

It was all Nick's idea. He thought we would look healthy with tans and have an improved chance competing for the better-looking whores and also Eileen Rush, in case for some reason one of us would be on a downtown Seoul street some day and have to share a cab with her.

"What a view," he said, pulling a beer from an ice chest one especially lazy weekend, celebrating something no one could remember. A half-dozen other officers, including a TDY guy from Japan, were spread around the tarpaper. Nick raised his bottle in a toast. "I'm happy we can all join the pleasure of the tropics today. Our own little South

Pacific. I mean where else can you get this kind of luxury. You know, unless you're one of those guys."

He was standing at the edge of the roof and pointed down below, at the VIP parking lot. Two sergeants were sweating and cursing under a shade tree. They'd gotten called in to fix a visiting colonel's Jeep. We toasted them, too.

The sergeants looked up, fingered us all.

"Hey, allow me to throw down some refreshment," Nick yelled. "Final offer."

"And fuck you for that," the younger sergeant yelled back. "Fuck you very much."

I pulled off my green T-shirt and sat in my cut-off fatigues in one of the PX canvas fold-up chairs we'd saved from the dump.

On the Armed Forces Korea Network, I could hear an old Beatles song. I tried to listen. Hard to, though, with Nick keeping up his wiseass interchange with the sergeants below. "So hey, lads, is it true? If you hold a sparkplug up to your ear, you can hear a deuce-and-a-half rolling in."

From below: "Fuck you." Several repetitions.

From the radio: "I wanna hold your hand..."

From the TDY guy: "Let's throw down some beers anyway. Misery deserves alcohol."

From Nick: "You got a friend up here, guys. And I'm with him. Whether you like it or not, it's raining Pabst Blue Ribbon."

He and the TDY lobbed down at least a dozen beers.

"If we drink 'em, will you fuckers let us get this done in peace?"

Laughter.

From the radio: "Oh, please, say to me. . . you'll let me be your man . . ."

The sun was making me drowsy.

I pulled my cap over my eyes.

*

I am back in college days, on a real beach towel on a real beach at a real lake. Beth is kissing my ear. Then my mouth. Her skin is soft and tanned and warm. I want to kiss her breasts, and move my hand up her stomach, lingering slightly along the cool cotton of her two-piece, rubbing upward in tiny circles, our bodies twisting to each other. But we have to stop. People are all around. But my old Buick is parked all by itself back in the treeline. So, we go there.

*

The Panasonic snapped me back to the present: "This is Armed Forces Korea Network, and that was the Beatles with 'I Want to Hold Your Hand.'"

I wiped sweat off my face. Funny how a song can sweep you back. Is that called radio-vu? Except back then it was with Beth, in just one part of a two-piece, running her finger through her damp hair and putting the finger into my mouth, and then, after far too much progress, "Tom, stop. We can't. I know. Just kiss me. Just kiss me."

45

In Korean tradition, the dead are buried in mounds. Big ones for royalty and the rich, and more modest ones, three feet high or so, for ordinary people. Sansoe told me that someone told him that the bodies are buried sitting up, but Cpl. Yu said that wasn't true, but it was kind of cool to think so. Mountains, at least the foothills, in several places around Suchow and Bupyeong and even up towards Seoul were often covered with the smaller mounds. Kim said they were called Happy Mountains.

"I don't know what's so happy about it," I said as we hiked up one on a Sunday afternoon.

"Why not happy?"

"Because they're dead." I reached for a tree branch to pull myself up a steep incline. She followed.

"You no think dead happy?"

"How should I know?"

"You the one say it no happy."

"I mean I don't think a graveyard is very funny."

"You mean 'ha-ha,' like that funny?"

"Yeah, funny ha-ha."

We were at a boulder, and I pulled her up and around it.

"Not Ha-Ha Mountain. Happy Mountain. Happy and Ha-Ha not same."

"Pretty semantic for a Korean."

"What semantic?"

"Never mind."

We reached the top and looked out over a wide valley.

"Hey, yobo, you happy?"

The valley was gorgeous, green with summer.

"Sometimes."

"You think everybody happy?"

"Of course not."

She picked up a branch and dug into the dirt. "You think I happy?"

"Are you?"

She paused. "I think so."

A breeze blew past us, cool on my sweaty back. Kim pointed the branch toward some mounds.

"You think they happy?"

The way she said it sent a dark flash through my soul. I don't know why. Only that I knew there was so much more in her than I could ever imagine. That I only caught glimpses of. "Are they?" was the best I could come up with.

She drew her arm back and swirled the branch out towards the mounds. It got caught in a tree. She dusted her hands on her pants, took in the view, looked me over. Slowly.

"I think so."

46

There was a virgin once I found among whores. She was Nick's yobo's friend. He treated her in his special midnight dental clinic. I helped him, watched with a queasy stomach as we pulled two teeth from Miss Seong's mouth.

"That's from diet, eating kimchi and rice all her life. And not much dental care, if any. Her teeth are barely making it. If we want to help these people for real, we could take care of this kind of stuff. Teeth, eyes, lungs, vaccines, schools, roads . . . fuck."

"Are you finished?" I asked, holding the vacuum hose that took the saliva and blood. "I mean, a little hypocritical. Given the fee."

The fee was a free fuck.

And the free fuck, Miss Seong, thankfully sedated, was different.

"Are you kidding? A virgin?" I asked two nights later in one of the large-ish hootches in the courtyard where Nick's yobo, Marilyn, and three others lived. It was the Korean equivalent of a whore house. We paid the yobos, the yobos paid the mama-san, the mama-san paid the rent.

Nick's yobo, Marilyn, had nixed Miss Seong's offer of barter for the dental work. Nick told her that was fine. Miss Seong owed him nothing. The whole idea of the payback was kind of a bad joke. He said, "I mean my yobo says Miss Seong is from a little village south of Incheon and only eighteen and only slept with one guy, a GI, and he was pretty rough on her and they didn't exactly finish, and she wouldn't take any money and she's scared and all. Like maybe not really wanting to get into the business. Except okay for getting her smile pretty again."

I rubbed my face, listening to that. It was too much. Things had a way of just turning nuts all the time, probably one of the reasons going into the ville was off-limits. On the other hand, there was never a dull moment. But fucking an 18-year-old semi-virgin so she could keep her teeth?

"You're right. A real bad joke," I said, and started out the hootch door.

Marilyn was right behind me. "Hey you, Hobbes, you wait."

Nick was right behind her. "Hey look, Hobbes. Just a damn minute."

I started to say something like fuck you, but Marilyn tugged at my arm. "You come back. You no need being mad."

I looked at her, at him. We settled into the wicker chairs in the courtyard, where GIs often waited. Marilyn said something and one of the bedroom doors opened. Miss Seong came out. Bowed slightly toward me.

"You can't be serious," I said.

Nick shook his head, like I was some kind of idiot.

I got up to leave again. And again, Nick stopped me. He put his arm around me, like we were pals sorting out a dispute. "Listen, man. You can't go now."

"But I can."

"Okay, but don't. Look at her. Could she be any more polite?"

"She's probably being scared. Fuck. Are we even having this conversation?"

"You just thinkee she ugly." Marilyn snapped, looking at me, then at Miss Seong.

"Not at all. "I tried to smile at Miss Seong, who seemed frozen in embarrassment.

"What she's scared of is being insulted," Nick said. "After all this, now you just walk away."

"Oh, for Chrissake."

"No, really," Marilyn said. "Miss Seong like you. You nice to her when you helping Dr. Nick. She hundred percent want to fuckee with you. Show she no cheat on payment."

"What?"

She nodded. "Like a trade, okay? She made deal for Doctor Nick. And Doctor Nick not want her. And she upset that the deal

183

not honored. So she say can she make sex with you instead? Payment all done. She rather fuckee you than someone like that GI that hit her before."

Miss Seong stepped forward. She smiled and pointed at her teeth. "I keep my word. This mean so much. Okay?" Her English was very good.

I looked at Nick. "You can't just call all this off now? I mean, the bad joke needs to be over."

"I've tried," he said. "She never took it as a joke, Miss Seong. Marilyn says she has a lot of pride. And you were the only way out so seeing me wouldn't be a freebie, or maybe she would owe me something else later. I mean, don't think of yourself, man. Think of her. It's not really for you to decide, sort of."

I know, I know, but Nick and Marilyn left, and I stayed the rest of the night with Miss Seong. Butterflying, Kim would say, but she would never find out. Or if she did, the butterfly ledger count was long in her favor.

Proud, gracious, beautiful Miss Seong. She was awake at dawn, watching me and stroking my hair. She wanted to talk, in English, so we did. I was glad I had stayed. I had no right, and I felt both wretched and pleased to be with her. It helped that I knew she had been glad I'd stayed, not for sex, but for re-thinking what a good, educated small-town girl was getting herself into to make some money. For her family. In a way, I was an experiment. Or maybe I just wanted to think of it that way.

We met Nick and his yobo in the courtyard. Miss Seong nestled against me as we made small talk. I thought we all might go to breakfast, but Marilyn made it clear the meter had run out.

Nick said something to Marilyn, and I attempted a good-bye with Miss Seong, but I couldn't remember how to say the words in Korean. She smiled, then hugged me.

"She likee you. She like see you again," Marilyn said.

"Yeah, sure." I gave Miss Seong a quick kiss.

I had left ten dollars on Miss Seong's pillow as a surprise. I hoped it would be the last money she'd make that way. And then I hoped I hadn't insulted her.

*

"Invest in youth," I told Coletti later, sharing the story and trying to pull a hollow laugh from something that didn't deserve it.

"The future of mankind." Coletti's look was what I imagined a priest would have after hearing a tiresome, self-serving confession. He held it uncomfortably long. "You're still a shit, you know. Like I said before. You just don't want to admit it."

I looked at him with a smile that quickly disappeared.

"You still want people to like you. Even if you fuck a virgin, or semi-virgin, whatever that is, just because she was raised to pay her debts and she wanted her teeth fixed so she'd look pretty and the only way she could pay for it was to fuck her dentist—or even worse, his friend. You know. You."

"You're judging me? I thought you were against that."

"I am. And I'm not. I'm more like calling you out. Like you volunteered to fuck her to seal the deal and also keep her from having to fuck somebody else."

"It wasn't like that."

"It was exactly like that, Mr. Likeable American. And you know what else? You're not just lying to yourself about who you are, because you're already one of us. You're corrupt and immoral just like the rest of us. Like I already told you and shouldn't have to say again, but I am."

"Asshole."

"Maybe, but you're exactly what happens here. What happens to the good kids and the jerks. High and mighty become the low and ugly. It's the way it works. We got no war, so we find other things to do. You just think you're above it. But you're not."

I started to respond but he held up his hand like a traffic cop.

"Just save it. Listening to this just now made me almost sick, and you know I'm no motherfucking angel. Not so much what you did as how you decided to tell it. Justify a truly slimebag move."

I slumped in my chair, tried to follow Hank Williams on the loudspeakers. Breathed out whatever had gathered in my lungs and ears.

He waved for the waitress. "Next round on me." Gave me a less disgusted look. "Maybe I went too far. Or maybe that's what a friend is supposed to do."

"But I did like her, for the record, and she liked me."

"And you showed by letting her pay for what she thought was her payment to Nick. And then dropping a tenner. As what, a tip? Payment to Nick?"

"Can we drop this? I just want her to be okay. Get the hell out of here."

The drinks came. We both sipped at ours so we wouldn't have to talk anymore.

Miss Seong did get the hell out. Within a matter of days, I found out later. To be a teacher, I hoped. Always would hope. Hoped that she would have a happy life. Maybe go to some university, like Cpl. Yu's friends. Never take a starring role in an endless soul-splitting vision like the one that was coagulating around me and spreading to Kim.

47

I, Hobbes. I come vanilla when I do. When I do, I do. Do you?

My teeth are Hobbes teeth. White. Summer comes. When it comes, I freckle. Do you? Freckle, not come.

My mind is Hobbes mind. Clean. In the morning, it is mine. Morning mine.

I can be president. Resident.

I can be rich. Itch.

I am twenty-two. Compared to eighteen.

I am a Hobbes. Compared to a Seong.

And what I wanna know is this, Mrs. Mother of Hobbes, if you were still around: What do you think of your blue-eyed boy now?

48

Twenty years ago, there would have been more to think about: Trying to stay alive. In a way, Sansoe said, that might have been less. If I had thought of it, fresh off the Stretch-8 at Kimpo that first day in Korea, I would have asked Col. Foster. He'd also been on the plane, but up in the front row, reserved for senior officers. But even green as I was, seeing him, I knew this wasn't his first tour. I would have asked him how he planned to handle his return. Did it seem different this time? Did he seem different? Not that he would have told me the truth.

Maybe that was why he had come to mind again. I'd been here more than half my tour. Was I anywhere near where I thought I'd be? Maybe the incident with Miss Seong, to put it that way, threw me into personal accounting mode. Not looking good. The ledger was all red.

That day in the Kimpo terminal, Col. Foster, like me, had walked quietly through the duffel bags, picking roughly at several until he found his own, then going outside toward the buses cloaked in white exhaust vapors. He did not, as did I, turn to gawk country rube-like at the yobos, at this cold land. He took the first seat on the first bus. Thinking it proper, as a fellow officer, I took the place beside him. Several officers outranking me came on and gave me snotty looks as they passed along to other seats. Like any of it fucking mattered.

When the bus had filled, the Korean driver breathed onto the inside of the windshield and wiped it clean with his soiled black glove. We lurched forward across the parking lot and rumbled down the pock-marked perimeter road, past the guards and the gun batteries, out into the first small Korean village I'd seen, huddled against the barbed wire for protection and sustenance.

Col. Foster, as I could see by his name tag, gazed out the frosty window. "Never should have come," he breathed to himself.

But I heard. We were all Americans here, weren't we? Friends, practically.

"I guess you've been here before, sir."

He measured me up quickly. "Yes, lieutenant."

"Oh, during the war?"

"Yes, the war. The Korean War." He turned his head away. "You must have read about it."

Then it was thirty miles of silence to the compound at Bupyeong.

But as the road narrowed to one lane at the sentry gate, we caught our breath. Others in the seats behind us mumbled indistinctly.

It was the woman outside the gate. My first look at her, which I already mentioned.

Not the last, when I was leaving and she was dead. Which might not have been real. Which I also already mentioned.

The bus drove through the gate. The plastic vinyl seat creaked as Col. Foster and I leaned toward the windows for a better view. I think she saw us, these new devils who were staring, and she made us know her, while she was still alive.

"Twenty years," Col. Foster said, turning to me as if I'd just shown up. "Have I been here before, lieutenant? Isn't that what you asked? Have I been here before? Jesus have I been here before."

He tilted his head back and inhaled as if drawing on a cigar. "Twenty years. And not a goddam thing has changed." He wiped flight sleep from his eyes. "Did you see the kids playing in the goddam potholes along the way?"

"I saw them."

He was grinning, his face hard, smooth. His teeth, which I could now see were tobacco-stained, were crooked. His gray hair was cut close, and he wore round, wire-rimmed glasses. Hawk-like, Prussian, were words you could use. Defeated, cynical, were others.

"Tch, tch, son. Too much for a gold bar?" I knew my face had reddened. "Bet they told you you'd fuck a lot over here, huh? Well, be my guest. Help yourself. I recommend that one highly."

I sat without responding.

His smile dissolved. He mechanically brushed dust from his attaché case. "Quite a sight, isn't it, your first few hours on the ground?"

"I guess."

"That damn whore pulling up her skirt by the gate doesn't even know who did it to her. Might've been last year, or ten years ago, or twenty. Can't even tell how old she is. Doesn't matter though. She won't last."

The bitterness was overdone, I thought, so I just nodded rather than speak. But behind all that, turns out he had a secret. The woman had triggered it, and he would confess.

"Could've been me for that matter," he said, arranging his things. The acid in his voice was gone. Now more just a low, steady stream. "I fucked her, or somebody like her. You will, too. You'll fuck them. We all do. I had a special one once. Miss Kim. My mouse. Miss Kim. I left her and never said goodbye." He snapped his fingers. "Just like that. A year together and just like that. Not even goodbye." He snapped his fingers again.

The bus pulled up in front of a large white building that said: Officer Billeting.

"I wonder, still, what ever happened to Miss Kim? How about that?" He pulled his briefcase against his chest and stared ahead in silence.

Kim was such a common name it was not impossible for it to be shared. Later, I thought of the coincidence, if that was what it was, but didn't tell my Kim. She was funny about those kinds of things.

The driver opened the bus doors. Col. Foster stood up, adjusted his uniform and saucer hat, and was a regular Army lifer full bore. I put on my own hat and stood in the aisle, blocking it so he would have room to get out ahead of the others. "Good luck, sir," I said, following as he jumped down the steps to the ground. He'd never mentioned that he was reporting for duty to be the commander of the entire compound, and I rarely saw him after that.

He only lasted four months.

On Groundhog Day, PFC Albert Owen, a mechanic in the Transportation Section, threw a hand grenade into Col. Foster's hootch. Owen admitted it, but said he thought it had been the hootch of Command Sergeant Major Albert Hite, a card-carrying racist asshole, and he hadn't meant to kill Col. Foster at all.

Owen signed a statement because they said if he did, he would go to Leavenworth instead of an Army prison in Korea. But while awaiting shipment, Owen died. They said it was pneumonia. His cell block was run by Sergeant First Class Joe Don Lawrence, who had once shared a hootch with CSM Hite.

After the fragging, Col. Foster's body was sent to Portland, Ore., where he was buried beside Grace, his wife. Zack Thiller, a doctor who lived in the White Elephant before the Evac went to Seoul, told me Col. Foster lived two hours after the explosion. Zack said the colonel slipped in and out of consciousness, smiling crazily under pain drugs, coughing blood, and babbling of the war. I told Zack of our bus ride. He said maybe that was why the colonel pulled him close and gurgled, "Tell Kim I know."

There was one other thing. Coletti once received a case of stolen hand grenades from a Korean in exchange for new, American-made winter coats. To get rid of the grenades asap, he swapped them to another Korean for some copper pipe. The copper pipe eventually went for plumbing in the new wing of the Officer's Club, in exchange for which Coletti received a large shipment of liquor, which was swapped to Koreans from Incheon, and so on.

Lee Hae-Sing was the man who arranged the pipe trade for the grenades and secretly received them himself. He gave half the grenades to PFC Albert Owen to settle a complicated gambling debt. Owen sent all but one to a gangster in Seoul. They disappeared.

Because Owen died, there was never a trial, and nothing could be traced to Coletti.

49

Nothing could be traced to anyone. I could begin to feel the distance and knew how the past became the future. Nothing traceable. Come, see, conquer. Go home. And then others can deal with it. Let them wait in busy, lonely military air terminals until it is 2300 hours and out through the cold ground fog the Red Tail doors open. And they are gone.

Time did pass—from my arrival in autumn, through icy winter, teasing spring, wet summer. Now autumn again. It had all happened and still was happening, measured by the battery-powered ticks of the headquarters clock. Tiny units, infinitely divisible. Nothing to be done to or for them. Just let them click, escape them as best we can. I'd be gone by Thanksgiving, most likely.

She came to me and said: "Yobo, I gonna have baby."

I reacted with a snorting laugh, the kind when you spew your coffee, expelling the entire content of your lungs but suppressing what you can because don't want anyone to know. "Sure, you are, and I'm gonna re-up and go to chopper school."

She gripped my arm with primitive force and didn't smile. And then neither did I.

"When?"

"You no worry. After you gone. You no have to see it."

We were in her mama-san's hootch, which she'd still been paying rent to keep. She said the yobos all did that for a while. In case they had to move back fast. She could have given it up, but now she just kept it so if she was out doing deliveries for Coletti, she could use it so I wouldn't know. Which I knew. Also that she sometimes sublet for the night to other working girls who needed a fast place to do business. But, to avoid another fight, I never said anything. Now, everything had to be said.

The sun fell on her face through the plastic patch in the window, and I could see her jaw muscles quiver. "I write and tell you whether it a boy or girl—" she began and then choked on the words. The quiver spread across her face and throughout her body and she dropped down on her knees, sobbing. I dropped, too, took her hand. "There, there." As soon as I said it, I remembered the line from Yossarian in *Catch-22*.

"I sorry, yobo. I no think I can have baby. I take the pills. So we don't use rubber like we should. For clap, too." She started to choke again. Her eyes wild. I could only look and listen. "You know. I only find out two days ago. I afraid to tell you, but my friend she say I should tell you and so I have to or she tell you, she say, but I am afraid and don't want to, you know, yobo." The words ran all together until her mouth hung open, unable to work and she just stared at me, no voice at all now, and a look I had never seen before.

It never occurred to me to wonder what look might be on my face. Whatever it was, it was in service of only one word.

Pregnant.

Pregnant.

I got her pregnant. Knocked her up.

And then I thought: You're a father. I would be lying if I said the thought wasn't intriguing. As in unbelievable. But it was only an instant. Knocked-her-up was the message that bullied its way back.

Followed by darker ones. Hurtful ones.

"Kim." One had to be tough-minded. "Kim, are you sure it's mine?"

She squeezed my hand so hard the knuckles cracked, then pushed it sharply into my nose and slid away from me.

"I mean, I'm just asking." I felt my nose. Not bleeding or broken. "I mean there have been times we were fighting, and I . . . and you might've . . . I mean I just wanted to be sure."

Saying nothing. Glaring. We were still kneeling, facing each other, but her body went stiff and upright as a steel beam. I reached for her. She pushed my hand away. In her eyes, anxiety hardened to hatred. Her mouth tightened, as if she were going to spit.

Then it all collapsed again. Her head dropped against her chest, draped with her hair.

I felt as bad as I should have, if that were possible.

"I'm sorry, Kim . . . I meant . . ."

And there was nothing my mouth could say, either.

Minutes seemed like years. Her body straightened, her head rose, framing a face that might hurt for eternity. "Hobbes-san, why I say it yours if it not?"

I reached for her again, but her arms were tight across her stomach.

"I don't . . . forget I said it. It was stupid. Stupid."

She stood. As did I.

"I know you think I sleep with toc sahn GI. All of them. You think I just whore. You only wanna fuck me. I know you no love me."

"No. That's not true."

"Yes, it is! I know. I know this, too. I woman. I have baby. I know it is us. Just us."

She looked out the window, possibly beyond the entire planet. When the clouds shifted, the sun rays spread back across her body. I followed it. I tried to see if her abdomen had grown.

She saw where I was looking and ran her hand across her stomach. I realized I had forgotten something important.

"How long have you been? I mean, when did it happen? I mean, it can't be that long?"

She started to say something, but instead moved closer to me and put her hand on my wrist. She guided it to where hers had been. "You feel anything?"

"No."

"Well then, you know it not been very long for sure."

"So?"

"So, about a month, I think."

"So, July, August?"

"End of July, early August. You care?"

"Of course."

"You just want to know if we together or having fights when this happen."

"Not really. I just wanted to know. And so about when it would be born?"

"April, probably. Or May."

"You've seen a doctor?"

"They know what I am. They won't see business girls until later."

"Why?"

"Never mind why. Just how it is."

"Jesus, Kim. This is a lot to think about."

She rolled her eyes.

I felt a half-smile on my face. The kind I sometimes got involuntarily. In school, teachers said I smirked, but they always had it wrong. This was more a daze. I couldn't see where I was. Like being in water, under a mirror, watching myself move. Like laughing when I thought I was about to die. Sort of.

"My baby," I experimented.

"Our baby," Kim said, still slowly massaging her middle. "Yobo. I want you to listen me. Okay?"

"I'm listening."

"Okay. Listen me. I tell you this last time. You understand this now or you leave, never come back." Her features hardened again. Like I'd never seen in her before.

"Yobo, this *my* baby. I have it. I grow it. In here." Patting stomach. "I care for it. I born it." She drew a long breath. "You no think it yours, okay. I know you think that." She moved so close her breaths were mine. "So you listen. I tell you again. If you think that, you just be oop-soh right now. Leave." She pointed to the door. "Get out, never see Kim again."

I stood like a pillar of dumbstruck. She went over to the boxes and mirror she had cleverly improved into a dresser to look at herself. She pushed back her hair, nodded, returned to me at the window. I had barely moved. It was a very small room. No place to hide. No space to evade. And she was not going to let me.

"You makee love here and in our hootch all this long time and now you be GI and say, okay, yobo, not *my* fucking baby. Maybe somebody you butterfly." I thought she was going to hit me again, but she didn't. "So I tell you and by damn you listen good mister. Like I say when I cry, but I not am cry now. It yours and mine. Ours. You don't believe, then nice knowing you."

A lifetime within two seconds:

In the first, something warned me—get out now. This is your chance. Leave now. The perfect chance.

Then came the second—I saw her. She made me. And she made me see me in her. You can help me, her eyes said. But also the reverse—I can help you.

"I want to stay."

I went to her. I showed no tears, but I kissed her, held her so tightly she finally said, "Yobo, I have to breathe."

50

Maybe she was mistaken. It happens. But no, she was right. Maybe it was right. The idea, the concept, bounced in my head. I could never precisely see the three of us: her, me, a child. But I sensed the concept. Part of the life-urge, the process. All that I'd heard about. And yet.

And yet there was the World. It crept through the mindless time-less urge and distorted it, sucked it out like marrow and made it empty. The World.

I wanted to tell Coletti. He was here when I stepped off the Stretch-8, would be after I had gone. Perhaps as an old man he would still be here, free from the Army, secure as an ex-pat, and king-like over his Mayor of Suchow empire. But for all that, all his cynical greed and no-questions deals, he did not judge me. He took what was given, and grifted. He had no more enemies than friends, for he had no allegiance and no cause. Once I had considered him a great hero, an eternal force, but Coletti was only a cipher.

So, I told him. "Kim is going to have a baby."

Even in the Homestead's dim lights, I could see his eyes widen and for an instant, the barest instant, show puzzled surprise. But he recovered immediately and used his mask of joviality to disguise all but a trace of concern.

"Magnificent, Hobbes. Another half-breed to civilize this pagan wilderness. If this progresses geometrically, we'll supplant the Korean race with blue-eyed Teutons in 1,816,753 years. Give or take. Or maybe the opposite."

"No, really. I'm serious."

He grinned like I had slipped on a banana peel.

"I mean, it's mine."

"I understand, me bucko."

"Well?"

"Well, what?"

"Well, what should I do about it?"

"What should you do about it? What you mean what should you do about it? What can you do about it?"

"Come on, man. I'm serious."

"So am I. What can you do? Nothing. Absolutely nothing. She's having a kid. So what? It's mother nature. Happens in the best of families."

He drained his glass, leaned forward, and looked to see if anyone was eavesdropping. "Tell you a secret, me bucko. I got one over here myself."

"What?"

"That's right. Had it a few months ago. The mother is down in Busan."

"Are you serious?"

"Yes, goddam it. Are you listening?"

"Jesus." I rubbed my face. It hadn't occurred to me this happened to other people. "Why didn't you tell me?"

"Why should I?"

"Well, I mean, the same thing's happened to me. I mean I told you, didn't I?"

"Sure." Coletti leaned back. The waitress plopped two fresh glasses of whiskey on our table. "But it's different. You're scared and fucked up. I'm not. I was surprised to get it, a little girl, but glad I did. I can handle it. I mean, look, it's not a problem for me."

"But it is for me?"

"That's for you to decide."

"Thanks."

"Oh, come on. Mr. Good Guy wants a little advice from Satan?"

"I was just telling you."

He raised his palms. "Okay, okay, peace." He looked around again. "Look, Hobbes—just take it, roll with it. Take the changes. What else can I say?"

My brain was a mass of mixed data. All this confusion wasn't about the baby. Beyond the birth, I wanted her. It had been on my mind anyway. Why did the baby matter? Did that really make a difference? Would I leave Kim without it?

"Did you marry the mother?"

He shook his head but didn't answer. Silence. Temptations on the speakers.

"What if I said I thought I should go ahead and marry her? I mean since she's having a kid?"

"Kim?"

"Come on."

He leaned back, silhouetted against the red lights strung across the walls. He seemed very quiet, my cipher.

"It'll never work."

I watched the lights flicker. "You really think so?"

Whatever he started to say, he took a breath instead, let it out loud, and rubbed his eyes. "Fuck, I don't know. You're stuck in your indecisive gear again."

"Well, it's a fucking lot to decide."

"How far is she?"

"A little over a month."

He looked out into the room, too early to be filled with drunken soldiers and prowling ville girls.

"Do what you want. Just . . ."

"Just what?"

He put his hands over his face, shook his head slightly. Brought them down. That smile was back. "Just know what you're doing."

"Damn." I took a long drink, and in a frenzied flash of Coletti's eye, I saw it. I could do it. Even if I didn't know if I could, or wanted to. Or I could completely fuck the whole thing up. It wasn't his call, and he didn't want to have dig into the angles again. The mom in Busan was more than enough. Not that he'd ever say so.

I wish he would have. But seeing his wound, even just a few stitches, was what I needed. It was the window to all those nights of wondering and pretending, the struggles to say I love you to the woman I loved. We'll have a baby. She will be the mother. And I will rescue her from this place, save both their lives. Kim will be my wife.

Fuck them at home, in the World, wherever we might go. The decision couldn't wait. Yes, I thought. Yes. I could really do it.

*

I told Sansoe about it the next day. He also was shocked but tried to be sympathetic.

"Sorry, man. What're you going to do?"

"I don't know. It's still early."

"You're not thinking about getting married?"

"No, no, of course not."

His eyes rolled. He had, after all, predicted this. "Don't do it. You wouldn't marry that Beth girl back in the World just because you knocked her up, would you?"

I shrugged.

"Would you really? Just because she was pregnant?"

"Not just because she was pregnant."

"Oh," he said as if it just hit him, "you mean you think you're—"

"No, no. I don't. I'm not in love with her. It's just something to think about. Come on, you've been to the orphanages with me."

That registered. "Yeah, yeah, okay."

"Well, I just don't know what to do. What would you do?"

"Unh, unh, don't ask me that. Talk to me all you want, but don't ask me that. Really."

Damn. Now I wasn't sure if I had made a decision after all. Talking to Coletti was just a rush—just an initial good feeling. Cheap and easy to stop. Happened all the time in the ville. No expense to anyone. Except Kim. The fuck was I talking about? Make a life, take a wife. Is that how it's supposed to go? So, it was my decision? Get a grip, Hobbesie. Real quick. Good lord, I was even going to Sansoe for advice.

200

"Hey, stop zoning out."

"Sorry."

"Really, just look at it this way. Who are you marrying? Her or the kid?"

Neither of us expected an answer, nor got one.

I wanted her now, to hold her now, caress her now, protect her now, keep a child out of the dusty orphanages now. But was it a dream? Or was it real? Does this place, this exact place and moment, exist? Or is it only a dream, maybe an opium dream, from something I had only ever read in history books or seen in movies and newscasts?

*

The embryo grew, or maybe it was a fetus. I didn't know much about that. But there was still time. Sort of. Three months until my Red Tail back to the World. Less than that to decide if she keeps the thing or not. Although I already knew the answer to that. With each minute, the offspring of Kim and Thomas grew, and rented out more space in her insides. When we talked, I saw desperation in her face, but I assumed it was because of the needs of the baby, not because of wondering if she wanted to stay pregnant. Here was her big chance, if you wanted to look at it that way.

How could I waffle when what was really inside her was me? Me and her. Us.

Her end game, to circumvent my indecision, was to find a way to come with me anyway. To the World.

What could I have done differently? Broken it off then and there, like a man? Nip it in the bud, painfully as that would be? As they say, better a small hurt now than big heartache later. Maybe I could tell her at a drive-in, like giving back a class ring to a gum-chewing cheerleader. Only there weren't any drive-ins. Or cheerleaders. Or rings. Still, I wanted to be sure I had covered all the scenarios. Fuck.

So just break it off. Then where would she be? She had seen this plenty of times. The GI waves goodbye, maybe sheds some tears for his yobo, maybe feels some guilt, but no real suffering. The yobo's life becomes a dead-end. She can only enter the sex-gladiator coliseum again if she wants to survive.

So, she couldn't tell me her Big Secret that everyone knew. Not the baby. The other one. She couldn't risk making it the truth by doing it. Better to gamble with the illusion. At least an illusion is real while it exists. With luck, and perseverance, she could turn the illusion to a reality. We would be settled in the World, in the New Mexico mountains. I could hardly shut the door in her face, kick her away. Especially with little Brett or Sherry in her arms.

The fetus grew.

With it, Kim must have reckoned her chances would improve. And yet. Jesus Jesus Jesus—and yet she could not shake her whore's intuition. That I would leave.

Her Big Secret plan remained practical. The deals with Coletti, and the money, would go on until she had accumulated enough. If I had listened, I could have heard the scream in her head. She had to leave with me. She and the baby had to leave with me.

She would not be lost. She would not be alone. She would not be abandoned with a half-breed, which wasn't even the worst name the child would be called. She would not be an unwed whore mother hiding unsightly stretch marks in bed. She shouldn't have to tell me. So, she wouldn't.

The fetus grew.

51

Nick was leaving. He only had the clap once and had performed an international trophy-worthy service on behalf of dentistry in the third world. Which I had witnessed. But he was leaving. Too soon. Not for him. For us. It could not be accepted. It was a time marker and bore the scent of death. But markers would come for us all. Travis already had gone his own special way. Coletti would stay maybe forever. Sansoe shut everything out and was drifting in his remaining months with the boundless current. I played whore's games, tinkered with love where I had no business. I would never be leaving. The thoughts became confusing, and then infuriating. I should have kept them to myself.

So, the hell with all that, we'd say a proper goodbye to Nick.

It started in the O Club with a few Happy Hour drinks around the bar and stories about each other's time in-country, from Suchow to the hospital fire. But it ended the wrong way. Nothing proper about it. More like "perverted," as Sansoe would summarize what we had done. What that was, was best to forget, which of course we never would.

Maybe I started it. That and the booze. Somehow the Happy Hour camaraderie slipped off the rails. Probably when I insulted Nick, in the midst of the yarn-swapping, with words and vitriol I didn't even realize I had in me. "Having fun, doc? I'll show you fun, goddamit, you fucking short-timer." I put my arm on his shoulder. "Stick with me pal, we'll go out to the ville later and it'll be the time of your life. The last time like this. For you. You're gonna miss the shit out of our little slice of heaven, all the pretty-girl mouths you get to stick your fingers in for barter."

Nick looked at the others, who caught my tone. His face crinkled, then smoothed like steel into a sharp stare. He held it for a few seconds, then threw off my arm and patted my shoulder. Not especially lightly. The steel face broke into a laugh and he raised his glass with his free hand. "Listen, First Lieutenant Thomas Jefferson Hobbes, thanks for all your bullshit concern. But fact is, I'm not really leaving. How 'bout that, chingu?"

Now it was my turn to stare.

"The American-International Dental Association is meeting here next Christmas. I don't know why but who cares. You know, party hats, important research papers, the works."

"Hell if you'll come back. Not after a year in the World."

"Hell if I won't."

"Well then, just extend here for a year and avoid all the travel. I can fix that up for you."

"You don't look that drunk. Are you?"

"I don't see how you can leave all these women with bad teeth."

Everyone watched closely. Like an intervention might be required. By now, the story of Miss Seong had gotten around.

"Just doing my duty," Nick said, finally.

As fast as it had lit up, my hostility went out. I was embarrassed. "Goddamn, Nick, you shouldn't fucking go if you're gonna come right back."

He figured it out, too, and did a fake smack to my chin. It was all I could do to squeeze back a tear. Later, Sansoe told me a lot of people got mad at short-timers because they wanted to leave, too. But weren't. He said it was a guy thing. Anger to cover up hurt, I guess.

I clinked my glass against Nick's and walked over to the bar. My shit needed to get back together. The club was rapidly filling up, and a pair of captains pushed past me to find an open spot. Pretty soon the meeting room, transformed with cheap decorations for Nick's soiree into the party room, would be open for us. That meant free appetizers and even cheaper drinks at least for a couple of hours. A whole new start-over for sullen goodbye-sayers like me.

But maybe not.

"Cocksuckers ought to be on duty," Nick said loudly, joining me at the bar, after one of the captains, probably temporary duty, brushed him too hard and barely mumbled an apology. Then, like a guy trying to start a fight, or a riot, Nick called out to everyone around us. "Why don't we liven it up a little with a Flaming Hooker before the adios-to-me party room opens." He was especially looking toward the captain who bumped him but also at a fast-growing clump of pilots in flight suits and grunts in Big Mac shades at the far end of the bar.

Charlie, the bartender, and a former patient, waved at his dentist to come over close. "Hey, doc, I got you, but lemme work up to it first, okay? It's crazy in here. I got to be careful." Nick gave him a thumbs-up, looked at me, rolled his eyes like he'd come to his senses. It was supposed to be a happy party. We waited for Charlie's cue.

Flaming Hookers were made from 180-proof Cuban rum, poured into a champagne or martini glass, a thin layer of cognac on top. You had to carefully light the alcohol, then delicately draw the rim of the glass to lip level and toss it back in one motion. Done properly, a bluish flame would linger inside the glass when it was placed back on the counter. Done improperly, it would burn the hell out of your face and mouth. It was a ritual, a rite of passage.

Nick wanted Charlie to pour one for me. But, perhaps to protect us, Charlie had already been setting up a Flaming Hooker at the other end of the bar. The pilot crowd was daring Andrew Blakson, a visiting lieutenant colonel from Seoul, and the son-in-law of the deputy commanding general of the 8th Army, to give it a try.

I will always love them for that.

As was the custom, everyone stopped whatever they were doing and watched. Nick and I eased up as close as we could get. Sansoe had come over, too.

Lt. Col. Blakson studied Charlie's every move, every pour.

Easy to tell he was West Point, boots polished, fatigues starched stiff, high and tight, strac. A rugged brown mustache, the kind you would call sporting, blended against his tanned face. He had seen much of this world, become a man in many challenges.

"So what now?" Blakson asked one of the pilots. "Just hoist it up and down the hatch?"

"That's all there is to it, sir. But don't hesitate. Just do it."

"Well, if I could drink a quart of goat's blood in Africa, I can bloody well do this."

Nick punched me. "What's this 'bloody well' shit?"

The lieutenant colonel stretched his arm over the bar and made a fist, thumbs up. "Light the sonofabitch!"

Charlie lit it.

The goat-blood drinker theatrically hoisted the beaker, brought it to mouth level, and tossed it. But anyone who looked at Blakson in the long bar mirror could have seen hesitation in his eyes. The fiery alcohol jumped from the beaker, spilling onto his mustache and chin. For a few seconds, the lower part of his face burned bluish. The officers around him found a towel. The flames went out fast. Not like the smile on Nick's face.

Blakson leaned heavily against the counter, dabbing at his skin. "Shit, shit," he mumbled through charred lips. His finely trimmed mustache reeked of singed hair.

"Is he going to pretend it didn't happen?" Nick said.

The lieutenant colonel tried to stand free, shaking off assistance, but his knees buckled. A major supported him under an arm.

"Get a Jeep," someone shouted. I looked around. Two or three junior officers, probably with Blakson's team, were bustling to find help. Most everyone else had returned to drinking at their tables, not really wanting to watch anymore. Afraid they might laugh. The pilots stayed at the bar, doing their best not to say anything.

"Tough act to follow," someone chirped as Blakson was escorted out.

Nick nudged me. "Your turn."

"Like hell."

It didn't matter. Charlie was in the back talking loudly to Tommy the club manager. You can imagine. Miss So, the head bar girl, served a few more drinks, but said she wouldn't make any stupid ones.

Before the night was done, a hand-lettered white sign would be taped to the bar mirror: "No Flaming Hookers." We found out a week later the quartermaster office had prohibited the import of 180-proof rum.

*

But the evening wasn't over. By 6:30, though, Happy Hour was. Cancelled for the rest of the week.

Sansoe and the rest of the Nick farewell contingent filtered into the party room. One of the tables had a cake with letters, "Last Dentist Out of Dodge."

"Ring the bell, short-timer," someone yelled. It was a tradition for the last night. It meant the nearly departed had to buy a round of drinks for the house.

Nick pulled the rope hard. "I don't even mind those motherfucking warrant officers getting free drinks off me." He rang the bell again.

"Leaving, eh, me bucko?" Coletti said, just popping in, high-fiving with Nick.

"You're goddammed right. The ville is all yours, you crooked cocksucker, every goddam slicky boy and yobo in it, too."

Nick turned to me. "Now, all I ask is that you keep an eye out for good-looking women with bad teeth. We could fuck our brains out if the cavities hold up."

I nodded back, signaling a truce over Miss Seong. He did the same.

Then he rang the bell again. "Short! No days and a wake-up!"

"You're not short, you're gone," said Sansoe.

"You buying the round again?" Charlie asked, popping in from a chewing out by Tommy, who probably only did it because he had to.

"Wait, it's on me," I said.

"Keeps us off the streets," Nick told Charlie. "Hail to Hobbes the big spender."

By 9 p.m., Nick had rung the bell five times, followed by Coletti and me with two each, and Sansoe with one, but he was on an enlisted man's salary.

The mood had picked back up. But somewhere near the end of the rounds at Nick's party, Lt. Col. Matthews, the new CO of my battalion, dropped in as a courtesy visit. He had taken Col. Samuels' place. We'd already had a "personality conflict." Hoping to get past his beef, I walked over to greet him. "Glad you could come, sir. Hope you can join Nick and the rest of us at Soul City later on. You know how those dentists love music."

I smiled. He sizzled. Seeing thirty drunk and boisterous junior officers celebrating a farewell, he just nodded, said to wish Captain Banyon well in his practice back in the states. Then he went across the hall to the dining room to have a drink by himself.

"Lifer!" someone muttered. The lieutenant colonel never heard. Probably.

It continued.

We drank more to the bell's chiming and danced with some whores who had come in, supposedly guests of Coletti. Around ten, the club was supposed to close, but nobody wanted it to, and Tommy said we could have the room for another hour for $40 U.S. to pay for the waitresses and overtime. Nick paid in full, plus a tip from Coletti.

We should have left at the end of the extra hour, but that was when Johnny Crowder, one of the pilots, was screwing a whore in a food storage closet. Tommy confronted Nick, who slipped him fifty dollars more to give us another thirty minutes. Tommy closed the main room and bar and locked the front door. He turned off the lights except in the party room. He looked nervous and happy with the bribes all at once. Also disgusted with what happened.

From there we went into double overtime.

Meanness, or at least stupid male aggression, brewed in the flowing alcohol. A half-dozen of us, including Nick, found drunken paths out of the party room and into the rest of the club, even without lights. But a light still worked in the game room, at the back of the hall leading to the BOQ, so we went in there. I usually avoided the room, because a framed replica of Rembrandt's "The Man with the Golden Helmet" hung on a wall.

It was a thing with me. I walked to it and threw up a finger.

"Are we gonna hear about this again?" Nick said.

"Every goddam club from here to Washington hangs this painting. It's an obscenity. To art, to the Army, to the world. And most of all to me!"

Nick moved up to it. "Off with his helmet!"

Just enough alcohol in me to allow me to pull down the frame and turn it over. "Aha! A fucking reprint. From the PX!"

"Not even the original?"

"Philistines."

I broke the frame on my knee.

Nick applauded. "A true critic. Bravo."

I gave the broken frame to Sansoe, who tried unsuccessfully to wear it on his head. I knew I'd get a nasty bill from the club. Maybe a reprimand. Fuck it.

"Time for the ville," Coletti said. "Our boy Nick ought to get laid once more."

Nick waved off the plan. "KPCOD." That meant: Korean Pussy CutOff Date, which was thirty days before you left, to make sure you didn't take the clap home.

"We'll see," Coletti said. "I'll take you guys to a new place."

*

En route to the gate, Sansoe and I half-supported our dentist, who was the definition of shit-faced. As we went through, past disapproving MP eyes, I saw an MP Jeep pull up. I started to joke that we should frag them for beating up Jackson while they were all together but didn't. I knew I was in no shape to hit the clubs. We all were dangerously, foolishly drunk. It was a rampage, and we knew it. Fuck it.

The MPs let us be, and we eased across the street to the ville sidewalks.

"See any snake-fuckers out tonight?" Nick asked.

"Snake-eaters."

"Fuck 'em, eat 'em, whatever."

"No."

"In here, in here," Coletti said, turning into a new club I hadn't been to before. It didn't even have a name yet. Inside, through beaded curtains, a gaggle of whores and dead-stoned soldiers made passes at each other. I started to think of Kim.

"I'd better have a drink," I said to Sansoe, who ordered two tequilas. We sat at a dance floor table, and I was aware that a woman was taking her clothes off in front of me.

"What is this, a strip show?"

"Very perceptive. That's why you're an officer," Nick said. A whore was already sitting on his lap, fondling him with her ass.

"Still thinking about KPCOD?" Coletti asked.

"What's that?"

The girl on the floor in front of me shed her red silk to jukebox tunes, psychedelic rock, "Time Has Come Today." Everybody loved that one. She danced in circles and thrust her crotch at the jeering GIs, who then applauded. Someone, maybe the club manager, threw a wooden dildo on the floor. She picked it up and threw it back at him.

Before I knew it, a GI was on the floor with her, taking off his clothes. She hand-jobbed him to make him ready. His buddies gave him encouragement.

I looked back to see Nick, but he was gone.

Then we watched the GI try to screw the dancing whore.

Sansoe grimaced. "She's a junkie. This is wrong. It's fucking perverted."

"Let's go," I said. "If the MPs come in, we're in deep shit."

"Wait for Nick," Coletti said. "He'll be right back."

I nodded. As they sank to the floor and the whore kneeled doggie-style, another GI was taking his pants off, looking at a different girl.

Enough. Beyond enough, I went outside. I leaned against a wall in the cool night air and tried to become sober. Nick was walking our way.

"Over here," I called out.

He made it to us, leaned next to me. "Get laid?" I asked. "That was quick."

"Jesus, can you believe it? Can you fucking believe I did that? What'll I tell my girl if I got the fucking clap?"

"Tell her it was a misunderstanding."

"Sure was nice, though. Goddam, I'm drunk." He looked at his watch. "I have to be at Kimpo in seven hours."

"Good luck."

Coletti and Sansoe came out of the bar, and we all started walking away.

"Adios, doc," Sansoe said. "I need to get stoned. This fucking place is getting to me. I mean, shit, what the hell was that?"

"Take it easy."

Coletti slapped Nick on the shoulder. "I promise to write every day, okay?"

Nick half-grinned.

Then, for no reason, Coletti grabbed my arm and we all stopped. "Hobbes. We're friends, okay? Tonight, we're friends. Fuck tomorrow. No judges. Right?"

"You're drunk."

"You're not?"

"I gotta go," Nick said. "Sure you guys don't want to ride out to the airport?"

"I can't make it," Coletti said, trying to keep his balance.

"Me either," I said.

"Yeah, sure. See you around."

He started towards the compound.

"Keep in touch," I yelled.

We both knew no one kept in touch.

Coletti said he'd go spend the night on the cot in his office at the Blue Dragon. I walked with him a few blocks until I peeled off for the alleys and the hootch.

I wanted something. To erase the night. I wanted her.

Just to be with her.

211

52

Things I knew: the fetus grew.

Things I wish I'd known: She continued to count her small fortune. Her efforts were nearly complete. She had arranged a visa, at a cost of hundreds in bribes and fees, and had secretly booked a reservation on China airlines, first to Hong Kong, and then to Taiwan, and on to Hawaii. All the arrangements were in her carved-bone box. I only put them together later.

My thoughts were still on The Decision. Such an important question. Should I marry her? So great my burden, I never saw her Fear.

The fetus grew.

To escape the compound and the questions, we took a weekend trip south. Away, we could pretend what we were not as the Hanjin bus rolled down the Seoul-Busan superhighway, the ground version of my earlier Huey trip. Now I could see more detail in the fields terraced on the hills. Peasants moved through them, hand-harvesting. Women waded up to their knees, wide-brim hats shading their eyes, skirts hiked to their thighs and folded against their backs. In one field, I saw a wooden platform.

"What is that?"

"It is where the rice-pickers sleep."

"Some kind of house?"

"Not house. You see any walls? it is where they sleep until the next job."

"They have no homes, then."

"No."

The field disappeared as the bus rounded a curve and a steep mountainside crowding the highway blocked the view.

I touched Kim's stomach to see if I could feel anything, but it was still early and barely bulging. She leaned against me.

"Yobo. What we do when you leave? November, still? Will Kim go with you?"

The mountain stayed hard against the road carved from its bulk. And then it was behind us, and I could see the fields again.

"I don't know. I just don't know yet."

"You want me sleep with the rice pickers? When I, I mean we, have no home." She put my hand on her stomach again.

"Kim."

"Take me, yobo. It will be all right. Take me with you. I love you."

I wanted to. I didn't want to. But it was more than just the two of us. Parting could not be such sweet sorrow because there could be no true parting. In my life, go where I would, part of me would remain in Korea. At an orphanage? Growing up to pick rice? Pick through garbage behind the mess hall? Dead at 35 in a drug den?

I could leave, yes. But not it. Not her. Not *us*.

Surely, she must have thought. Surely the child would keep us bound. If nothing else.

Save the Children!

Fuck the children! They grow up.

But Jesus I wanted to tell her. To say: Kim, let's get married.

I would have said it to Beth. But that was in the World.

Now what? Coletti said I lacked the guts. That was why he didn't think it would work. Not because her eyes were slanted, but because mine were jelly, like my brain. Ashamed, stupid. Me, First Lieutenant Thomas Hobbes, adjutant and master personnel officer in charge of quashing marriage certificates and observer of all human foibles. Me, in my own trap.

*

The bus went on, and I remembered. It was only last week in the Acid Bar when I had lamented with Sansoe yet again. I told him I was going crazy. "Do I love her? Jesus I must be out of my mind. And shit, shit shit, she's having my kid. How can I possibly take her with me. Don't you see that?"

As if he hadn't all along. Which he reminded me.

I drifted away, mumbling and numbing myself with bourbon. The purple walls glowed under black lights. Rock music crashed from five-foot square box speakers suspended from the ceiling. On the dance floor a Korean whore and a black GI spun dervish-like and a stoned GI hippie with a "Stop the War I Want to Get Off" T-shirt swayed alone to "Let the Sunshine In" from *Hair*. Magic neon rays flashed in their teeth and metal-tipped shoes sparked on the concrete floor. The bartender smiled as the metal shaker in his hands arced in a freak whirl, emptying gin onto ice. A waitress in a tight blue jumpsuit put glasses on her tray and pushed past the MPs getting paid off by the manager, then zigged among round tables in the confused dark to us.

"Ah, what service," Sansoe beamed.

"I think about something today and something else tomorrow. It's impossible. Im-fucking-possible." I rifled my hair. "What the fuck am I into?"

Sansoe leaned to the waitress, who asked to meet him later. She set our drinks on the table, and I gave her 300 won.

"You're going to marry her, aren't you?" he said. "Let's just stop going over it all the time. Just do it. Stop brooding. Who the fuck knows, right?"

We took long drinks.

He wiped his mouth. "I mean it's not the end of the world. I mean you could get a divorce or whatever once she's in the States."

"Would you?"

He laughed.

"I'm serious."

"I can tell."

*

Kim was looking out the bus window. Tiny hamlets and more fields and groves. I didn't have to wonder what she was thinking.

"Maybe you could have the baby here and, uh, meet me in the States later. Who knows? We have some time left."

She wouldn't look at me. My idea was so impossible it didn't deserve an answer.

Again, she took my hand and placed it on her abdomen. Now I could feel it. I kissed her and moved my hand up, across her breasts, her neck, to cradle her glorious face.

53

I had a Tuesday afternoon off, and, having nothing better to do, went to Seoul to take a few last scrapbook pictures. Squashing the ridiculous thought that my child back in the States would like to know where he or she came from. Papa-sans in billowing white at the Imperial Palace. Mama-sans in clean pastels. Children, not mine, or hers, in black school uniforms walking hand in hand. At Seoul station I saw a cartload of puppies on the way to the butcher and felt no remorse.

Back in Bupyeong, I was waiting in line outside the station at the circle to catch a kimchi cab to the compound. I noticed four slicky boys, probably in their early twenties, eyeing my camera. I tried not to look at them or signal any concern. There were no cabs, incredibly, and five Koreans were in the line ahead of me.

"Hey, GI Joe, what you got there?" one of the slicky boys taunted.

I said nothing. I realized I was the only American in sight. Still, I thought, I am an American. A soldier. They won't hassle me in broad daylight.

"Hey, you got nice camera there."

They were small, but muscular and street tough. Black belts for all I knew. They swaggered to me and one of them tugged at the camera case. I clutched the strap and glared.

"Whatsa matter, chingu?" the second one asked.

"Beat it," I said. The businessman ahead of me glanced back to see what was going on. I hoped he would intervene, but he turned and read his paper.

"Hey, lemme see camera," said a slicky boy in all black.

Another chimed in. "Yeah, we give it back. Hey, numbah ha-na Canon. Hey, lemme see."

What was this, Panther Detour re-imagined? I felt a rabbit punch to my kidney and lost the grip on the strap. One of the slicky boys jerked it from me. The pain was enough that I gasped awkwardly and watched as he took the cover off and started clicking the shutter.

"Come on, man. Give it back." I could barely speak.

"Hey, film in here!" He opened the camera and exposed it. "Ooops! No good now. Numbah ten on that for sure." He laughed at me and threw the film away.

The taxi manager saw what was happening and approached me, but the biggest slicky boy drew a blade from his pocket and flicked it open. The taxi manager stayed put.

"Nice camera," one of them boasted again, and then spoke to the others in Korean. He swung the camera over his head by the strap in a wide, slow arc.

"Goddam it, give me that ba—" I was demanding, when the camera zipped through the air and cracked into the side of my head. I dropped to my knees.

"Sure, all yours."

I teetered with one hand groping for purchase on the pavement. I wanted to get up, at least get the camera back. It took a minute. But when my vision cleared and I was on my feet, it was gone, and so were they.

54

All those long months had come to this, and here I was, another idiot GI with a whore. A pregnant one. And Jesus Christ I swore I wouldn't drive to Kimpo in a PX taxi with her, not to hear the turtles laugh and ask: Is that a yobo? As their pricks tingle with premonitions of vermin beds.

Travis gone, Nick gone. In five weeks, me. And, I was deciding, with her. Easy to say now. I would do it.

One of the last things Nick had done before leaving was arrange a doctor's appointment for Kim with an obstetrician at a hospital in Seoul. Kind of a favor for the Miss Seong "bad joke." She was probably almost two months pregnant when Nick left, and he said she should see a doctor right away and not to trust her to do it on her own. So, he had called Dr. Browne at Yongsan. It was illegal for a U.S. Army physician to treat a Korean who wasn't a dependent, but Nick said Dr. Browne owed him a favor. Seems like half the transactions among GIs involved paybacks and favors.

We took a cab to Seoul and Dr. Browne saw her at once.

A lean young man with thick eyebrows and a too-long auburn mustache, he talked briefly of Nick and promised to give Kim a complete check. He said Kim was very beautiful and I trusted him, but still, in the moment of first meeting, he looked at her and at me in a way that made me think of Benson and where the yobo might be that he left behind.

I waited in a visitor area outside Dr. Browne's office. The yellow plaster walls, lined with white mortar, smelled of antiseptic and all manner of bad breath. I slumped in a folding chair and thumbed through an old *Newsweek*. Two GIs sat next to me. I tried briefly to deduce why they were there, but lost interest. GIs, American children, Korean wives, doctors, nurses, aides, admins—all hurried by in an endless stream. I could never tell the inside of one hospital from another. In their coldness, I felt a sense of home.

In the *Newsweek* was a picture of President Nixon. The caption said, "Can He Bring Peace?" He was stepping from an airplane. I tried to see him in the harness of a door gunner, swinging out like Halua to get just one more. Or maybe get his.

I finished the magazine and began to doze. After more than an hour, Dr. Browne asked me to come inside.

"Thanks for seeing her," I said, following him through the paneled door. "I hope I can do you a favor sometime."

"Forget it," he said and walked into his office. He sat behind his small desk and told me to take one of the chairs in front. "Is Kim getting dressed?" I asked.

"Yes." He wrote something on a form. I sensed he was trying to avoid me. It was a bad feeling, like a phone ringing at 3 a.m.

"Is there anything wrong?" I tried to sound cheerfully inquisitive.

"Kim will be here in a minute. Let's wait for her."

When she entered, I saw her look at Dr. Browne. She had been crying.

"Please sit down, Kim," Dr. Browne said. She sat next to me, gripping my arm. Her skin felt cold and her face was pale. I placed my hand over hers.

"Lieutenant Hobbes," Dr. Browne began, looking at Kim instead of me, "I've just examined Kim very carefully, gotten a second opinion, and I'm afraid there's some, uh, bad news. I have told her, but she asked me to bring you in and explain to you, too."

I squeezed Kim's hand. She tightened her grip on my arm.

"She, uh, ummm," he cleared his throat and looked at us both. "She apparently has had a venereal disease, I think gonorrhea, during or before pregnancy. Or even maybe long before. It was treated and is gone, but, you know, these STDs, they can have lingering effects."

We squeezed each other harder. She wouldn't look at me.

"And . . ." He cleared his throat again. "And from my observation, which I admit had to be rather hasty—but, as I told Kim, I'm still sure of it—she probably will carry a, um, fetus that will never make full term. It's early, I know, just a couple of months, but we have a lot of this thing over here and can diagnose it pretty well, and uh, well, it's my experience . . ."

He was saying something, I don't know. God, it was just like that. Bam. Kim cried, hard. Dr. Browne nervously clicked a ballpoint pen but gave us time to let it sink in, at least on the surface.

I nodded. "Oh, I see."

Kim stopped crying but said nothing. She let go my arm and pulled away her hand.

Dr. Browne leaned forward on his desk and cleared his throat again. "So, this is the part Kim wanted me to tell you both together. And I'm sorry I have to. So nearly as I can tell, there is almost certainly going to be severe brain damage. There may be missing or deformed extremities. It isn't uncommon in such cases." He paused, as much for himself as for us. "I know how difficult this is, but this is the important part. I think this pregnancy could do some real harm to Kim. I'm not sure she could take it, either physically or emotionally. She doesn't have a large hip structure, and if she goes full term, and things go badly at birth, which is highly probable, she could be in serious trouble. Especially if she goes to a midwife, which is often the case here."

A freak. We're having a freak, a two-headed monster with scales, six legs and one eye. Oh, man, oh man. Jesus. Neither of us could talk. "What do you recommend?" was the best I could come up with.

He looked at us both. We must have appeared frozen. "Under the circumstances, as you can probably guess, I really don't think there's any choice but a pregnancy termination. An abortion."

It was all swirling now in my head. Lightning speed but also in super slow-motion, every word and image distorted. Kim? Kim? You are here with this inside you, poisoning you. Shall we give it birth? Let it be brought from the womb, cackling and flapping its wings?

Purple-veined eyes and gelatin nose? It's a boy! Look, Mrs. Hobbes, see your grandbaby? And here's the nice wife your son brought home. Isn't she lovely? Please don't touch her legs. They'll drop off. War bride? No, hell no, dad, no war, no killing, just good old-fashioned fucking! And see, see why they say how much better it is to fuck not fight?

"I suppose you're sure?" I said, breathing again.

"He sure," Kim said, almost angrily.

"Yes," the doctor said. "I'm sure."

"And the abortion?"

"Just listen, yobo. Stop looking over there. Pay attention here. He just said that."

"I'm sorry."

He nodded, let it settle. "Yes, I would recommend an abortion. I know there's a problem there. There's no way I can give you one here. You'll have to go to a Korean hospital. But there's a doctor I know at one here in Seoul who is very good, and he can take care of you. I'll be glad to call him." He began writing on a slip of paper. "Here's his name."

Kim shook her head. "I know doctor already. I go there. By myself."

Dr. Browne gave me the paper. I put it in my shirt pocket. I helped Kim to her feet and pulled a tissue from a box on Dr. Browne's desk to wipe mascara from her cheeks. Our eyes glued to each other until I was done.

"How long can we wait?"

"Not more than a few weeks would be best."

Her head fell against my chest. I could feel it all draining. What had been there was gone. She could never be Mrs. Hobbes now. Just another Korean yobo saying goodbye.

I thanked Dr. Browne. He offered Kim his sympathies, and we left.

In the cab, she rested against me. "Maybe we try again, huh?" She tried to laugh, but it would not come.

All the way back to Bupyeong, I stared at the passing fields and mountains, held Kim, cursing myself for having briefly, between the agonies, felt relief. She said not a word.

That night at the hootch, we argued briefly about how she got the clap, had to be late last summer, when the rains were still coming down, and I stayed in the BOQ instead of getting wet going to the hootch, and she might have earned some extra money, and that was why she wouldn't fuck me for a while. Or it could have been a year ago. Or it could have been me, from that one time, but I'd already been treated.

It didn't matter now, and neither of us cared.

55

All the words had not been spoken, nor tears dried, but it was obvious without further stating, dissecting, clarifying. She almost had you, Hobbes, old boy. Yep, by God, fucked around a little too much, there, didn't you? Lucky old shit. Saved by a germ. And it would replicate, and infest, and suck the good life from a woman's belly.

I was walking around the compound perimeter just before dawn. I had risen early at the hootch after hardly sleeping. We had lain together cold in the night, deserted by speech, victims for the Fear.

An idiotic phrase, "so near and yet so far," popped repeatedly into my mind, reducing the future to a cliché. I'd been ready to take her back, marry her, face the shit in the World. And now? It was revolting to confront my own shallowness.

I sat on one of the worn-out sand bunkers on the far perimeter of the compound, where we had waited to expel the entire North Korean invasion. Through the barbed wire stretched over a concrete drainage ditch, I could see an old woman in the countryside a hundred yards away, busy in the morning stillness.

She worked quietly in a rice field outside the house where her family lived. It was in the opposite direction from the ville, providing a rural clearing of hundreds of acres between the compound and the mountains. Living there was probably noisy and unpleasant, but it was safe to assume that the family stayed because there was nowhere else to go.

She set a pot next to a brown earthen crock as high as her shoulder, opened the top of the crock, from what I could tell, dipped out kimchi, or maybe was preparing a winter batch. In the evening the family would gather and eat bowls of kimchi over steaming rice. They would eat it forever. I thought of Kim's story about her own family. But they didn't last forever.

Suddenly everything annoyed me. The air, the sky, the mountains. Even the old woman. Fucking people, living like that.

Goddam, Kim, you knew what you were doing. Hell, you could've gotten some pills or something. Instead of trapping me. Of course.

This could not possibly be happening. My mind raged with rage and contorted with contortions, and it was no use. Yes, I loved her. Admit it: Thomas Hobbes loved a whore. He might've held out for a princess, but he went for a dark-eyed working girl, queen of the alleys, whose only claim to culture was liking Joan Baez and speaking passable English when she felt like it. Nonetheless, he knew that he loved her. And he knew that now—now that there would be no child to bind— he would leave.

56

I felt the whirlwind in my bones again. You could almost lay out the days, they were so short. Dr. Browne had said a few weeks, but Kim said she would go as soon as she could. I said yes, do it now. In no time at all they'll be loading me into a Red Tail.

But for days I couldn't find her. I would leave work, go to our hootch. Not there. Then to her mama-san hootch and hammer on her door while the whore in the next hootch smiled as if to say, hey GI, it's okay, you come over here.

Sansoe got sent down to Daegu for TDY for a week, so I couldn't talk to him, not that I wanted to. I got stoned at night and slept alone in the BOQ. I did practically no work. My turtle, a captain from Fort Benjamin Harrison in Indiana, was due in two weeks. Sgt. Frye's turtle, Sgt. Billingsley, was already here and avoided me. He knew the new colonel didn't like me.

This could not possibly be happening.

I couldn't find her again that night.

She was around, of course, but I didn't always know where. She knew exactly where she was. Shuttling to Seoul and crisscrossing the ville alleys for her business deals, or Coletti's. She had things to do. So, losing a baby, comparatively, wasn't that bad. Losses beyond that had to be avoided. Her travel fund, especially.

Kim's earnings finally had been channeled to the proper crooked hands. Mostly through Coletti. She would not slow down on getting what she needed even now that everything had changed. Coletti's black market and government bribes arranged her passports, visas. She had to cancel her old airline reservations and throw away the tickets and lose the deposits because the dates had all changed, but she was getting new ones. Just had to wait for her yobo's firm departure date. It cost a lot of money but there was still enough left to carry her through a few months in the States. Still hidden in her bone box in our hootch.

Again, none of this known to me. Guessed at. Asked about. Denied. Not known.

I am sure she had no idea that her stealth and desperation fueled my own. We shared little, thinking it wise not to ask questions we didn't want answered. Thinking this could all end with minimum damage.

Sunday afternoon, she opened the door to my room in the White Elephant. I was sitting at my desk. She didn't come in, just stood in the doorway. She wore an incongruously maidenly flowered dress, slightly loose. "I go to doctor now."

I stood. "Where have you been?"

"Do you care?"

I kicked the trash basket into the corner. "Goddam it, Kim."

She shut the door behind her, walking past me untouched, perching ladylike at the edge of the unmade bed. I closed my eyes and felt a swirling void, a tightness in my chest. My eyes took in her beauty in the sunlight.

I saw something hard in her, like the night I followed her through the ville. But this time it was the Fear. It was only to be accepted. No stupid questions.

But I had one. "I said where have you been?"

"It doesn't matter."

I changed pants and shirt for the trip. She didn't move or speak. "You might've at least told me."

"Oh, my poor yobo, you worry?"

"You wouldn't believe it if I said so."

"Then don't say so."

I slammed my hand against the wall. "Stop this shit, will you?"

She pitched me the belt I was looking for.

"We have to go now."

"What time?"

"Now."

"Why did you even come back for me?"

"You say you want to come."

"You have to believe I'm sorry."

"You never mind. Now you no have to take Kim stateside. Just to my doctor."

I forgot to put on my shoes until she pointed at my feet, then my black sneakers.

As soon as I tied the laces she started for the door. I stopped her, took her arm. She let me hold her, loosely.

"I—I love you. I really do."

She pulled back, looked into my eyes. I drew her to me again.

"Let's talk about it later, OK? I'm with you."

Though her arms were across my back, there was little pressure. Then none.

We left.

A kimchi cab in line at the gate pulled up. Kim gave instructions.

57

The "doctor's office," the one Kim had told Dr. Browne about, was an L-shaped wooden house, painted brown and green, with what looked like at least three add-on hootches, on the east side of Bupyeong. It was near a nightlife area. I looked at Kim to see if this was okay, but she got out of the cab, and I paid the fare. I followed her to the front door. She pulled the cord on a square-shaped bell, and an old woman greeted us.

"Annyong hashimnikka," she said. Kim entered. The old woman blocked me, said I couldn't come in. But I insisted and Kim said it was okay, so I was allowed.

We waited in the small entry foyer as the old woman went down a hall, to tell the "doctor" we had arrived. I could see several doors down the hall before it made a turn to the right and presumably attached to the extra hootches. The floor was clean, but paint was peeling from the walls. I could tell the building was at least partly heated by charcoal stoves. I thought I could hear voices and laughter, women and men, coming from behind closed doors. The old woman came back. She motioned for us to follow, and we went back outside, across a modest courtyard, to the far end of the add-ons.

"This is a goddam mama-san house," I whispered. "A midwife at best. Just what Dr. Browne warned us about."

We stopped at the end of the last hootch, which actually wasn't a hootch. It was bigger than the others, a separate building altogether. Judging from power lines, it had its own utilities. And its own entry bell. The old woman rang it, opened a door, and beckoned us into what looked like a waiting room, and indicated we should remove our shoes. Framed and yellowed posters of mountains and streams and clouds in blue skies hung on the walls. The smell of incense came from behind a teak door with carvings of birds.

I stood in front of Kim, took her by the shoulders. "Why?"

She said nothing.

"I know what this is, and it isn't a damn doctor's office."

Her eyes were moist. "No."

"But why?"

She shook free. "Yobo. We must go inside. Doctor be here soon."

I took her wrist, maybe too firmly. Again, she pulled free. "This not for you. It for me. Right? Right? You got baby in your stomach?"

"It's not a real doctor's office."

"So? This be quick, all done. All girls come here. Mistress Yung famous. No other place to go."

"So, we're in some slicky house where they use Coke and coat hangers. You could die of bacteria before you could get your dress off. Goddam it, Kim. Please."

"You not live here. You know nothing. I do. Be quiet."

She sat on a padded metal folding chair. I didn't want to but took the one next to her. It was done. She would not need me after this. Or even right now. I had not considered that.

After about ten minutes, she began taking deep breaths. She gripped my arm until I looked at her. "Yobo, yobo. I know I trick you to come here." Her voice husky, as if she could barely talk. She didn't want to cry but did. "I know I say we go to doctor. But yobo, if we go to doctor he ask questions, maybe put me in hospital. Maybe, maybe find out other things."

I don't know if you can really feel your heart break, but I think I did.

Another woman, different from the one who had greeted us, opened the teak door just as Kim was leaning into me and I was trying to hold her, awkwardly from our chairs. I guessed it was Mistress Yung.

She watched us. As if it were part of her job to evaluate incoming patient behavior. Probably was. She looked like death in black scrubs and cap. Kim stopped crying but continued to squeeze my arm. She wiped her tears and nodded at the woman. They exchanged names. Then Kim looked at me and stood, making a slight head bow to the woman. She returned the gesture with a look of professional sympathy, I would call it, and then touched Kim's shoulder as a sign of comfort. They said something to each other in Korean. Kim glanced at me.

"Mistress Yung, she just say we ready to go, and tell me not to worry, that she never talk about those who come to her. What she do, she never remember to anyone else. She not write down what happen, or put what she find in jar, like I see one time at hospital."

Mistress Yung, apparently with some English, nodded in affirmation. I did the same because I didn't know what else to do.

"What this mean is that soon we leave here," Kim went on. "Only us. Me. You. Nothing more. Everything burn, like with dead people. Bury ashes. Then we forget. She forget. Then nobody know no more."

I nodded again.

The midwife—a fair description of Mistress Yung—looked on calmly. It was likely her special quality, disinterest. It unnerved me, but Kim was right. No one would ever know. Mistress Yung would do her job without pity or disapproval, as she had with a thousand other women on a thousand other visits.

I reached out to stroke Kim's hair. "I'm sorry. I love you, and I'm sorry." Words hung in my throat, but I had to get them out.

She squeezed my hand, looked at me again, then turned her head down. "It okay, my yobo." Barely audible but my broken heart had good hearing.

Mistress Yung said something in Korean. Kim dropped my hand. "It time."

Mistress Yung led us through the ornate door into another small hall leading to an office and, at the very back, what looked like a basic hospital room. Again, Kim had insisted on my presence. Mistress Yung didn't object, although I got the feeling it was unusual for the man to be present.

At least the room seemed medical. A table and shelf with medical instruments and various supplies, a bed that might have been liberated from a regular hospital, and a gray plastic bin with "Waste" stenciled in English. An orange-tinted curtain hung across a small window.

Mistress Yung said something, gave Kim a bottle of pills. She said to take one now. Kim undressed, put on a hospital gown, and lay on the mattress, which was covered by a rubber pad and a sheet. She adjusted her head and hair on a pillow. The lighting was poor, and Mistress Yung said it was being repaired. For now, a bright bulb in a jerry-rigged metal cover dangled from a cord overhead. Mistress Yung pulled the curtain back on the window and that helped.

I stood at one of the side walls to keep out of the way, but I had a good view. For example, my first good look at Mistress Yung's face. Middle-aged, deep brown, creased. I wondered how long she had been doing this.

I stepped forward to squeeze Kim's hand, but Mistress Yung motioned me back to the wall. She gave me a firm look that things were about to happen.

Then she took her position in front of Kim, put on her gloves, said something, and Kim's legs spread wide. Mistress Yung moved in closer, pulled Kim's gown up enough to touch and examine. Kim closed her eyes. Some instructions followed, and Kim responded. I realized no one else was there to help with the procedure. And I realized why.

Before long Mistress Yung was reaching into Kim, delicately, then twisting and turning what might have been a scalpel, forceps, maybe more. I had intended to watch the whole procedure because of what it was and tell Kim if she ever asked. But I couldn't. I didn't.

But I did look when Kim began to cry and scream and shake in pain. Her body arched and Mistress Yung said things to encourage her to try to stay more still and perhaps to help with the pain. I wondered why she hadn't waited for the pill to kick in, but for all I knew, it had. Just not enough.

In what seemed both forever and no time at all, Mistress Yung said something to Kim, and I saw her withdrew her hands, red and sticky.

On the sheet between Kim's trembling legs, it lay. So tiny, I could barely make it out as human, but I knew that Dr. Browne had made the right call.

Mistress Yung quickly cupped her hands around the fetus and set it on a thick towel on another small table, taking care that Kim would not be able to see it. I knew because she glanced at me for a second, nodded towards Kim, shook her head and softly mouthed, "No."

I asked if I could come to Kim's side and Mistress Yung said I could. Kim seemed exhausted, barely conscious. When I took her hand, her nails dug into my palm. With the other, I tried to hold her steady on the mattress. But she pushed me away.

Mistress Yung did some cleaning up as she watched, and then brought another pillow to prop behind Kim's shoulders so she could sit up and keep her head raised. I guess she didn't think it would give Kim a vantage to see what had been inside her. But it did.

Kim screamed even louder than during the procedure and shook violently. Her mouth convulsed with no words forming. I had to keep her from falling off the bed. She began to vomit. Mistress Yung blocked the view of what Kim had seen, then nodded at me towards a stack of paper towels. I grabbed them and wiped up what I could. Kim fell back against the pillow, her body completely limp.

I held up her head to make sure she didn't choke and wiped her mouth and face. She breathed in like a diver coming up from the water, then spewed out more vomit and, dropped her head back again, looked only at the ceiling. I used another paper towel to clean what I could from her mouth and face, turning towards Mistress Yung and yelling harshly. "Pick it up! Jesus Christ, pick it up!"

The subtlest flash of contempt crossed Mistress Yung's face. But she did pick up the bloody fetus. Actually gently. She wrapped it in the cloth towel and looked at me to see if Kim wanted to see it again. More openly. I shook my head, probably with a contorted expression. Mistress Yung nodded, took a look at Kim just to be sure, then eased the fetus down into the waste can. Being sure Kim couldn't see.

"Girl," Mistress Yung said to me. "If she want to know later."

Kim convulsed again. I tried to hold her. She flailed the air, striking me, scratching me, pounding herself. Crying although she was hoarse. Mistress Yung said something to her I didn't understand, then looked at me like I should handle this, and continued cleaning up.

I managed to pull Kim back to a sitting position and propped up the pillows that had been knocked to the floor. I crossed her arms as if with a strait jacket. I watched. She went limp again, bending forward toward her knees, sobbing softly, completely withdrawn.

I cursed us, first to myself and then to us all: Me, her, God, the "doctor," until it became useless.

Mistress Yung had left the room, as had the waste can. It's content supposedly bound for cremation. No one would ask.

"Kootchie-koo" kept coming in my brain, "kootchie-koo, little baby." As if she were a person. With a name. Or even close.

I coughed. My voice wouldn't work. I cried.

We remained there until Kim had enough energy to let me wash her off better and help get her dressed. We had no more words. They would only bring to life what happened and it had to remain dead. She didn't even ask to see the remains again. Such was our new lover's bond.

We returned to our hootch.

She bathed more fully in our tub. I helped her towel dry and put on her nightgown, which was really a large yellow T-shirt with a drawing of the sun. She took more of the pills she'd been given. I held her carefully as she eased onto our bed. She was asleep within minutes. Stayed that way all night. I sat in a chair and watched, mostly.

In the morning I went to get her some breakfast and coffee and water, but she only nibbled, without talking. She took another pill, said she just wanted to go back to sleep. She pointed to the spare cot we'd bought for the nights one of us came home too late. She asked me to sleep there from now on.

She said she wanted to be alone.

58

And so. Meanwhile. Behind the big curtain . . .

Maybe it was the next night, Coletti had a visitor. "I expect to receive what I pay for," Lee Chae-Sing said.

"Meaning?"

"If I give you $5,000 for a pound of junk, I expect a pound of junk."

Coletti's mind raced. He was smarter than Lee and had enough friends to withstand cheap extortion from a third-rate pusher. He stifled his anger and smiled. "How much are you short?"

"About five hundred each delivery. U.S."

"I assume you can prove it."

Lee nodded. His semi-bald head glistened slightly in Coletti's Blue Dragon office. He produced a small ledger showing weights of heroin delivered and amounts paid. It could have been forged, but Coletti knew Lee wouldn't do that.

They haggled briefly as Coletti tested the computations, but in the end Coletti accepted Lee's position that he had lost at least $3,000 worth of various kinds of dope, street value, much of it stolen from military dispensaries.

"I want it back." He said, lightly fingering a silver-tipped walking cane, the kind he sold to the brothers. Coletti leaned back in his chair. "Let me see what I can do first," he said.

Lee smiled. "I'll have her tits for breakfast if the money isn't back in two weeks. You'd better tell your friend."

"Don't fuck with me. You'll get the money. Just don't fucking you dare fuck with me."

Lee smirked. "She'll be here when you've gone."

"Beat it."

Lee left, with a smirk.

Coletti sat alone in his office and closed his eyes. It hurt, somewhere. He would have to settle it, of course. But he could do it. He was the Mayor of Suchow.

He called out to Miss Yu, just starting her shift at the bar.

"Tell Kim I want to see her."

All this he told me later, as if it would count.

III

The Fear

(The World)

59

Sometimes I thought I had missed it. I had seen this, that, and done those things, with Kim capping the list, but when the young buck sergeant came into headquarters during my last weeks to ask directions and I said, "Hey, your hair's down over your collar, don't you think you ought to get it cut," and he said, "Yeah, I guess I forgot, I just got sent over from Nam," all I could say was, "Oh." Even though I knew he was Namming me.

It took SFC Sawyer, who had been there, to jump in: "Don't give us that Nam shit, sarge, just get a goddam haircut."

When Nick was here, he didn't cut me any slack, either. "Jesus, I can't believe you feel guilty about not going to Nam. I thought you were against the damn war anyway."

"I am, you know that. I just can't get it straight, though. I mean why Halua or Sawyer or Jones or any of those guys and not me. Or you. It's like, almost getting a free ride."

"I thought you were over all that shit. But you're still a world-saver, aren't you?"

"That's not it. It's not that, exactly."

"Then what?"

"I don't know. It's all so random. It just doesn't make a lot of sense. I mean I didn't want to go, and that fucking war is wrong, and it makes my time as an officer a bitch right now, but you know, I almost think I'd have felt better if I'd had to go. See for myself. Now I just hear about it, and wonder, you know."

He shook his head. "If you expect some sort of perverted sympathy from me, forget it. That's the biggest load I've heard in a while. You hate it and you feel bad about not going. Pick one, dammit. I'm off to the ville."

"Go on."

We all had the stories. Mine was Scotty Dawson.

When he was 18 and I was 20, in college, we met a girl named Barbara. She was what was known as a gang bang. Scotty had trouble in school, and was failing, and had joined the Marines. I told him he was crazy. He hadn't even gotten laid yet, ever. So, I thought I'd fix this up for him and we picked up Barbara and went to a $4-an-hour motel and signed in using fake names, John Gretschwasson or something so bizarre it didn't sound phony. So, I waited in the bathroom while Scotty lost his virginity to Barbara, and then he waited while I had a turn. When we were leaving, Barbara asked me for $20 each and I realized she was actually a hooker, and it was a good thing I had the money.

Nevertheless, Scotty was terribly excited, and in the car afterwards Barbara said he was the best and Scotty managed to work that into conversations an amazing number of times. When he went to Nam, I knew he would be back. He wrote on U.S. Marine stationery and said he was a sniper, and he'd tried smoking heroin. Heroin. Scotty. Hell, we'd just started drinking beer. And then his sister called me about 6 a.m. on a Tuesday, crying so hard, so hard, that I knew before she said it. I couldn't ever ask the details, and at the funeral I had to leave because his mother was hysterical, but a guy told me Scotty had been shot in the eye up in his sniper tree.

The guy that told me, William Watson, worked at the funeral home. He wanted to tell me all the details about the body, what body bags were, and all. He had been over there, too, a Marine, and before that we had called him Billy and he played the guitar. He came back not long after Scotty left but didn't tell anyone and we found out by accident. William, he was very strict about being called, found a job working at night at Green Meadows Funeral Home to finish his way through college. He said somebody had done a good job on Scotty's face.

And there were more stories. Fred Jolson, a poly sci major like me but who couldn't keep his grades up and got drafted, faced off a VC about three feet away in a jungle clearing and shot his head off with an M-16 on automatic, but not before the VC's AK-47 made him like Hemingway's Jake.

Barster and Holmes had gone to Canada. They said I should go, but I was already in ROTC. Not that I would have gone anyway.

Such a helpless generation. Not like the World Wars, so nihilistic and brave and foolhardy that if you went it was assumed you wouldn't be back. Those wars, that produced such strange men we called our fathers and grandfathers, but who won the fight.

For us, it was just happening. To be or not to be, to do or not to do, made no difference to anyone. No difference. Winding up in the jungle was beyond my decision, rested on a stroke of fate, a birthday, a random pick by a computer or somebody's hand in a big glass jar.

Sansoe knew what I felt as much as anyone, but he didn't think we'd missed anything.

"Look at what we are, man. Look at this fucking place, what we do, what we talk about. What we've become. Have you ever met anybody from Nam who said you should've been there? You think your friend Scotty found out something you haven't just because people were killing him? And look at that goddam Frye. At the colonel. At Travis. At Coletti. Shit, man, the way I look at it, the only secret of war is that people get killed, and you can find that out on the goddam freeway."

60

We had lost it. Just as we had grabbed it. Right there in that room. On that table. A great love. Strong, firm, committed.

Every time I thought that way my stomach knotted up. Our love, if that was the right word, could not even survive the horror of a single night. But I needed something to get past it. Even if more lie than true. So did Kim. We couldn't give anything else to each other anymore. Maybe that's all that was lost.

I had thought, after Dr. Browne, that nonetheless we could overcome the endless, bottomless funk. Anyway, she still could come home with me. I had convinced myself that I could hardly be that chickenshit.

But the exit ramp was too wide, too easy. One day I'm gone. Nothing to worry about from then on. No orphanages, half breed outcasts, hearts in the trash. Just me to leave. Kim to stay behind. That simple.

I went to see her often to make sure she was—what's the word? —OK.

She was still staying in our hootch, and by agreement I stayed at the BOQ. But I knew she needed to get up and get out of that gloom-laden cavern I went to see her the second night after the abortion. Not good timing on my part. It was nearly midnight and I'd been at the bars. But I knocked, and she let me in. She wore a robe and her long hair was beautiful on her golden shoulders. She was holding a full glass of makgeolli.

"You drunk, yobo," she laughed as I came in, tripping on the doorstep.

"Look who's talking."

"How come you see me when you drunk, huh? You afraid of Kim?"

"I didn't know how late it was."

I put my hand against the wall to steady myself.

She sat on the bed with her chin tucked on her knees. "Always late for us, huh yobo?"

I tried to smile.

She held out her glass. "Here to you, Hobbes-san. A real GI bastard."

I toasted with my empty hand.

She held out the glass again. "Here to our baby, Hobbes-san. Hobbes-san, junior." She hesitated. "And to Mrs. Hobbes." She swallowed the wine and tossed the glass onto a rug.

"Don't, Kim." I went to the bed and sat. Slouched, more like. The room spun wildly. "It will only make it worse."

She inched over to me, her brown eyes staring into my blue. All four still reddened with grief and lack of sleep.

"What you mean, worse? Worse? I think it only worse if I come to States. Right? You better believe it."

"I came to see if you were okay." I lay back.

"Numbah hana I feel great. You just no be fuckee me tonight, GI." She laughed, darkly.

"You're not bleeding . . . or anything?"

She lay back, too, but angled so her crotch was close to my face. "Am I?"

I turned my head.

"It's okay, yobo, I know lots of yobos do this. Get rid of what up in their pussy. Their tummy. What got to come out. Then back in the ville in a just couple of days! Make money again! Whatsa big deal." Her words started to slur.

"I'm sorry."

"Goddam!" she yelled and threw a pillow toward the door. Her eyes accidentally caught mine, and for a horrible instant, I felt it. Beyond love, remorse, not to say happiness. In those perfect eyes, seizing my soul, opening to me because of the bond, the dead baby bond, I felt the Fear.

I could not say so because I couldn't. And we were both drunk, and what would it matter? Beyond the eyes, I could feel her body throb. Not over embryonic garbage, but over a vanished future, a life-loss not for a half-formed nothing person, but for a grown, terrified woman. Who had found the chance, maybe her last, and lost it.

Lost what? Me? I was repulsive.

"Goddam you bastard."

"Look, Kim."

"Shut up, you."

"I didn't come to fight."

"Yeah, you say that yobo. That what you do. Fuck this shit."

I turned to my side. She kicked my leg hard.

"Hey, yobo. Answer me this, OK?"

"Answer what?"

"You just say yes or no, okay?"

"Okay."

"Look at me." I rolled over to see her.

Cold, cold stare.

"When I have baby. I mean back then, before . . . you tell me, you say you love me. Yes?"

"Yes."

"And you say, you say we be marry."

I looked away.

"Well?" She pulled me back by the chin. Her wine breath blasted my face.

"Yes."

Another night, I would have tugged her to me.

"And now what you say, my yobo? You know what the girls call you that know I was pregnant? Ping-pong head. One time this. One time that. Back and forth. They also call you dick head."

I said nothing.

"You know what I think? I think you never want to marry me. I say you marry yourself. When baby still in me, you think it yours, and you take it stateside for yourself. Yeah? And me? Me, your pregnant yobo? Me you only take like, like package, package with baby." She took some irregular breaths. "So now, baby oop-soh, all gone. Now you not need me. So, you say, 'We gotta think about it, Kim.'"

She pushed my face away roughly, moved to the edge of the bed, and sat up. "So maybe you just go find somebody else fuck. You do that, yobo. You say you not like other GI, but you, you—"

I moved next to her. I could only watch her cry. When I tried to touch her, she pushed my hand away, and then slapped my face.

The sobbing stopped. We sat.

"I'm sorry. I am. I'm so sorry."

She looked at me, tears covering her face.

"Why you sorry, GI? I not sorry." She lay back, rubbed her hands across her breasts, then down to her legs. "Nice, huh, yobo? I not sorry. Next week I be in Officer Club, find new yobo and fuck-suck him. Numbah hana, you betcha!" Her smile became a leer. I could see her white teeth, courtesy of Dr. Nick Banyon. But they seemed like fangs now.

I lay back, too, and closed my eyes. If I could have held her, I would. I could hear her hand still rubbing her body, funny sounds from her mouth, and then nothing but breathing.

I sat up. She was staring at the ceiling. I touched her cheek. This time without objection. Then I pulled her up so I could hold her in my arms. She was shivering. I hugged her for a long time.

"Please no leave me, yobo."

I held her tighter. My heart was pounding. I eased her down on the bed, our bodies closer than they had been since that day.

"I love you," she whispered.

"I love you, too."

She let me kiss her on her swollen lips.

"I'll come back tomorrow. Or stay tonight if you want."

She was asleep.

Slowly, I slipped from her arms, covered her with blankets. Watched to be sure she was breathing regularly. Not vomiting. I knew I couldn't sleep and that she had to. Probably better without me. I checked her again and went outside, locked up. It was still cold and dark. No dawn, no birds to sing of the coming day.

An intense sensation of superfluousness swept me. Beyond Kim, even Korea. An enormous feeling of not mattering. I was still drunk but got back to the White Elephant. I fell asleep on my bed without meaning to or even taking off my shoes.

61

Startled, I awoke in terror. Someone was in the room.

I lay frozen, peering frantically into the darkness.

It had been a sound. I had heard it, somewhere in my sleep and came rushing full to consciousness. I would not move. He would not know I was here.

But I could not see him. Quiet. Still. He will go away. But I couldn't see him.

Good god, perhaps he will come rushing on me, laughing savagely, and plunge a jagged knife into my throat, ripping me apart to drain, gurgling with a final question.

I waited, telling myself it was nothing, that this was too silly, too absurd, yet knowing he was there, he could take me, and I could do nothing.

In an hour, when my eyes had adjusted to the dark and I was sure it had been nothing, I went back to sleep.

Next day, I mentioned it to Capt. Plato. I thought it meant something about me, or the war, or Kim, or the illusion of mortality.

"Maybe you should get a night light."

62

Capt. Plato lived in the room beneath mine. I met him about a month after I got here. My stereo had arrived from the PACEX store in Tokyo. He came upstairs and said it was a little loud. He was 29, a philosophy major who stayed out of the Army with deferments, including going on to law school at NYU. Slim, nearly handsome in his brown mustache, his real name was Francis Franklin.

He didn't mix with the usual gang much and rarely went into the ville, although he did go to Seoul almost every weekend or opportunity. He said he had a real girlfriend back in the World and also a small apartment in Seoul so he could just feel normal as often as possible. Travis thought he had a secret yobo. There were other rumors, but nobody believed them.

He was always fun to be around and loved to talk about anything remotely intellectual. Once, at the O Club, his main hangout, he had been in a loud argument with Sam Townley, a doctor, about, of all things, medical care and socialism. At one point, Townley slammed his fist on the bar and yelled, "Who the hell do you think you are, goddam Plato?" It stuck, and no one ever called him anything else. It was ironic, though, given Francis's view of his namesake.

"Plato was a fascist," was the way he put it.

Now that I was staying in the BOQ instead of the hootch while Kim recuperated, more emotionally than physically, Capt. Plato and I spent more time together. But she was ready for me to come back another day. She would stop drinking and taking the pills and I should, too.

So, I decided to just stay in, to drop in at the O Club for a burger and a beer. Just one. Then Capt. Plato showed up and we started drinking and talking and somehow got into philosophy and ended up in his room where the whiskey was free and other officers couldn't eavesdrop. We kept at it until midnight. He had no patience for small talk. Which was good, because all I could really think about after Kim's abortion was the meaning of anything.

The ideas went back and forth. I was looking for some kind of reason for being. He wasn't. I said I needed some kind of guide, even a yardstick. Any truth that would make sense about what happened. At least life on earth had to make some kind of sense, I said. Finally, he'd had enough. He drained what was left in his glass.

"Okay already, you're never gonna give up, are you? So, look, man, just think of it as a synthesis."

"A synthesis?" For the record, that's really hard to say when you've had one too many.

"Yeah, you know—a common thread of the things you want."

"And?"

"And bingo, young lieutenant. Big truth to the whole bag is definitely needed."

"And?"

"And the thing is, the synthesis is kinda like your namesake saw it. Poor, nasty, brutish, and short. Really, you don't know that?"

I just shook my head, took a sip, let out a heavy sigh.

His expression turned wistful, pragmatic, the kind philosophers often front before dropping the big one.

"Okay, I'll put it another way. It's all bullshit."

I looked at my glass, made a very slight effort at a toast. "It's late. I gotta be up early."

We'd worn the subject out. He held up his glass, too. "Here's to at least fucking trying, though, eh, lieutenant? And especially for our friends on the Z and in the jungles of Southeast Asia. Man do they ever got this shit figured out. Hobbes—I mean your long-departed predecessor—would've made a helluva grunt."

We fell silent.

The dream about being attacked popped back into my head. No idea why. I was just drunk enough to run it by Capt. Plato. I mean who else in my little gang would have a better take. Did the dream have to do with where we were? Where we could have been? What was going on with Kim?

"You're just worried about dying, man. That's all it's about. Who the fuck isn't?"

"You?"

He smiled, barely. "First let me tell you a story. I know, we all know one. But mine's different. Remember when they had the war here, the one in the fifties. Killed about fifty-four thousand Americans. A few million of everybody else? I had a brother, quite a lot older, in it. On patrol, his squad ran into an ambush. Everyone was killed except him and his sergeant. The sergeant had been hit in both legs, but my brother dragged him to cover. It was nearly dark and when night came, my brother put his sergeant over his shoulder and carried him back to his outfit. It took most of the night, climbing those damn hills and trying not to be heard. He finally found his platoon, but when he stumbled down the mountain, somebody opened fire with a Browning and shot them both. My brother lived a couple of days in an evac hospital, like the one that was here. Cinch for a Silver Star."

"I'm sorry."

"Comforts you, doesn't it?"

"Not very much."

"It should. It shows the purpose of life."

Long pause.

"Do you believe in God?" Don't really know why I asked.

"Are you serious?"

"Yes."

"No. Of course, I don't believe in God."

"I guess I don't either."

He gave me a studious look. "You say you want a truth, but seriously, do you believe in anything?"

"I don't know."

"You ever been in a VA hospital?"

"No. Why?"

"You ever been to a home for retarded old people?"

"No."

"Ever seen anybody dead?"

"Of course."

"That's what I believe in."

"That's all?"

"Is there anything else?"

"Then life has no meaning?"

"No. It has a meaning."

"What?"

"To amuse someone."

"You mean God?"

"No. Us."

For some selfish reason, I told him Kim had had an abortion. No details.

He didn't ask for any. His face went blank, and he sat with his hands on the arms of one of the old vinyl chairs he'd sneaked for his room. "It's late, like you said. And I'm not a priest."

"I just mean . . . I just mean who the hell are we?"

He tapped his finger and stared away. "Really?"

I got up, went to the door. He gave me a fake salute, with a "Mañana."

I returned it and went back upstairs.

I got maybe four hours sleep, cleaned up, and dropped by the battalion office to check the mail before anyone would be there, so I could sneak back to the White Elephant for breakfast. Cpl. Yu was already inside, the KATUSA day almost always starting earlier than ours. He was killing time, seemingly transfixed at a photo spread in *National Geographic*. I peered over his shoulder. A cheetah was gorging on the carcass of a gazelle.

"Eat or be eaten," I said.

He flipped the page. "No, sir. Eat and be eaten."

63

I was getting so short I was down to counting the days and a "wake-up." I would leave and never know Korea again, or Kim, or Coletti. All would be gone, 7,000 miles and twenty years of war and occupation behind. Like Col. Foster. No one I will know will have known who I knew now, and the past will make no difference. Forever locked out.

That would be good, I thought, but everyone will also be forever locked in.

It was going to be dark soon, so I made myself stop staring out the window and get on with the usual diversion. Pot. I scooted off my bed and steadied myself against the cluttered desk. Closing my eyes for a second, I saw her. In our hootch. Asleep.

I put on my shoes, flicked some ash off my shirt, and headed out to see my girl. The hall was empty, and I stumbled clumsily down the White Elephant steps.

Outside, the late October chill numbed me. Shit, it was autumn, and my coat was inside. I stood nearly a minute trying to decide if I should go back for it. Maybe I'd get sick without it and go to the pneumonia ward in Seoul.

A business girl passed me, probably on the way to the Elephant. What we called a house call.

"Toc sahn cold," she said.

I nodded, resisted an urge to strip naked and sit against a tree by the gate. It was a stronger urge than I wanted to admit. I made it across the street into the ville and turned toward the Blue Dragon. I could feel warm tears on my cheeks and felt my hand quiver when I wiped them away. It was annoying, but they dried in the evening wind.

My mind wheeled with the dope and the lights flashed and the ville was black and white and fuchsia. Music coming from everywhere. I passed through the old alleys, the shops and smells and Koreans and GIs. Coletti was in the Blue Dragon, as I had figured, talking to girls at the serving bar. The Fat Man, I thought, from that movie about the bird. With Bogey.

"Hobbes, me bucko!"

"Yeah."

"Drinks, Miss Oh."

"No thanks, I'm stoned."

"Ah, bad stuff in the ville these days."

"You're asking me or telling me?"

"Bad stuff," he repeated.

"Yeah, bad stuff."

I wanted to talk.

"Look, Coletti. Let's go over there to that empty table in the corner, OK?"

His right eyebrow arched as he tried to interpret my motive. "Sure."

I picked up his drink and tugged at his arm to follow me. He started to complain but came along. I must have looked like a wreck.

We sat. I told him about the abortion.

When I finished, his hands were in a fist, rubbing together, on the grimy tabletop.

"Are you listening?"

He was weighing something in his mind. Slowly. He looked away. "She hasn't told you, has she?"

"I just got through telling you, didn't I? Of course, she did. I was there. It was fucking awful. Weren't you listening?"

"That's not what I mean."

I could feel the Fear.

"What do you mean?"

I was sure he was going to say he was the father.

He leaned close. "Are you straight enough to get this?"

I nodded. Nothing like stark anxiety to sober you up.

He took a long breath.

"I promised not to tell you." I could see muscles working his jaw. "But somebody had better pretty soon, me bucko. Tell you."

"What?"

"Kim is in bad trouble." His eyes flashed. "She's fucked somebody over on some deals and she's damned close to getting wasted."

"Kim?" Now I had to take a breath.

He said nothing.

"Do you mean killed?" Another breath. "Do you?"

"Shut up," he looked around the room. "You're louder than the fucking stereo. Of course, that's what I mean."

He told me how in addition to the usual business, she had delivered dope and drugs for him for months. I took it in. His conclusion: "She was one of the best. She knows everyone in the ville and half of Seoul. And she begged for the work."

"What the fuck?" I inched my chair back, like I was about to get up and either leave or attack. "You dragged her back in? She told me she wasn't doing any more drug hustles for you."

He slapped the table. "Did you hear me? She asked, man. She said she needed money. What do you think you've got there, a goddam nun? Kim's been around, Hobbes. Your little fairy-tale bride knew what she was doing."

"Fairy-tale bride? What the fuck?"

He put up a palm to calm me. "Sorry. I shouldn't have said that. But look, I have to be honest with you."

"Damn right."

He leaned in again. "So, don't ask me how, but I came into possession of a lot of skag. I couldn't turn it down."

I sat frozen in my chair, a little from the drugs, a little from what the person I thought I could trust was telling me. He was looking around the room again, not yet packed.

"I mean it really was a lot of the shit, man. More than I'd ever handled. Now you know I'm not usually into that kind of business, but, well, the product was there, and no real risk to me, and well, why not? Somebody else would do it if I didn't, right?"

I stared.

"I mean I had this stuff and I wanted to move it. So, Kim hit me up at the right time. Don't give me that look—I mean even if she let it go for a while, she couldn't turn it down, either. That's when I gave her a few deliveries, and she did them, and I got my money and gave her a fair cut. No complaints either way."

"Then who—"

He seemed to chew on his lip. "So, she started getting ideas. You know? But I didn't know. Somehow, she skimmed off some the smack on this deal before she delivered it to my customers. Even worse, she cut it and sold it on her own on the street." He shrugged. "It had to happen, right? Sooner or later the main guy on the other end found out."

He seemed to be sweating, even though the bar was plenty cool. "So, this guy came to me a week ago real pissed off and wanted the money he had lost. But look, he wanted to go after her on the spot. But he couldn't risk it. Then he thought I should pay for the skim. So, I talked to him until he settled down—what a fucking temper—and I got an extension. I didn't tell him, but I thought I'd be able to get the stolen bucks back from your lady. But now . . . now . . ." He turned his palms up. "Time's running out."

By then I was rubbing my eyes, shaking my head, trying to get off the planet.

"What guy?"

"You know."

"Lee? You got to be shitting me."

"I'm not."

"Kim knows?" I said when I could barely mouth the words.

"I told her."

"What did she say?"

"She said okay, but she needed some more time."

I flashed back to the doctor's office, the abortion, the nights since.

"Did she say what she was doing with all the money?"

"Guess."

"What's that supposed to mean?"

"Grow up. You know."

"Well, can she pay it back?"

"I don't know."

"Can't you do anything?"

"That's not for me to say."

"What does that mean?"

"It means I'm out of it, man. Look, I got her a lot more time than the situation calls for. But I've done all I can. But I'm telling you this. You'd better talk to Kim."

"Fuck, I thought all that was over."

"I don't know if you're going to marry her or what, but I know damned well she's playing with some bad fuckers. She owes them, mostly Lee, and if she doesn't pay up, she won't make it. I don't care if she's Mrs. Thomas Hobbes or what. She won't make it."

"And you won't stop it."

"Not won't. Can't. I mean this is their turf. Their fucking country."

"You've got connections."

"Give me a break. I can't do everything. I mean who could?"

"I did you a favor. Remember. A big one."

"Fuck you!" He stood up. "Listen again you hick Texas bastard. Kim fucked over some dealers. She didn't cheat at monopoly or kick a john in the nuts. She fucked over some guys who make a living turning people into junkie trash. They don't give a shit about your infantile love life problems. They just want the money. They want it back and I can't hold them off any longer."

He slammed his big fist on the table. Some heads in the bar turned our way. He put up a hand to indicate all was well and sat down again. And lowered his voice. "The only reason I told you is so you could help her. And if you don't, you can kiss her good-bye in a slicky ditch. You know what Lee and his guys are into?" He gestured as if a knife ran across his chest. "That's how you'll find her. Carved like salami. Take that home with you, all-American boy."

It was hard to sit still. To control my voice. I wanted to curse him into the roach-filled woodwork, to cut out his entrails and say, "Barter these, motherfucker."

Instead, I sat still. "How long?"

"A week."

"I'll make you responsible. You!"

I waited for him to punch me. He shook his fist furiously enough, but controlled his temper, made another signal to the eavesdroppers and the waitress that all was okay. "You just watch your ass talking like that."

"We'll see whose ass gets watched."

"Goodbye, Hobbes."

I stood, pushed back my chair. Too hard. It fell on the floor. I picked it up, only to save the waitress from coming over, and crossed the empty dance floor to the front door.

Out in the street, I shivered again in the cold. A week. What a coincidence. My Red Tail would be here in two.

64

It was the horror. The Fear. It lurched through my pitiable veins, arteries, capillaries, became the ear-piercing bass line of my mind. When I smiled, I knew the canines were there, gleaming in front, hungering for the meat, the kill, and the conscienceless sleep of the predator, who takes and need not explain.

I could not accept that she hadn't told me. *Hadn't even told me.* She could have fucked the most clap-ridden scumbag and not telling me could not have been worse. When she clutched me in our last nights, what did her pelvis whisper?

Why had she kept the secret? We had some secrets, but nothing like that one. Could she have wanted me so much? Was it me she wanted? How could she?

What do they say about accepting love? That it just happens, and you let it, and it makes you feel better? I said I loved her. But then, even with the raw fetus meat on the sheets and the "doctor" ripping my soul, I did not know that what you accepted, and what made you feel better, had no limits and could burst your brain like a swollen melon. It was a horror, a Fear, a revelation as sacred as death. Knowing it, I became life-sick.

I had gone back to the BOQ but as soon as I walked into my room, I knew I had to get out, and started back to our hootch. I was obviously stoned. What would I say? What did it all mean? Is there a more stupid question than that? What does it all mean? Christ. No wonder Capt. Plato wearied of me.

I'd no sooner crossed into the ville, turning up a semi-lit backstreet, when I spotted her. Walking alone. Instead of calling out, I ducked into a shadow. To watch. Unseen. It was all wrong, but I had to know. If there was anything to know.

She stopped at a dingy food and convenience shop and bought something. I saw the old man give her a sack and her change. She counted it carefully and put it into her pants pocket.

Back in the World, when I was a small boy, and went to the grocery store, and the cashier gave me change, I stuck it into my pants pocket, too.

Wow! Kim and I were soooo alike.

I had no doubt, thanks to Coletti, that there were dozens of nights like this when she had slipped through the alleys and arranged her escape to the World with the deliveries she had cut out for herself. I realized it had not been a risk. A risk implies something to lose. Maybe something to win. And most of all, is real. What she could win, or lose, as a working girl, all rode on finding one insulated, naïve American GI fool who thought fucking and dope were the joys and secrets of life, and he was a better man for having both. And with him, if you were the right girl, came a ticket, a certified passage from what, if you told anyone else, could only be assumed to have been a pipe dream. As in not real. But I was real. And I was the fool.

I shrank, watching her. I perceived her continuity, and my lack thereof. The random insignificance of my presence, perching on the brink of nothingness.

The Fear was strong. It was in my mouth and on my skin. I laughed years ago when someone said animals could smell fear. How could you smell something like that? You could and did. And this was not even an immediate fear, not like being cornered in Panther Detour or a slicky-boy ambush. There, I felt no fear, or was beyond it. I knew there would be another day. The real Fear, this one, was more than that. A drain of the soul, an intimation of worms. The Fear is helplessness, and neutrality, caring nothing of its victims. It is beyond denial.

I felt it, watching her navigate the darkness of her world, and her pain was mine. I felt dizzy, maybe from being high, maybe from trying to stay surreptitious. I felt cottonmouth, cramps, wild-eye fever. Jesus don't let her die. For me.

I started running now, bumping anything in my path. She turned back in surprise at the quickening footsteps, and at my cry: "Kim. It's me. It doesn't matter."

I half-panted as I caught up and took her by the shoulders.

"The baby doesn't matter, none of that shit matters. Come with me. Please."

I was talking rapidly, desperately. But she understood.

She dropped the paper sack from the shop. "Yobo? You run here?"

"Yes, yes, yes."

It was a century before either of us said anything, and then we kissed.

I opened my eyes as two loud, drunk GIs walked past. One of them said, "Fuck her, buddy, I did."

I started to yell back but I realized that summarized me in Korea.

"Stupid GIs," Kim said. Also, a summary.

We held each other closer, where reality, existence, was nothing but us.

"Yes, yes, yes," kept coming out of my mouth.

I would take her. I wanted her. I wanted to escape in each other. Our true home was miles away, minds away, and I would take her. It was done.

That simple? Maybe not, but it sufficed, and it broke the Fear. In later years, if they asked, I could tell others what I learned, that to live requires not the thought, merely the act. Before the act, the thought has no meaning, and dies from the Fear. Between the shadow and the substance is nothing. When the act comes, we pretend to understand, to smile and say ah, yes—but still we understand nothing, heeding only the imperatives of Neanderthals.

We pulled apart, so we could see each other's face. Brain. Heart. Soul.

She knew that I knew.

"Coletti, dumb bastard, he tell you."

"Yes."

She looked away.

"Kim, Kim, Kim. Marry me. I want you. Please. Let's get the fuck out of here."

So quick, so final. That she could have risked everything for me.

Who needs bells and music when your spine-rattle is the clue?

"You say same tomorrow and I say yes."

"Say yes now."

"We in the alley."

"Who cares?"

We kissed again.

"Yes," she whispered. "But also, tomorrow if you be same."

We kissed again.

She picked up the sack and we walked back to the hootch. She turned on the electric floor heater and we sat on the rug. She told me, with almost no emotion, about the deals, how she skimmed, used talcum powder and flour and other things. She thought they would never find out. She told me about Coletti telling her that they did. She was frightened of Lee, she said, and was going to give him all the money and plead for her life. But now, for me, for us, she would just stall him until she could get another flight change as soon as she could.

I barely knew what to say and just nodded my head through most of the story. I told her I could barely take it all in and I didn't know how she had kept it hidden for so long.

She looked at me in a way hard to describe, something timeless, and then the quiver came back into her voice. "I think I lose you, my yobo, like with all the other GIs. This is why. So I get all that money. So if I have toc sahn money, I can go, too. Airplane from Seoul. I buy my own ticket. Maybe catch you up stateside."

She kissed me again, also in a timeless way. I felt it head to toe.

"I mean that was what I thought, my yobo. Now, all different."

"Kim, Kim . . . I can give you the money you owe to Lee. I can get it from the bank right away from my account. It'll be okay. Coletti, that son of a bitch, I'll get him to take care of the payoff. You don't even have to be there."

261

She looked down. "It cost lots to take me."

"Fuck it. They pay me too much anyway."

She hugged me around the neck. A long time.

I had a strange, irrational feeling that her thoughts were elsewhere, but I ignored it. I had been lost and found by her.

She said we should eat something and opened the package of ramyan she'd bought at that store and cooked it on the hot plate. We sat at the tiny table, and talked about plans, dredging up half-forgotten promises from lost nights. Then I said, "So when will you return the money?"

She tried to hide the look on her face but couldn't. "Maybe two days. No worry, Hobbes-san."

"Do it tomorrow. Why wait? I mean he's not going to wait much longer, a week at most, from what Coletti said. I can go to my bank for cash first thing in the morning."

She frowned. "I think we need one more day anyway. Maybe it take longer to get all my money together. No bank for me."

"But you don't need the money. I can take care of it, like I said. I mean, it's the fucking least I can do, right?"

We looked at each other.

"Maybe, yobo, but I got it all planned. No worry, no problem."

She reached out to tap her finger against my nose, as if I had been a bad boy but no longer. She leaned across the table to kiss me. "I understand, Hobbes-san, man I love. You give me all that later, okay? When we married and stateside. If you want to. Don't worry, I take care all this while you at work."

"Tomorrow?"

"Tomorrow. Same day you have to ask me to marry you again."

We laughed.

"So, while you do that, I'll meet the movers at the BOQ for my hold baggage and then start clearing post. Probably take all day. So, we'll get everything ready."

"And we stay at hootch rest of time."

"Except when I have to be at the office."

She looked at me as plans and options careened in her head.

"I'll catch Coletti at the O Club at breakfast or at his office to set things up, whatever you need."

"Yobo, I not need him. I can get message to Lee. It will be faster."

"But Coletti can do it all. Just give him the money and then it goes to Lee."

"It not work that way here. Lee already hate me enough. I have to say sorry when I give him money and ask him forgive me. He keep his pride. You know?"

"But you don't even have to see him. Coletti will handle it. That's what I'm saying. You can pack up and we can put you on a train to Seoul right away. You can stay at a hotel as long as you need to get a plane to San Francisco after I'm gone. I mean, all that money should take care of some gangster's fucking wounded pride. And you'll never hear from him again."

We could have argued over it, but she stroked my cheek softly. "You so American, huh? So you not see what I say."

"I do."

"You don't. But okay."

She kissed me again, then got up. We put the dishes in the tub in the sink.

"Yobo, where we live back stateside?"

"Tomorrow. Okay?"

"Okay. Okay. Where, yobo?"

"Oh, probably back in Texas. Or maybe New Mexico. or Colorado."

"What Colorado like?" She said it: Cor-o-rado. I loved her for it. I could barely pronounce kimchi. "Mountains, snow?"

"Like here."

"But no slant-eyes," she laughed. "Except me."

"That's right. Just you."

We sat on the floor rug again and talked about what it would be like. We could have had a drink or a hit but neither wanted to escape from anything.

"Yobo," she asked, stifling a yawn, "yobo, why you decide marry me now?"

"Because you will make me happy."

"I tell you secret."

"What?"

"Maybe you already know."

"What?"

"Yobo, I think you go away after . . . after baby die. Like all GI."

"No," I said, a second too late.

"Maybe that why I keep money."

"Why?"

"You know."

"No I don't."

"Never mind."

"What?"

"Nothing."

"What, Kim?"

She moved across the rug and kissed me. "Nothing, yobo. Nothing. You with me now. We be stateside most skoch. Live in mountains, make babies. I be good wife for you."

The hootch was warm, but nothing compared to the feel of her cheek against mine. I felt the years pass through me. The ones ahead. I also felt death, but it was warm, too, full of promise.

"We'll be happy," I said.

Later, we made love. You could really call it that.

65

Seagulls swarm, diving at suicide angles for stranded fish in the mud. The Incheon harbor tide, out now, rises and falls two dozen feet each cycle. MacArthur knew that, made it work. If fish or fishermen do not, they can get caught in the deep, oily goop.

A jumbled mass of boats sits there now, masts nearly level with the shore wall. They rest by design, not accident, as part of their in-and-out-to-sea routine. Some for fishing, some for cargo, are so cluttered men walk from one to another as if on an Atlantis arcade. On the decks, tired sailors sleep in the sun. Others have crawled to the shade to eat or carve figurines. The strong smell of the harbor stings my nose.

My time is running out, and Sansoe will be stuck here until January, but by his own choice and my finagling. We got him a six-month extension in Korea that would in turn let him out of the Army nine months early. GI math. You grabbed what you could. We decided to squeeze in our goodbye with the photoshoot we'd put off too long. I'd even bought a new camera from the PX, to replace my stolen Canon. Much cheaper than waiting to get back to the States.

Kim is okay with our outing. I'd asked her to come but she said she wanted to stay to do her last-minute packing and cleaning at the hootch and whatever else she needs to do that doesn't involve errands for Coletti. She has gotten the money to Lee as we planned and says everything has been taken care of. So, we'll get her to a hotel in Seoul by the weekend and I'll be on the Red Tail a few days after that.

Kim says another reason I should go with Sansoe is to just relax a little and also see real Koreans. Same as Corporal Yu wanted. They're more than right. The harbor is too cheap and working class to be labeled a paradise, like the ones in the travel ads in the *Times*, full of Caribbean harbors of bikinis and drinks on the beach. But this is a beauty in its own way. It is where you live because it is your job. Your way of life. It is life itself.

The sun is almost too bright, so we set our cameras at 1/500. On the plus side, the sea is unnaturally blue, the children lively and happy. All kinds of tradesmen and craft masters at work. The best shot is of workmen balancing delicately up the long, trembling planks from ship hatch to shore, dropping 100 lb. grain sacks at a weight scale. "Aiee," they exclaim as they let go their burdens. Wiping the grainy sweat from their faces, they stretch tightened muscles and lope off again for more. The boss at the scales checks each sack quickly, arguing whether it is too much, too little.

Sansoe and I change film rolls often. It seems important to get this.

Toward the center of the harbor piers, we see an old man in a threadbare green suit, surely his only clothing, sitting cross-legged, making a yellow fishing net. His fingers weave a bone needle in and out, lace for the sea creatures. Seeing us, he smiles toothlessly and beckons in Korean. Come here, come here, he must be saying.

"Go on," I encourage Sansoe. "He wants you to do it." Sansoe kneels at the man's side and touches the net. Smiling, pleased that we are interested, the old man weaves two more squares. Sansoe studies the movements, then picks up the bone needle. He draws the thick twine in and around, in and around.

We thank the old man. He wants Sansoe to stay, keep him company. But there are more pictures to be taken, saved. Only a little ahead is the anchor-maker. Small, muscular, his arms and back glisten in the sun. A headband keeps the sweat from his eyes.

He is straddling a 50-foot log. With his axe and chisel, day after day, he will turn the rough timber into a sturdy anchor. We watch him. He speaks rarely, mostly to give instructions to his apprentice. Then he measures the timber and begins sawing. The apprentice batters a heavy bolt into a finished crossbeam for a different anchor, nearly finished.

Hewing and pounding, waking undaunted each morning at the new sun, they will be lucky to live past fifty. Here, as in so much of Korea, there are few questions, only necessities. Sansoe says that is what his grandfather said about Mexico. I say maybe that isn't so bad. We snap more shots. I remember what Kim said about Happy Mountain.

I need to get back to her.

66

"Whatsa matter, yobo?"

"Nothing."

"Well, smile, then. We almost there."

"I'm glad."

Her happiness was nearly more than I could bear.

While I was out of her hair in Incheon, she was able to wrap everything up. Hotel, flight out of Seoul at the end of next week, everything settled with mama-san. And Lee. I'd be gone a few days before, but she would be safe while I waited in San Francisco.

No more decisions, traumas, guilt. She had done it. I had done it. We had done it. It was peaceful.

That night I told her she was so good at real business, forget business girl, that she'd do great in the states. She said when we got there, I would call her Anne. She spelled it. She'd used her real first name, Ahnjong, on the passport and everything else and wanted to be that girl again. I said it was perfect for her. We would be Tom and Anne. With an "e." That brought on a long kiss. For the first time, at least with me, she was truly happy and optimistic. We slept the entire night in each other's arms.

In the morning I dressed hurriedly to get to the compound clearance office for some final paperwork. Sansoe was helping me, even though he couldn't believe what was happening.

"Meet you about six tonight." I kissed her goodbye.

"And tomorrow we in Itaewon hotel."

"And you can just relax and get ready for the trip."

"To America."

"To our new life."

268

67

I had been here all my life, watching newbies, turtles, come fresh, more or less, into the distant land and leave as dirty-dick old men fifty times their actual age, ravaged with needle-dotted arms and shattered smiles. Or blank, stupid indifference. So, what if I was leaving it all behind?

Sansoe had been here even longer. He was the one guy I knew I'd see back in the World.

Nick and I agreed to look each other up when we got back, too. Which would never happen in a million, trillion years. I'd never see Coletti, either, but neither would I try.

As for Travis, I was still upset that he'd gone and got himself killed. What a prick. A real jerk. But I would not remember him that way.

As for that day in Bupyeong, that day in the midwife disassembly line while I held Kim and tried to drive everything out of that sight? As for the waste bin? As for the waste? I would not remember that day, either.

None of that would prove true.

"Lieutenant?" I snapped back from my miserable thoughts.

"Hobbes, Thomas," I told Spec. 5 Croker. We were standing in the warehouse where everyone turned in gear and winter heavy clothing. I was glad Sansoe was helping me. There was a lot of paperwork clearing the post, and a lot of waiting time, and a million distractions on my mind.

But everything was in order. And my hold luggage was already gone from my room. All I had left to take on the plane was my trunk and a duffel bag. And Kim. I could only think of San Francisco—we would reunite there in no time. Thomas and Kim Hobbes. Tom and Anne.

"All there, sir?" Spec. 5 Croker asked. I wasn't sure if he meant my brain or my turn-ins.

"Yeah. Sure."

Sansoe flashed an OK. "Don't worry about his stuff. I already checked."

"Good for you. I don't give a shit," Croker said, and scribbled something on Form 3035. "Kay, sir. See ya in the World." He passed a carbon copy to me and went back to reading his *Playboy*.

"See you." We both said it at almost the same time.

I had lied to him. I had kept most of the winter clothing allowance to use back in Colorado.

Next stop, the armory. Took about five minutes. I never even checked out a weapon, except for the time we thought we'd been invaded.

We had plenty of time left, so we dropped into the PX snackateria for lunch. "I'm sorry I couldn't tell you more about all this before," I told Sansoe.

He waved away concern as we found chairs at a small table.

"I mean, what can I say?"

"It's okay, man. I really believe it. What you said about Kim. You guys will make it." He grinned in a way that made it all seem clear.

I smiled back. Sort of.

"Look at these bozos," he said, glancing around the room. "Fuck them. There's all the stories and bragging and bullshit, but you know how all that is. And it's not you. You'll make it. I have to admit, I didn't think it was much of an idea, at first, I mean you getting married, married to a . . . to Kim, but I finally figured there wasn't any way out of it. I mean you were bound to do it."

We had a laugh about the muck at Cherry Hill. And then I maybe went too far. I told him, making sure no one could hear, about Kim's dope and gangster Lee.

As I talked, he shook his head and nodded in that unconscious spaced-out way he had. But serious. When I was done, he let go the breath he'd been holding,

"Holy Jesus. All this while, you never said a damn thing."

"I only just found out myself. Really."

"She never told you?"

"No. It was Coletti."

Sansoe's expression changed to stunned. His mouth actually dropped open. "Fuck me to tears, Tom." He never used my first name. He stared down at the table, started to swat his coffee to the floor, but pulled up his hand at the last second. "Shit!"

"Yeah."

We both looked everywhere except at each other. He finally broke the silence. "I mean that's really fucked, I mean everything else and now this. It's a court-martial if you don't get killed first. And her." He shook his head again. "It's a good thing you're getting out now."

"Getting out of what?"

"Just Korea, man. Just Korea."

We went about the rest of check-outs. For all practical purposes, I was logging out from my time as an Army officer. Forever. I had to report to battalion one more time, maybe, but my turtle, Capt. Bernard Humbert, whom I annoyed by calling Barney, had finally arrived so I wouldn't have to actually do anything. And neither he nor LTC Matthews were desperate to see me again. Ever. They'd probably just let me hang out at the White Elephant.

Either way, I was all but gone. Oop-soh, outta there, see ya, don't forget to write. I was about as short as it gets. A handful of days and a wake-up. I had my ticket: Mil Trans Flight 938, dep Kimpo 0845. I had my orders. I had my bags packed.

I told Sansoe I'd try to catch him later at the Homestead and asked him again not to be pissed off at me. He gave me a funky left-handed salute as we split up and I knew he wouldn't. And he'd still help with anything I'd still need taken care of.

I went back to the BOQ, changed into civvies, and went to meet Kim. Halfway to the gate, I turned to rush back to battalion HQ before it closed, having almost forgotten some State Department forms to show I was her sponsor and responsible for her. They were on Barney's desk, used to be my desk. He was surprised to see me and flashed a look somewhere between condescension and indifference.

68

The sun was nearly setting when I left the gate. Kim asked me to meet her at her old hootch she was still keeping at mama-san's and then we'd go to our own place. The rent was finally up and she'd cleared out her things but had forgotten a set of expensive combs. Mama-san had sent word for her to get them before tomorrow or they'd be sold.

I passed the usual shops filled with tailors, food sellers, cigarette hawkers, games of Go, unhappy children, mixes of locals and GIs going who-knew-where to do who-knew-what. So different from the port at Incheon.

The outer door to mama-san's courtyard was unlocked, so I wouldn't have to ring the damn buzzer. Judging from the noise of tape decks and laughter and moaning from other rooms, some of the girls were already in business. Extended afternoon delights. I was so glad this was Kim's last day as a tenant. We'd argued about it every month.

Crossing the cobblestones, I could see Kim's door was partly open, and hoped she was ready to split. "Hey, Kim, it's me," I said, then did the ritual knock. Hoping she'd be in there with a bag full of combs and a hug.

I heard nothing, pulled off my shoes, and stepped inside. A small bed lamp was on. For a moment, my eyes wouldn't hold what I saw. A thought zipped through my brain: I must be in the wrong room. Eyes—look again. Send me other information.

She lay sprawled across the quilt on her bed.

I gawked, gaped, stared.

She was breathing softly, sporadically, as if she couldn't stop.

I hadn't breathed myself, or moved, and finally did.

Her body was sliced in so many places. Blood and vomit streamed from her face to her thighs. My god, her face. She convulsed and choked. The jagged flaps where her breasts had been pulsed up and down.

If I yelled and cursed, I didn't know. I didn't know anything.

I dropped to my knees at the side of the bed. My right hand trembled as I reached to touch her, but drew back, reached again, hovered and then ran a finger along the blood from her cheek. I'd never seen anything so pale, and so beaten.

Her eyes half-opened. Through the horror, the dumb-struck fear and horror, I knew she saw me. I smiled. I don't know why.

Her eyes closed again, and the choking came back.

My mouth was so dry I couldn't shut it. Or speak. I studied with embarrassed terror the way they had carved her.

I closed my eyes. Not to hide but trying to find a way to get even a little control. And keep breathing. I heard another curdling scream. Had to be mine.

I stood. Wiped my hands. My shirt and pants now covered in blood. Same as my face, which I also had wiped. I looked around the room. It was hard not to stay locked on her, but I had to. It hadn't even occurred to me someone else might be there. They weren't. The ransacking was ferocious. Did they think she had more money somewhere? Drugs? Or were they just butchers from the Seoul mob?

I closed the door, not having had the presence of mind before. First making a quick visual sweep outside. No one. Nothing. All hootch doors shut. It struck me as odd, but I didn't dwell. Then I moved to the other side of the bed and pressed the baseboard slit on the wall, as she'd shown me, not unlike her hiding trick in our own hootch. At first it stuck, probably glued, until I kicked it open.

I thought there would be money left over after the Lee payoff, or maybe family keepsakes. Instead, only Miss Han's Colt .45. All this time, I thought it was hidden in our hootch with her bone box. Did she come back for this more than the combs? She'd never be able to get on a plane with a weapon. Or was she that scared? The Fear that strong?

I had to stop wondering. There was no time. I had to suck it up.

I went back to the other side of the bed and knelt. Her eyes half-open again, looking nowhere. She breathed, but not enough.

I leaned, kissed her. Her lips were blue and bloody and vomit-caked. They tasted warm and salty in my mouth.

I looked at her again but made myself stop. I pressed the pistol muzzle to her temple.

I couldn't.

Not Kim.

I pressed it one more time.

Not Kim.

But I couldn't let her stay like that, either. Dead but alive. Maybe she was past pain, one foot already in the universe. But maybe not.

I put the gun on the floor, kissed her again, like it would bring her back to life. Like the fairy tales. This time as her lips parted I could see broken teeth and strands of blue cloth. I pulled the cloth out, smoothed her lips and chin to cover the damage.

"I love you," I said. I mean I think I said.

I do know that I pinched her nose with the thumb and forefinger of my right hand and sealed the palm of my left over her mouth and bore down hard enough to stop any airflow. I leaned across her torn chest in case she began to heave or convulse. She didn't.

Her eyes opened, but not in fright. I like to think she was in there, but beyond suffering. Then the eyes closed, and I knew she was gone. I held my hands in place until I was dead certain. I remember that phrase bullying its way through my head.

I couldn't cry. I couldn't speak. Nothing. Nothing,

I let go, sat next to her, looking only at her face. I didn't want to look away or leave her side, but I knew I had to. So, I got up, sucked it up, made myself look at the context. This time I saw more of the room than I had earlier. Drawers were on the floor, mirrors broken, the bed stand shattered. A blue hand towel, bloody and wadded up on the quilt. That's what was in her mouth. They had gagged her. There had been a fight.

Had no one even heard the noise? No one?

Just another drunken brawl or beating in a hootch? Happened all the time. GIs knew when to stop to avoid court-martial or SOFA and how much to bribe. Then I realized. Mama-san never called the police. But she did call Kim to come over for her combs. And the body was left with an open door. Anyone could see. Any of the business girls. As an example.

Fuck, I really had no idea.

An idiot instinct told me I should shoot mama-san.

Another instinct said I should leave. Most skoch.

I took one last look at her, seeing only the times we had shared that bed after we first met, before we moved in together, before we fell in love, and I tried not to admit it.

They are only dead, she had told me on Happy Mountain. That's why it was happy. Could I ever think the same of Kim?

I had almost forgotten the .45. I tucked it in my pants under my shirt.

Finally, I left.

I hurried down the mud alley. I cut through Panther Detour, then turned up towards the Blue Dragon. The vision of Kim was replaced by that of the Colt. I sang as I walked: "I got a fucking gun. A fucking gun." I passed a few people, then more as I neared the back side of the bar district. If anyone heard me, they chalked it up to another drunk or speed freak all bloody and messed up from a fight.

Just a few more blocks to the Blue Dragon.

69

When I got there, I stopped the death song. But I still felt the Fear. That is, I had sensed it, imagined it. Fear had turned to something else. I pushed a whore or maybe a waitress aside as I caromed through the rear exit, rarely locked. It was the unofficial entry to the unofficial office for the unofficial Mayor of Suchow. A girl in the hall yelled at me out of habit but didn't really care. I swung open Coletti's door, walked in, and slammed it shut behind me.

The unofficial mayor looked up from his unofficial metal Army desk, startled, from the unofficial daily grind of cooking his extremely unofficial books.

I pointed the .45 at his nose.

"What the fuck—"

"Shut up, cocksucker." My arm and hand trembled from rage. Along the gray-blue muzzle, I could see his heavy features. The front sight wavered. I put my other hand under the grip to help steady my aim.

"What the hell is this? Good lord, were you in a fight?"

"I said shut up, you bastard." I used my left hand for a second to rub my eyes to clear my tears and her blood, then steadied my aim again. Then I thought someone might come in behind me. I stepped away from the door and braced myself against a wall.

"You killed her."

His head cocked like a dog's, looked down, breathed hard, tightened his expression, looked back up. "Kim is dead?"

Somehow, his awkward reaction told two things: He wasn't surprised. And he hadn't done it. I let him live.

"Oh Jesus. Jesus, Hobbes. Oh Christ. I knew it would happen."

"Of course, you knew it would happen, you bastard. You set her up."

"You know better than that."

"Do I? Is that what I know? Tell me, Mister Mayor, me fucking bucko. Is that what I know? Were you just helping us out and we blew it? Is that it?"

I let the pistol drop low for a moment.

Coletti started to stand.

"Hold it," I snapped and put the muzzle on target again. "Just don't move."

He stayed seated.

"I thought she gave the money back to Lee. Didn't she give it back?"

"You know."

He studied me. "Yeah," he said at last. "I know."

"Jesus, Coletti."

He rubbed his face and shook his head. "Who knows why these people do any of this shit? Man, I don't know. I mean she knew Lee wanted her ass—with or without the money. He's a real bad fucker. You know, a rough dealer. But he said he wouldn't hurt her if she paid up. In person." He slammed his palms on the stolen Army desk. "He said he wouldn't."

"He did."

"I tried to talk her out of it. Swore not to tell you. She was so excited about leaving. And she knew she had to deliver the money. I mean, she was right about that. About having to give it to Lee herself, to apologize. And she did. She told me. So, I'd know if I saw him. But she was wrong that's all he wanted. Whether he'd come back."

"You could've told me."

"She begged me not to. You know. She didn't want you in it. Or find out she'd been lying to you. And she thought it was all over, paying him to show respect."

"You could've told me."

Coletti nodded and slumped back in his chair. "Did . . . did he cut her?"

"She was still alive when I found her."

277

"Then—"

"I shot her. With this." I lied just to make him feel worse.

He stared, dumbstruck. "Do you want some paper towels? I mean—"

"Where is Lee?" I shook the pistol at him.

"I don't know."

"You'd better fucking find out."

"Don't." He gestured at the Colt. "You'll never make it."

"Make what?"

"I mean they'll kill you. Assuming the MPs don't spot you first."

It was kind of funny. Between him and me, across those few feet of green floor tile and gray desk were the visions. All of them. Summarized. Ready for the personnel files. The days of Kim, the nights of sin. Of love. Of nightmares. I shook my head to drive it out.

I stepped against the desk, leaned forward. He watched me like you'd watch a rabid dog. I waited for him to break. Something to show he shared my agony. Even just imagined it. He stayed put, not moving a muscle.

I pushed the pistol as close as I could to his face. Maybe he could have swatted it. Maybe not. I wanted to see the blood spatter; his brains fly onto the wall. Watch his fucking Mayor of Suchow deals leak out his gasping mouth like sewer spit.

He didn't yield. The Fear was in him, but it didn't show. Something else in there, too. For me. I could hear our silent interchange.

I felt the trigger tighten, but in a blind, black instant I swung the pistol to the right and shot the wall.

I stumbled backwards, then caught my balance, rambling in words I can't recall.

Coletti didn't even duck. Nor did his eyes stop drilling into me. "Well . . . You'd better stay in the Elephant until your flight," he said, looking through the smoke at the bullet hole. His voice stayed even, calm. The kind of response we got in training for handling freak-outs. I thought, Jesus, I'm that guy. He stood, very slowly, testing my response. Which was none.

"If they find out she's dead, they'll send the MPs. It'll go really bad. Maybe not just for you."

"I don't care. For you, either."

We held eye contact. Then I was done. I dropped the Colt to my side. I had a hard time identifying where I was.

I could almost hear his relief. "And look, I'll see that she's taken care of. Buried, whatever it takes. Shit, Tom, I liked her a lot, too. You don't have to believe me. But do."

Not that it mattered. Blood was caked in her ears and her mouth. Self-preservation had the only meaning now. The only truth. Coletti was all about reality. He'd often bragged that he'd been to Rome. He knew the drill. Let the dead bury the dead.

He stood up slowly from his chair, watching me closely, and held out his hand.

I gave him the pistol. He put it in a desk drawer, upper right.

"Can you get back to the Elephant by yourself?"

I said I could.

"I'll get someone to follow you. You look like hell."

"Do what you like."

"Just to be sure."

"What does it matter?"

"I'm really sorry."

"Will you get Lee?"

"I'll do what I can."

I opened the door. The bartender, Mr. Oh, was standing in the hall, blocking me.

"It's okay," Coletti said.

Mr. Oh scanned me hard, then took a step into the office. He gave it a look, waved off the smoke. "No shooting in club."

Coletti bowed, held up his palms in peace. "Nobody hurt. I'll pay for everything. It was an accident. I'll explain later."

Mr. Oh stared a little longer, especially at me. "What wrong with him?"

"Just let him go on. Please. I'll owe you."

Mr. Oh flashed serious disbelief, then stepped aside so I could leave.

"Always here, my friend," I heard Coletti shout as I headed into the hall for the main room and front door, Mr. Oh right behind me.

I made my way through the yobos and GIs on the dance floor and Creedence blasting on the loudspeakers and never wanted to see any of them again. No doubt the feeling was mutual.

Outside, instead of going to the White Elephant as advised, I took to the alleys again. I don't know if Coletti's tail had gotten to me in time to follow, but it didn't matter. Nobody bothered a guy who looked deranged.

Cutting through Panther Detour, I broke into a run. In no time I was back at Kim's hootch. Still plenty of noise, but no one in the courtyard. Her light was still on, too. I hadn't remembered to turn it off. I hadn't locked the door, either. She was on the bed, as I had left her. I dropped to my knees. It was some time before I could stand. But I did and pulled her body upright. For a second, an insane second, I clutched her to me. All that left me was more blood and gore on my clothes and face.

I propped her up against the backrest, in a sitting position, as if she faced the sun. I wrapped the quilt around her, bloody as it was, because there was nothing else. I made sure her eyes were closed. It occurred to me they had not been gouged out.

It had been wrong for me to have just left her, as though her body had become a ghost and would have disappeared all by itself. But there was nothing more I could do. Coletti was right that I couldn't be caught by the MPs. Kim was gone. I was lapsing into insanity.

I left the hootch, door closed but unlocked again, this time on purpose. I wanted Mama-san to find her before the body decomposed and take care of it or call the police. Or maybe she would call Lee, which I hoped, because he might kill her, too, as another kind of example.

I knew I had no idea once again and walked fast to the compound. Running would draw too much attention, especially the way I looked. When I got to the gate, the MP smelled my breath and gave me a close once-over and asked what the hell had happened. I told him there was a fight in the ville and I'd given first aid. It was pretty messy. He shrugged, said something about "fucking morons," waved me through, and listened to his radio.

280

I went up the outside fire escape to my almost empty room and saw no one. I sat on my bed, which still had a mattress, pillow, blanket, and sheets. I stripped, put everything I was wearing into a laundry bag, and dumped it in the big green trash bin on the way to the shower. No one was around. I made sure all that was left on my body of what had been done to Kim washed completely into the drain. I had forgotten to bring a towel but walked back to my room anyway. I didn't care. I made myself laugh with the only thing that came to mind: "Tomorrow's another day."

70

It took hours to fall asleep, so late the next morning I called Sansoe from the wall phone in the Elephant and asked if he could come over. I must have seemed crazy when he saw me. Babbling? No, not foaming at the mouth. But high. I felt so high. Light and laughing. It could not possibly have happened.

But I told him. And I made him promise not to tell anyone. That I had to get out of the country like I was invisible. That there was nothing he could do.

He said okay—in a bewildered manner, trying to take it in. To make sense. Was I crazy? Was? What about *Is*?

I asked him to take care of whatever I forgot and let me know of anything he learned about Kim, after I had gone.

When he left, we shook hands, as I had with Capt. Plato, except more difficult, surreal.

"I'll see you in the World," he said, and hugged me instead of a handshake. It was embarrassing, and he left quickly.

I still had a couple of opium-laced joints in the desk drawer. I'd bought them in the ville and was pretty sure they weren't laced with LSD. I smoked them throughout the day. Later in the afternoon, buzzed but seeking anything to keep my mind distracted, I walked down the hallway and talked to some of the mama-sans in the laundry and shower room, telling them goodbye.

"Why you stay here?" one smiled. "They already take your things to go to States."

"No problem. I oop-soh most skoch."

"Ahhh," another said. Of course, they already knew. Not about Kim. About me having to wait out the flight. Rumor was officers who had to wait more than a day or two after their personal baggage was boxed up had pissed somebody off. I thought it was my turtle but could have been LTC Matthews, whose last disappointment in me was that I wouldn't re-up to go to chopper school in Alabama.

I thanked the mama-sans again for everything and pulled a ten-dollar bill from my pocket and left it with the one we called Madam Clean. I went to the head and then back to my room. Evening came. What was real ceased to matter.

I would not think of it. That was the way. She was not there. I had not known her. Send her to me in another vision.

But what to do with the boredom/Fear? I went out the back way to the ville. I walked aimlessly for an hour. I didn't want to see anyone but remembered I had another favor to ask Sansoe. I found him in the Acid Club. He waved when I came in, surprised I'd ventured out. Lifting his glass like we'd be having that last drink after all.

I said all I really wanted was if he could take care of her body. Maybe Kim II would know, or Miss Han or probably Coletti for sure. I wanted her cremated and the ashes sent to me. I wanted to sprinkle them in the New Mexico mountains. So she'd really get there and we'd really be together. Not that I knew where her body was.

Sansoe knew it sounded insane, but said he'd do it. I told him I'd get the money for the cremation wired to him before I left or soon as I hit the World. Maybe he didn't want to get into how impossible my request seemed. No doubt he could tell I was high and knew he'd just figure it out. Or try.

I went back to my room, ran into Capt. Plato. He was in a hurry packing up to head to Yongsan for a week on some kind of legal thing. I told him, like I had told him about the abortion. No warm-up, just the gut punch. I probably shouldn't have, but I had to.

He listened, like a friend, but also like a lawyer. I mean what else could he do with that kind of shit from my mouth, that kind of stupidity from my actions, that kind of horror. That kind of crime. I asked him to keep it quiet. That the only others that knew were Sansoe and Coletti, and they were helping me. That they'd keep it to themselves. He agreed that was the best thing.

He usually avoided Coletti, but said it was okay for Sansoe to get in touch if anything was needed. He said I'd probably get out of country on a Red Tail because if I was in real trouble I'd already be in custody. When we shook hands goodbye, I could tell he was having a hard time processing my situation. He said as far as he was concerned, we'd never spoken about this. We had a phony laugh at how that sounded like something from a spy or mafia movie. But it wasn't funny. We'd never talk about anything again. I was leaving.

For my last day, I stayed in my room except for a few walks to stretch my legs and stave off the memories, and to eat at slow times in the O Club restaurant. It didn't mean I had to talk to anyone. The boredom was more like torture. Nights almost sleepless. I was living out of my trunk and duffle bag. I didn't even have any books, but I ventured to the PX early and bought some magazines, careful to dodge anyone.

Sansoe dropped by after work to fill me in. He had gone to Coletti, who turned out to be more helpful than I would have thought. Even said to tell me good luck. But the real news was that Kim's body had been picked up by the police after all and taken to a Bupyeong funeral home because the police morgue was either full or being cleaned. Coletti had gone over there and set up the cremation and paid Mr. Lim, the owner. He said nobody treated it like a big deal.

Sansoe hung out with me for a half-hour, and we laughed, more or less, at our third goodbye. I felt so much better even if I couldn't be there for Kim's ashes. I actually slept.

*

It was a month later, after I was long gone, that I got the letter. Sansoe said he hated to send it but thought I'd want to know. I guess I did. He said Kim's body had disappeared and the funeral home wouldn't give the money back because they'd already paid for the cremation service. No one knew who took her remains or why.

I felt like catching a plane and tracking down Coletti in one of his fucking bars and putting the Colt back to his head and blowing it off. Nothing that big happened without the Mayor of Suchow knowing about it. Or if it was something best left unknown, or investigated, he'd know of that, too.

I wrote back to Sansoe and asked if it was possible that maybe Coletti had stolen the body as a friend to bury her in the mountains. Even if it was also to hide the evidence. Or maybe Lee took her, but I hoped not. Sansoe wrote back and said no one knew, or much talked about it, and he was leaving in January so he was sorry he couldn't keep asking.

Thus was I freed of them. It. Her. Freedom? Just another word for nothing left to lose, according to the song. Which was written by Kristofferson, an Army guy, and he would know. It also was a word from the books, the teachers, the politicians. From the lies of the World. Now my only freedom was me, and look, I am nothing.

71

That final morning, my "wake-up," I was going to take a PX cab to Kimpo to go back to the World. But I cancelled after Cpl. Yu dropped in to say goodbye, because I'd stopped coming to HQ. He said he would take me in the battalion Jeep and didn't mind it being early. He was a KATUSA and up anyway. He said I looked sad. I hadn't told him anything about Kim, and he thought it was just about leaving my friends: "Even me."

*

Oh-dark-thirty. Cpl. Yu pulls up at the White Elephant. I'm waiting in my class A's. Haven't worn them in a while. Only a Jeep ride and a few time zones to go.

We ease onto the highway and pass the Shinjin motor factory, ringed in gray walls and barbed wire. Teenage girls in white blouses and blue skirts on shift change are already walking through the guarded entrance. What if Kim had worked there?

We hit a pothole in the road. For some reason, the jolt reminds me of meeting Col. Foster the day we both arrived. Did he really know another Kim, as he said on his last day, on the surgical table after the fragging, dying with steel slivers in his chest? He knew, and he told them under anesthesia, the gossip said, and then was gone.

We are at the Kimpo entrance. A few yobos are waiting outside the fence. I remember when I wondered what a yobo was. Now, even pre-dawn, I can't look at them. So why do I see her? The ravaged one from my first day? I almost say something to Cpl. Yu, but why drag him into it on our last time together? Or make him wonder if his American friend can't even get home without seeing things and tripping out.

The sentries wave us through. Cpl. Yu drops me near the terminal doors.

The Red Tail is on the runway. It is real. Finally, something. I will ascend the ladder and fly away.

"Write me. Tell me if you go back to your father's farm or to college," I say, pulling my luggage from the Jeep. "Tell those girls I really am sorry about being such a dork."

"You will miss Korea?"

"What do you think?"

"Remember us."

We shake hands, salute out of respect.

"I already do."

I go inside to line up for the boarding call.

In two hours, I am in Japan. Waiting in the airport lobby while the plane refuels. I am restless. Where is Kim? A skeleton at the bottom of Incheon Harbor? A body with no one to mourn in a shallow grave, not the real graves on Happy Mountain? Will she ever be happy? I must look mad to soldiers and Japanese alike.

High over the Pacific, closing in on Seattle, the mystery unravels. Kim is with me. It is winter and I am naked in a ville alley. She is beside me, wrapped in her bloodied quilt. My teeth chatter as rain freezes in my hair and eyes. She opens the quilt, pulls me in, presses her lacerated body to mine.

I hold her forever.

ABOUT THE AUTHOR

Award-winning writer, Rod Davis is the author of *East of Texas, West of Hell*, the sequel to *South, America*, described as "a triumph of Southern noir." He is also the author of *Corina's Way*, winner of the fiction prize in the inaugural PEN Southwest Book Awards for 2000-2005, and of

American Voudou: Journey into a Hidden World, selected as one of the "Exceptional Books of 1998" by Bookman Book Review Syndicate. A long-time journalist and magazine editor, he is a member of PEN America, the Texas Institute of Letters, Mystery Writers of America, and was formerly on the board of directors of the National Book Critics Circle. He served as an Army first lieutenant in South Korea in the Vietnam Era.